# I MARRIED KROGAL

*Prime Mating Agency*

## REGINE ABEL

# CONTENTS

I MARRIED KROGAL

**He is the cuddliest of teddy bears.**

A year after fleeing an abusive partner, Farah's welcome in the refuge sheltering her is ending. With no money, no job, and no options, she's floored to be presented with a marriage of convenience to an alien behemoth as a solution. Considering her recent ordeal, entering a relationship with a four-armed giant with herculean strength is the last thing she wants. But the sweet, respectful, and cuddly male she discovers behind that intimidating façade makes her feel safer than she has in years.

**She exceeds his wildest dreams.**

As the biggest and strongest male on Xoccoris, Krogal struggles with his people's expectations that he should lead a warrior's life instead of caring for wounded and helpless creatures in his veterinary clinic. When the Prime Mating Agency finally finds his soulmate, Krogal is mesmerized by the stunning and delicate little human she turns out to be. While her previous hardships stir his protective instincts, Farah's inner strength and compassion dazzle him.

But as their bond grows stronger, will the ghosts of her past destroy the future they're trying to build together?

# DEDICATION

*To those who refuse to be defeated by adversity. There is no greater pain than to be hurt and betrayed by those who should love you the most. Never give in, never give up. And above all, never forget that you are worthy of true love and respect.*

*To parents who love their children unconditionally, who stand by them in their time of need, and who support their dreams and aspirations, even when they clash with your own preferences and desires. Your children aren't tools for you to achieve your missed opportunities.*

*To loving families, the greatest gift anyone could ever have.*

# CHAPTER 1
## KROGAL

As soon as the latest panel ended, I snuck out of the auditorium, praying no one would try to stop me or engage in yet another mind-numbing conversation. I loved veterinary medicine and to exchange with the greatest minds in the field. Sadly, since helping to save Ferach, my cousin Bayron's stone wolf, I'd become somewhat of a celebrity. Where Bayron would thrive under the adulation and flattery that came with it, I had no interest whatsoever in attracting so much attention.

Anyway, I had somewhere far more important to be.

I didn't travel off-world too often. This year, I even considered skipping the Intergalactic Veterinary Medicine Summit. Finding out it would be held on the Eldar Space Station located a short distance away from my home world Xoccoris helped. But learning that Kayog would be transiting through here during those same dates convinced me to come.

Since my cousin married his human mate, thanks to Kayog matchmaking them through his Prime Mating Agency, I heavily weighed whether to also avail myself of his services. Granted, it was Belle, not Bayron, who had retained the agency. Still, despite the improbable odds stacked against them, Kayog managed to unite these two halves of the same soul separated by entire solar systems.

As much as I doubted I'd enjoy the same blessing, I finally accepted that it could only happen if I set things in motion.

I hastened back to my hotel, where I had rented one of the smaller boardrooms to meet with the Temern. By all accounts, he was reputed to be pretty laid back, but it felt disrespectful to simply invite him to my room.

To my dismay, he was already waiting for me inside when I arrived.

"Master Voln!" I said, slapping my fist to my chest in greeting while my stomach fluttered with nerves. "Apologies for making you wait."

"Not at all! I just arrived myself," he said reassuringly while rising to his feet... well talons.

A noble and majestic aura swirled around the Temern. He possessed large maroon wings, the same color as the feathers covering his body, except for the golden down feathers on his chest and head. A long fluffy white tail with the same golden yellow at the tip trailed behind him. Despite the stiffness of his beak, his gentle smile and the warmth in his silver eyes immediately put me at ease. Although in his late seventies or early eighties, Kayog Voln could easily pass for someone in his mid-forties, especially considering how fit he kept himself. But then, he had been one of the top athletes in his school back in college.

"Please, remain seated," I said, gesturing at the stool he had risen from, glad the hotel had honored my request to have it added to the room.

With his wings, regular chairs with backrests could get uncomfortable. He bowed his head and resumed his seat while I settled across the table from him. The small room was mostly barren aside from this round wooden table big enough to seat six people, a giant vidscreen, a medium-sized console, and large reflective windows that gave us a pleasant view of the concourse outside.

"Do you need some water, food, or other refreshments?" I asked, pointing at the water pitcher and glasses on the console. "I can have room service—"

"No, my dear Krogal. I do not require anything," Kayog said in a slightly amused tone. "Stop fretting so much. It's only me, Kayog. There's no need for you to be nervous."

"Right," I said, the pointy tips of my ears heating with embarrassment.

As an empath, the Temern knew exactly what an emotional mess I currently was.

"I hope it's okay for me to call you by your given name?" he asked.

"Of course," I replied.

His smile broadened while he gazed upon me with a contented expression. "I'm glad you finally reached out to me."

I blinked, taken aback by that comment. "Finally?"

He nodded. "Since her marriage to your cousin, Belle keeps telling me that I need to find you a mate."

Heat spread down my ears to my cheeks. "Apologies if she pestered you about this. Belle can be a little enthusiastic and blunt at times."

Kayog laughed good-heartedly. "She is a true delight, and she cares a great deal about you."

I smiled fondly, my chest warming for the little human. "She has a very big heart," I conceded.

The Temern cocked his head to the side in a very bird-like fashion. "You like her," he mused aloud.

"Who doesn't?" I asked in a self-evident fashion. "Belle is always so positive about everything. You cannot help but smile in her presence. And she's so small and fragile compared to our females, you just want to hug and shelter her."

He nodded slowly, a strange glimmer in his eyes. "Fragile in appearance but not weak," he countered.

"Definitely not weak," I replied with a snort. "There is great strength and determination in her. You should have seen the way she fought for Ferach when none of us thought that stone wolf pup had a chance to survive his wounds. It's extremely hard to tame a wild beast and earn its trust. Belle went beyond that. She not only won his heart, but she helped create a bond between his species and my people. Stone wolves no longer attack the Zamorians they encounter or who accidentally wander into their territory. All thanks to her."

I smiled wistfully as images of Belle playing with the pup through his various stages of growth flashed before my eyes. When I refocused on the Temern, it struck me that he had been observing me quietly while my mind wandered off. The intensity of his gaze immediately unsettled me.

"I'm not in love with her, if that's what you're thinking," I blurted out, horrified he might misconstrue my words. "I do love her, but she's a sister to me."

He nodded, his face unreadable. "But you would want someone *like* her?"

I hesitated. "In many ways, yes. Our women are too strong and independent. Don't get me wrong, I don't want someone weak or submissive. But I would like someone sweet and affectionate," I said, my cheeks burning.

"Can you define sweet and affectionate?" he asked in an encouraging tone.

I grabbed the single long braid my hair was plaited into, bringing it in front of me, and ran my fingers over its length in a way I always found comforting.

"Belle proudly holds Bayron's hand in public, which is something my people don't do. During assemblies—which are regular clan gatherings where we sit around a fire and talk—she won't sit on one of the benches like everyone else. She insists on sitting in his lap and cuddling with him. The clan often teases her about it—not in a mean way of course. Deep down, all our males envy her mate. She gives him a plethora of cute pet names and supports him and his dreams, however wild. In the short time they've been together, Belle has made Bayron an even better man than he already was, without him losing himself. And above all, she made the rest of the world realize who he truly is and why he deserves their accolades instead of their disdain."

"And you haven't found something like this with your own females?" Kayog insisted in a gentle tone devoid of any condemnation or judgment.

I snorted bitterly and shook my head. "I'm Krogal, the Mountain. Because of my size, strength, and battle prowess, everyone wants me to be a warrior or hunter. Even now, my parents remind me how disappointed they are that I became a veterinarian. It's only gotten worse since Bayron achieved great fame by saving that Atreall Queen. As the biggest and strongest male on Xoccoris, I'm expected to pursue a career related to combat. Everyone asks why I'm not more like my cousin, and why I don't use my natural talents to bring honor to our house and our clan."

"But that holds no appeal for you?" Although he worded it like a question, it was more of a statement filled with sympathy.

"As a Zamorian, I enjoy fighting like every one of our males. But it's merely for entertainment. I only hunt to provide for our needs. Slaughtering animals should never be a sport. I'd rather heal than kill them," I said, a sliver of anger entering my voice.

"May I ask why you became a veterinarian instead of a medical doctor?" he asked with genuine curiosity.

I waved a disdainful hand. "There are medical doctors everywhere. With technology—especially the new advanced medical pods—people can mostly take care of themselves. And when they can't, they're still able to express what the issue is and request specific assistance. Animals are very limited and often helpless. In most cases, they can only treat basic problems like eating grass to force themselves to vomit when they have an upset stomach. Some will eat certain plants or minerals to fight an infection or a toxin in their system. But what else do they have? They can lick their wound, rest, fast, or seek a warm area, and that's pretty much it."

I nervously peered at the Temern, bracing for the usual confused or even disappointed look my people gave me for being so concerned about animals instead of seeking fame and honor. My throat tightened at the sight of the almost paternal way he was smiling at me, encouraging me to continue.

My own father only ever looked at me like that when I won a battle in the arena.

"When it comes to serious illnesses, they're completely help-less. What can they do about an open wound or broken bone? Sometimes, it's internal injuries they have no way of identifying. So they simply suffer in silence until they die," I continued. "I can fix that for them."

"And I'm sure they are grateful for it," Kayog said.

"They are, Master Voln! They *truly* are," I said with fervor. "Animals are the most honest beings in the universe. Unlike people, they don't fake or exaggerate illness for attention. They don't trust easily, especially when they're wounded and vulnerable. But once you earn their trust, it is the sincerest thing you will ever experience. You would have to do something truly horrible to lose it, if ever. No words can describe how they cuddle you to express their gratitude, even when they're beyond help and know their time is near. Deep in their hearts, they know you tried your best."

I shifted in my seat and ran my hand over my braid again with a nervous laugh. It was a little mortifying to have allowed myself to become so emotional in front of him. But the Temern had a way of making you feel safe and like he genuinely wanted to hear what you had to say.

"Sorry. My parents and our females hate when I speak like that. It makes them question my virility. I should be bragging and making plans to compete and dominate," I added with self-derision.

Kayog chuckled. "Ah yes! Winning and outwitting the competition is a huge thing for Zamorians. It got your cousin in quite a bit of hot water," he said teasingly.

I snorted. "It certainly did. But I also like a bit of competition and outwitting my opponents. I just like doing it in my own time, and when I'm in the mood for it. Otherwise, I would rather look after injured animals."

"Basically, you are a giant, cuddly teddy bear," Kayog said with a mischievous glimmer in his silver eyes.

I burst out laughing. "That's exactly what Belle calls me," I said, affectionately shaking my head. "While it's not exactly flattering for a Zamorian male, I can see why she would say that."

"And I see exactly what you need," he replied in a more serious tone. "Just understand that finding your soulmate will not be easy."

My shoulders slumped, and the little voice at the back of my head that had warned me from the start that this was a pointless endeavor came back with a vengeance, cruelly mocking me.

"Do not despair, Krogal," Kayog said firmly. "I'm determined to find your mate. However, you are not eligible for the Prime Mating Agency services. Your species is far too advanced, and the UPO will not benefit from our involvement."

"I'm confused. You say you're determined to find my soulmate, but also that you cannot get involved?" I said, baffled.

He gave me an indulgent smile. "While the agency itself cannot get involved, *I* can personally look for her on your behalf," Kayog explained. "But when I find her, we will not be able to cover her relocation costs."

I waved a dismissive hand. "That won't be a problem. I have more than enough wealth to cover all the expenses."

"Excellent!" Kayog said with enthusiasm. "I don't know how long it will take, but I will do everything in my power to find her for you."

# CHAPTER 2
### FARAH

I wandered around the faire hub, intense stress stiffening my back as I drowned in a sea of indecision. Calling this a faire struck me as incredibly callous and insensitive. Khendis—a major galactic shelter in the Chabor region—organized one every three months. This was my fourth time participating. The shelter took in a wide variety of people. It included victims of domestic abuse, people battling most forms of addictions, the homeless, disaster victims, and even ex-convicts.

Their massive compound was divided into distinct sections to avoid exposing certain groups to other ones that might jeopardize their welfare or recovery. But with the constant influx of new people seeking assistance, they needed to make room. Therefore, they held this faire to get rid of those who, like me, had overstayed our welcome.

Like in the shelter, clear sections offered different options. On the left-hand side, one huge room was dedicated to mating agencies. Two bigger ones were devoted to job seekers and recruiters. The central area of the circular room offered family reunion services, mostly for the displaced following a disaster or people rescued from pirates and flesh traders. On the right, a surprisingly big section had been reserved for the detox and reintegration programs. And last, the section I had just left offered volunteer work opportunities.

As I wasn't a junkie, was not an ex-convict, and had no family to reunite with, those three options wouldn't apply to me. As far as mating was concerned, that entire section could take a hike. Fleeing an abusive relationship had landed me in Khendis to begin with. Therefore, being paired with some random partner was the last thing I needed, regardless of how dire my current situation was.

That left me with finding a job or working as a volunteer.

As with the three previous times I participated in the faire, the volunteering opportunities totally sucked. Granted, they provided free food and lodging as well as a minimal amount of credits on top. As I didn't seek wealth or luxury, I would have been more than happy to settle for that, so long as I had a warm place to lay my head at night and a safe environment to live in. But the good volunteer openings always got snagged first. In truth, I suspected that some of the agents kept them for their buddies or even sold them.

The remaining ones equated to a life sentence in places where no one in their right mind would want to go. Even the prison planet Molvi sounded like a luxury resort in comparison. No wonder they never filled those openings.

Depressed, I walked past the impressive crowd lining up outside the intergalactic matchmaker section. Many of the big agencies had their names plastered on the holographic display outside the room. Even more hopefuls sat patiently in the adjoining waiting area.

How desperate did one have to be to gamble their future by being blindly paired to someone they'd never met and who could be a complete psycho? Sure, most candidates had to undergo a thorough psychological examination on top of a background check. But considering ex-convicts were also allowed to sign up for those matches, how safe were they truly?

*They have served their time and are trying to reintegrate society.*

True. It still unnerved and baffled me that anyone would put themselves in such a vulnerable position. Then again, before meeting Liam, I used to be a lot more adventurous. He had crushed the dauntless flame that once burned inside me.

I headed over to the jobs section. Inside the rooms, people who found interesting postings were undergoing live interviews. Outside, sitting at small tables lining the walls, many agents were having one-on-one talks with other would-be candidates. They generally were counselors helping guide people with many options towards the one best suited or most beneficial to them.

After my previous humiliation the first time I sought such counseling, I knew better and stayed in my lane. I walked up to one of the countless self-service kiosks in the large open area in front of those consultation tables.

Tears pricked my eyes as I flicked through the list of openings. As always, none of the jobs appealed to me. The only ones I even stood a chance of being hired for involved hard physical labor or took place in hostile environments. All the nice, well-paying jobs were out of my reach. I wasn't even being picky or a diva. I simply didn't qualify for any of them.

It was both my fault and Liam's… but mainly mine because of my poor choices.

I had no degrees, no experience, and no professional qualifications except for my voice and my dancing skills—neither of which I could use. Liam was too well-connected in the entertainment industry. Even if I changed my name, the minute I started performing again, someone would recognize me and tip him off. The thought of what he might do should he find me again terrified me.

I tapped on a maid job offer. My stomach twisted, and my

throat constricted with an all-too-familiar sense of despair. The requirements: one year of experience and references. I had no experience. Even if I managed to sweet talk my way past that—which others had successfully achieved in the past—I would never overcome the security clearance.

Technically, I didn't have a record as I never committed any crime. But Liam had been neck deep in shady businesses that I'd been too blind—or too dumb—to see until it was too late. While the Enforcers hadn't found anything to pin on me, they'd flagged my file as me being a possible accomplice.

*Even lightyears away from me, Liam continues to ruin my life.*

Around me, countless people were walking away from their chosen section with a glowing smile. They found something good. Both recovering and still struggling addicts also sauntered off with a pep in their steps. A lot of great programs existed for them. As much as I rejoiced for their good fortune, it only added salt to the wound of my own despair.

Fighting the tears stinging my eyes, I dragged my feet to one of the benches in the waiting area between the jobs and matchmaking sections. I needed a moment to think, regroup, and make a decision.

*I have too few options.*

Any way I looked at it, my only hope would be to apply to a different shelter. But why couldn't I just stay right here? Why couldn't they let me finish my current studies so that I could have a decent future? I more than pulled my weight in Khendis. I wasn't a mooch, worked hard, and had undeniably proven my dedication to making something of myself.

With the back of my hand, I angrily wiped the lone tear trickling down my face.

What was I going to do? If I took a volunteer position or a brutal job, they wouldn't let me come back here once it became clear I couldn't physically handle it. But if I didn't make a choice quickly, they would make it for me.

"Are you okay?" a gentle voice asked, startling me.

I jerked my head up, stunned to see a tall Temern standing next to me, a concerned look on his face.

"Sorry, I hadn't seen you. Yes, I'm fine," I said, my voice a little shaky.

He gave me a 'Don't be silly' look. "In case you haven't noticed, I'm a Temern. I *know* you're not okay."

"Right," I said, clumsily wiping the wetness off my cheek while feeling stupid.

He sat down next to me, the compassionate expression on his face turning me upside down.

"My name is Kayog. Will you tell me yours?" he asked gently.

"Farah," I replied automatically.

As I usually went under a fake name here to cover my tracks, it shocked me how naturally it felt using my real name with him.

"Do you want to talk about it? It could help," he insisted when I scrunched my face. "I could feel your pain all the way inside the other room and would love to help ease some of it, if possible. I'm happy to listen."

Something broke down inside me. Tears gushed from my eyes, and words tumbled out of my mouth. I couldn't tell if this unexpected kindness after months of feeling abandoned and isolated or the excessive stress weighing me down was the cause. Either way, the dam burst wide open.

"I don't know what to do. Khendis is going to kick me out any day now, and I have nowhere to go. The volunteer roles and jobs I could qualify for are way too harsh for me. Even with the best of will, I won't last long. The jobs I could and would be more than willing to do, I don't qualify for. There's always something: no degree, no references, or no experience. The one thing I'm talented at, I can't do without putting my life in danger as it will allow my abusive ex-partner to find me again. I'm trying to better myself and learn a new career, but Khendis won't give me enough time to finish my studies."

"I can see why you are feeling so distressed," Kayog said with compassion. "But there are great programs—including educational ones—for victims of domestic abuse. Have you looked into those?"

I sniffled and wiped my face with the back of my hand in the least elegant fashion. "That's the first thing I looked into when I arrived. But once again, I don't qualify. It was all psychological abuse and control. He never physically hurt me, but he would mistreat others to punish me," I said in a shaky voice. "Publicly, I was living such a princess life that nobody believed me once I escaped. Worse still, he turned out to be involved in terrible criminal activities. Since I met him through his very lucrative legitimate businesses, it took me too long to finally grow suspicious. I was just too naive and too blind."

"I see," he said, a frown creasing his feathery forehead. "If you're fearing for your safety, I'm assuming he was not arrested?"

My shoulders slouched as I shook my head. "They didn't have any proof that would stick enough to get a formal indictment, let alone win a trial. As I had been his partner for seven years, the cops—and then the Enforcers—thought I was hiding what I knew and covering for him. They even had one of yours present during my final interrogation," I added angrily while waving at him. "The Temern confirmed that I was being truthful by saying I didn't know anything. Honestly, him vouching for me was the only reason they allowed me inside Khendis. They didn't trust my words or the fact that I fled and asked for help. Only a male Temern saying I should be believed swayed them… and partially, at that."

A slender woman in her late sixties timidly approaching us interrupted me. My companion turned to see what had caught my attention and a spark of recognition laced with guilt fleeted through his silver eyes.

"Sorry to interrupt you, Kayog, but we need you to return soon," she said sheepishly before casting an apologetic glance my way.

I responded with a quivering smile, feeling a little stupid for making such a spectacle of myself and pouring my heart out to a complete stranger. And yet, although none of my problems had been solved, talking indeed helped a little.

"Of course, Isobel. I'll be there shortly," he said with a gentle smile to the woman.

She smiled back, nodded at me with the same guilty expression, and walked away.

"Sorry, I didn't mean to hog you," I said as I watched the woman head back towards the matchmaking section. "But thank you for—"

I froze, struck by a sudden realization. If she was waiting for him to return to that area, then he had to be one of the matchmaking agents. My eyes flicked to the holographic panel listing the agencies present. As far as I knew, only one of them had a Temern.

My heart lurched at the sight of 'Prime Mating Agency' listed in third place.

"Oh, my God! You're *that* matchmaker!" I breathed out.

He chuckled, a strange expression settling over his features, intense and yet laced with amusement.

"Don't sound so horrified," he said teasingly.

I lowered my eyes with embarrassment. "I didn't mean it that way. It just took me by surprise. For some reason, I pictured you... Well, not this 'normal' and polished. Or this young," I added with a sheepish expression.

He burst out laughing. "Thank you, especially about the young part, although my aging bones would disagree. As for my general appearance, you would be traumatized by some of the ways people who have never met me think I look. For most of them, I'm short, plump, beyond ancient, and with crazy eyes."

I snorted and bit back the fact that I, too, had pictured him as an eccentric, funny-looking, old birdman. Whatever response I had planned on giving him died on my tongue when his smile faded, and he took on that same intense expression but this time laden with seriousness.

"Have you ever considered—?"

"Don't even go there!" I interrupted him sharply, guessing where he was headed with this. "Have you not heard a single word I just said?"

"I heard that you were with the wrong partner who was abusive to you. The right person can help heal you and be happy. It so happens that I know exactly who it is," he said calmly.

As I gaped at him in disbelief, shock and anger warred within me in equal measure. "You don't even know me!"

"You're correct, I don't," he conceded in the same soft tone. "But I know who your soul belongs with. Since you have heard of me, then you must know that I'm never wrong on that front. This would also give you the fresh start you need."

"Fresh start or not, considering what I'm going through, this is a highly inappropriate thing to suggest," I exclaimed, baffled that an empath could be so clueless, not to say callous. "I'm not ready for a relationship. Doesn't your agency require couples to bang on the very first night? I'm not *that* desperate!"

"Peace, my dear Farah. The rules would be different in your case. Krogal does not belong to a primitive species. Therefore, the two of you would not be subjected to the PMA's strict guidelines. There would be no sex requirement, no minimum trial period, and no penalties should either of you decide to call it quits at any point in time," he explained in a reassuring voice. "In fact, you would not even be forced to marry."

I blinked, totally confused. "Really?"

"Really," he said gently but firmly. "Listen, I must go. But with your permission, I will contact you later tonight with a proposal that you should find acceptable. Krogal is a wonderful male, with a heart of gold. He's the greatest warrior among his people, and yet he chose to become a veterinarian because of his strong nurturing and protective nature. He's been waiting for five years for me to find his soulmate. And I know beyond the shadow of a doubt that you are the one. Fate brought us here this day."

"Wow!" I whispered, unsure what to think.

"My former client, who married his cousin, describes him as a cuddly teddy bear," he added in a slightly teasing tone, while extending a holographic card to me. "Here's my card. Please keep an open mind and message me later tonight or as soon as you are ready to talk. Believe me, this will be the best decision of your life. Goodbye, Farah. I look forward to speaking to you again soon."

My hand still clutching his card, I watched him walk away with determined steps, his gait elegant and effortless as his fluffy white tail gently swayed behind him. Males and females alike sitting in the waiting area by the entrance of the matchmaking room looked at him with hope and excitement.

As soon as he vanished from view, I glanced back down at his card. What madness had taken root inside my mind that I would even consider this? Sure, the Temern and his agency had a stellar reputation. But after my past experience, even though an entire year had gone by since my escape, hooking up with a new man was the last thing I needed or wanted.

*He says no sex, no formal marriage, and no minimum trial period rules.*

That meant I could bail the moment things went sideways. But could I really? Or would I be trapped on some primitive world with no way out and no one to rescue me?

*He said he wasn't a primitive alien.*

I had too many questions and too few answers. As much as I

refused to let myself get sucked into this fairy tale, the seed of hope had been planted. By all accounts, Kayog was never wrong. If that Krogal was indeed my soulmate, a great protector, and willing not to rush me into anything I wasn't ready for, going to him could exceed any other alternative plans I might come up with.

*Let's wait and see his detailed proposal.*

# CHAPTER 3
## KROGAL

Since receiving that impossible call from Kayog four days ago, I'd gone through the entire spectrum of emotions, from intense joy to extreme stress. After waiting for more than five years, I had lost hope that he would succeed in finding my soulmate.

Discovering that she'd been a victim of abuse had my blood boiling with the need to crack that wretched male's skull. Saying that my protective instincts were firing on all cylinders would be quite an understatement. As much as it distressed me that those traumatic events made her not overly keen to marry, I was looking forward to being the rock she could lean on to get back on her feet. She was my soulmate. I would bring her the stability, love, and support she needed to heal.

Granted, it stung a little that she only agreed to come here out of desperation. At the same time, it filled my hearts with pride to be the one to provide her with a safe harbor in her time of need.

We wouldn't have a real marriage at first—which also meant none of the cuddling I craved. But I had no problem with that.

Having our happily ever after once she was ready was more than worth the wait.

*And she's so incredibly pretty!*

Since Kayog sent me a 3D hologram of Farah, I'd been unable to tear my gaze away from her. By Zamorian standards, at 5'10, she qualified as small, especially compared to my 8'. Her slender body possessed all the right curves in the right places. Generally speaking, I liked females with a bit more meat. And yet, I could find no fault with her. Farah's skin reminded me of golden desert sand kissed by the reddish lights of the setting sun. She had the cutest bud nose, generous heart-shaped lips, and big, brown, doe eyes that screamed of innocence and vulnerability, which sent my protective urges into overdrive.

Kromor's teeth! I would have to shackle myself to refrain from smothering her in hugs the moment we met.

Unfortunately, for now, a highly disagreeable task forced me to cast all wistful thoughts of my woman aside. My stomach knotted with tension as I rang the chime to my parents' dwelling. I'd delayed this confrontation for as long as possible and was determined to keep it short. Considering I already knew the unpleasant outcome, I tried to enjoy a sense of normalcy until it couldn't be postponed anymore.

With Xoccoris being a matriarchal society, I couldn't marry without my mother's blessing. My father left town for a few days for a hunt. As he didn't have a say in the matter, his absence was irrelevant. Even should he disagree with my mother's decision—not that he ever did—she could never be swayed from whatever path she had settled on.

The door parted before me with a soft swish, the mechanism likely activated by a vocal command as my mother stood a few meters from the inner set of doors to the antechamber.

Talinsaya Skortheatis embodied the beauty, elegance, and strength of the Zamorian females. From her, I inherited my black hair and eyes. At fifty-six, she could easily pass for my older sister rather than my mother. Her greige skin, a paler shade than mine, was flawless and luminous. As was fashionable among our females, she was wearing a colorful sleeveless crop top with a matching ankle-length skirt with thigh-high slits on the sides.

She gracefully wiggled her fingers at me in a beckoning gesture, an inquisitive expression on her face.

"Krogal, there you are. Come in, son."

I crossed the short antechamber into the open space living area of my mother's dwelling. As I closed the inner doors behind me, she gently caressed my single braid Zamorian males always plaited their hair into. It constituted both a gesture of affection but also of status and dominance. Children belonged to their mother until she released them to their mates. The braid—often referred to as the leash—was the symbol of that ownership. No female but your mother, and later your wife, had the right to touch your braid.

"You wanted to talk?" she asked, curious but not worried.

"Yes, Mother. I have an announcement to make," I said in a formal tone.

"Oh? Should we take a seat then?" she asked, gesturing at the set of comfortable, dark-brown cushioned chairs and couches in the living area.

I shook my head. "If you don't mind, I would rather stand."

She narrowed her four eyes at me, tension seeping into her previously relaxed demeanor. I only remained standing for unpleasant discussions.

"Very well. I'm listening," she said, her voice a bit cooler.

"Kayog Voln contacted me to let me know he found my soul-mate," I said, relieved that my voice didn't reveal how nervous I felt.

My mother stiffened, and her eyes widened in shock. "What?! How?"

I cleared my throat and ran a hand over my braid. "A little

over five years ago, I contacted Kayog to look for her. He's been searching ever since. And at last, his efforts bore fruit."

"Why in the world did you not mention this to me before?" she exclaimed, disbelief laced with a sliver of outrage filling her voice.

"What was the point?" I asked with a shrug. "I doubted he would be successful. There was no point creating expectations that would likely never be met."

"You still should have told me!" she insisted with an irritated gesture of her primary right hand. "This whole time, I was looking for a mate for you!"

I nodded. "Correct, and you might have found her. There was a real chance she would be a Zamorian, right here on Xoccoris. Until my soulmate was found, we couldn't know where she would be. It would have been foolish of me to eliminate any option."

Mother huffed, not fully mollified, but unable to argue with my logic. "So what is she like?" she asked in a grumbling tone.

I couldn't help the wistful smile that blossomed on my lips. "She's a breathtaking human. Although taller than Belle, she's a lot more delicate."

The way my mother scrunched her face and rolled her eyes immediately had my hackles rising.

"Figures," Mother said, unimpressed. "Ever since Bayron's mate came here, you've been pining over humans. She's nice enough and a good mate for your cousin. But what's so special about her to make you shun your own people?"

"I have not shunned our females," I ground through my teeth, instantly aggravated to have her bring back that same old refrain. "The ones I met simply weren't for me. And the fact that Kayog found my soulmate confirms what I felt all along. Belle's arrival only helped me identify what I wasn't finding here."

She shook her head at me as if I was an oddity that defied any possible logic.

"Why are you so strange?" she asked, more to herself than to me. "Why can't you just be like your brother and the other Zamorian males? Where did I go wrong?"

"I am not strange," I snapped. "The fact that I have my own desires and ambitions—which happen to differ from yours— doesn't make me weird. It only makes me an individual. Why should I be a copy of my brother or someone else? What's wrong with being me? And above all, why is it so hard for you to just love me for who I am and the way I am?"

She waved both her primary hands in a dismissive gesture while giving me an annoyed look. "No one said I don't love you. That's all in your head."

"You certainly don't act like it," I countered, crossing my primary arms over my chest and fisting my secondary hands by my sides.

She ran her fingers through her long black hair cascading loosely over her slender shoulders, looking discouraged.

"It's just that you could be so much more! As your mother, it's my duty to push you to be the best you can be. It's not that I don't love you, quite the opposite. I try to reason with you *because* I love you!"

"Why is it so hard for you to understand that I already am what I *want* to be?" I exclaimed, exasperated and wondering why I was allowing her to drag me down that tired old slippery slope that never resolved anything. "I don't want those other things *you* wish for me. Fame, trophies, and bragging rights have never held any appeal for me. You already have Demar fulfilling your wishes and ambitions and bringing plenty of honor to your house. Why can't that be enough for you?"

"Because you are the strongest male on this entire planet!" she spat angrily. "You are my firstborn. You should be setting the example instead of laying it on the shoulders of your younger sibling. Your name could go down in history as our greatest warrior of all time! Instead, you're wasting your potential slapping bandages on animals."

I was so tired of hearing those words from her. Knowing replying would only send us down a pointless spiral of resentment, I merely stared at her, my face devoid of any expression.

She sighed and shook her head in discouragement, understanding that I was done with this topic. "There's just no reasoning with you. But fine, we'll organize your human's clanning. When will she arrive?"

"Tomorrow," I said in a cold voice.

"TOMORROW?! Seriously, Krogal, you could have given me more warning!" Mother exclaimed, throwing all four of her arms up in the air in disbelief. "Grrr, by Khivolt, you never make things easy. But fine, we'll sort it out. I already have brumar sweat for her. You must go hunt a grummoll today. And I need her measurements for her sacrificial gown."

While speaking, Mother's eyes flicked from side to side as she tried to inventory all the things she would need to organize a traditional claiming and bonding ceremony. The part of me that still loved my mother felt grateful that, despite my rudeness of dumping this on her at the last minute, she would go out of her way to make it the most spectacular wedding she possibly could. Sadly, as much as I wanted to believe it was out of devotion to her son, I knew her too well. This was all about *her* image.

"That won't be necessary, Mother," I said in a neutral tone.

She stiffened, an understandable confusion settling over her noble features. "What?"

I sighed and braced for the next and even bigger storm to come. "There won't be a bonding ceremony tomorrow or in the foreseeable future."

"But... I thought you said she was your soulmate?"

"She is. However, she survived great trauma and abuse from her former mate," I explained, not wanting to go into too much detail as it wasn't *my* story to tell. "Farah is scared and will need time to learn to trust me. We will simply have a legal marriage by signing a contract so that she can enjoy all the protections of citizenship. A formal wedding will have to wait."

"I see," Mother said, visibly displeased, not to say disgusted.

She always pictured me marrying one of our few battle maidens who would have elevated our status even more. The prospect of me choosing what she perceived as a weak and feeble woman distressed her. One more proof she truly didn't understand me.

"However, once my mate is ready for us to proceed, be fairly warned I will not have a traditional bonding ceremony," I said in a tone that brooked no argument. "I will not slaughter a grummoll in our arena."

This time, my mother gasped and visibly recoiled. "That is our way!"

"It is barbaric and uselessly cruel!" I snarled. "Proving my worth as a mate shouldn't require making a spectacle of killing a wild beast, and making it suffer for the amusement of the crowd."

She rolled her eyes in exasperation. "You and your obsession with animals! Grummolls are feral beasts that need to be culled to protect our cities. And the kill is not gratuitous or wasted. The entire beast will be used to feed the guests."

"I will kill a grummoll for the feast. But it will be a swift, clean, and merciful death during a hunt."

"It's tradition! It's our way!" she repeated as if she thought I'd lost my mind.

"It's *your* tradition, not mine. And I have a pretty strong feeling it won't be Farah's either."

"You would truly dishonor our house like this?" she whispered in complete shock.

"Mother, I'm not trying to dishonor you or our family," I said in a reasonable tone. "I specifically came to you hoping to get your blessing for an alternative ceremony when the time comes so that I do not make unrealistic promises to my mate when she arrives tomorrow."

"There will be no alternative ceremonies," she said in an icy tone. "I forbid it. You will follow our way or not marry at all."

Despite knowing it would come to this, my hearts still broke at the finality of it all.

I nodded slowly and sighed with resignation. "Then I have no other choice but to renounce my house."

My mother visibly blanched and gaped at me in both shock and horror. "You would dare? For a human you've never even met?!"

"First off, I don't need to meet her to know she's the other half of me. If Kayog says she's the one, then it is an irrefutable fact. Second, even if she had been a Zamorian or any other species, my decision would be the same. My wedding day should be about *my* happiness, not *yours*. It will happen according to the rules my bride and I set for ourselves, not those imposed by others."

She snorted with disdain and looked at me as if I'd said something stupid. "And where exactly will you take that so-called soulmate of yours once you've been banned from this clan?"

I gave her a sad smile. "I haven't been banned. And should that occur, that will be Feidin's decision to make, not yours. As I highly suspected this would be the outcome of our discussion, I've already set a meeting with her to address my status within this clan."

My mother paled even more. This time, true fear entered her obsidian eyes.

"When?" she breathed out, flabbergasted.

"Now," I replied, matter-of-factly.

"I forbid it!"

I shrugged. "You are free to make your case to the Matriarch, as will I."

Despite the hurt lacerating my twin hearts, I plastered a mask of stoicism on my face as I exited her dwelling and made my way to the lift. She followed in my wake, berating me the whole time. I ignored her and remained silent as I entered the lift's cabin and as it raced down to the ground floor of the giant fortress that housed the closest families sharing our ruling clan's bloodline.

When we stepped into the hallway, Mother lowered her voice as she continued to feverishly whisper for me to get back to my senses before I caused myself and our family irreparable harm. We merged into the main hallway leading to the Gathering Hall where the clan's Matriarch—my aunt Feidin—and her mate Ugrul were currently hearing requests and grievances. A few people loitering outside the imposing, intricately carved doors leading into the massive room glanced our way with curiosity at the palpable tension surrounding us. The unusually panicked expression on the face of the control freak that was my mother fanned the flames of their curiosity.

The doors parted before us upon our approach, revealing the immense octagonal room that served multiple social functions of the clan, from dining hall to audience room, and meeting hall. Lining the walls, an elevated section contained enough dining tables to host all the clanmates living inside the fortress, but not those living in the other fortresses within our city walls. A few short stairs led down to the central area where performances were sometimes held or, like in this instance, where supplicants could make their requests to our leaders. Surrounding the central floor, a series of cushioned benches formed a mini-amphitheater where clanmates could bear witness to the proceedings. And right now, many of those benches were occupied.

My hearts constricted further. As there had been no major issues to be discussed today during the open hearings, I had hoped few people would witness what would inevitably be an embarrassing moment for my mother. Whatever our differences, I did not wish her ill.

Kraslo, one of our clan's most talented chemists, was currently standing before our Matriarch, pleading his case. Feidin—who was an even more beautiful, slightly older version of my mother—was sitting on the dais, on a stone throne next to her mate Ugrul. My cousin Varkuth—who was her firstborn son—was sitting to her right. Although he also had a smaller seat on the left side of his father, Bayron had not taken his rightful place there, but settled instead on one of the benches surrounding the floor, his mate blissfully snuggling in his lap.

When Varkuth lifted his head to see who just entered the hall, I nodded at him to signal that I was ready to speak with his mother once she concluded the current matter before her. He smiled, and blinked in acknowledgement, having no clue what was about to go down.

Realizing the imminence of the inevitable, my mother gave up any pretense of restraint.

"Enough of this nonsense. You're coming with me!" she hissed.

Simultaneously, she grabbed my braid and pulled on it hard to force me to follow her out of the room. It stung, but I didn't move an inch. Instead, I closed my hand around my braid above hers, and yanked it right out of her grasp.

"My braid is no longer yours!" I snapped. "You don't get to touch it anymore."

Her startled gasp resounded loudly in the deafening silence that had descended over the room. My stomach sank as every eye turned towards us in disbelief laced with horror. Normally, if a male could not be reasoned with, his mate—or in my case my mother—merely had to take hold of our 'leash' to end any discussion, and the male was expected to submit. Refusing her command indicated the type of rift that would be deemed grievous if not irreparable.

"Kraslo," Feidin said in a gentle tone, "if you don't mind, we will continue this later."

The chemist nodded graciously and cast a concerned look my way. I gave him an apologetic smile to which he responded with a nod meaning it was all right. That didn't erase his troubled look, reflected on every face as he went to take a seat on one of the benches near the dais.

"Krogal, approach," Feidin said in the same gentle tone while her mate's gaze flicked between my mother and me. "You had requested an audience. It seems that it is indeed needed."

"My son is mentally unwell and clearly unfit to speak right now," my mother interjected preemptively as she hurried to stand in front of me, blocking my path.

Our Matriarch's features hardened as she stared at her younger sister. "He doesn't look confused or delirious," she countered before looking at me behind my mother. "Come, Krogal."

Undeterred, my mother once more blocked my path when I tried to circle around her. "*I* am his mother! And I say he's not fit!"

"Must I remind you that *I* am your Matriarch?" Feidin retorted in an icy tone. "I say he is fit. You would do well to mind me, Talin. Now, Krogal, speak freely."

My hearts bled for my mother, but I steeled my resolve as I successfully circled around her this time and came to stand in front of the dais.

"I wish to emancipate from my mother's house and sever my blood ties with her," I said in a calm tone.

Loud gasps and shocked whispers resonated throughout the room. Even the ever-stoic Feidin and her mate appeared shocked by my declaration.

"You see?!" Mother exclaimed. "He has lost his mind!"

"Quiet, Talin!" Feidin said to my mother menacingly before turning back to me, her expression softening. "That is an extremely serious decision, Krogal. Maybe family mediation—"

"With all due respect, Matriarch," I said in a soft but firm tone, interrupting her, "we are past that. This decision was a long time coming, and now we're out of time."

"Out of time?" she echoed, her confusion reflected on many faces.

"Kayog has found my soulmate, and she will arrive here tomorrow."

"Oh, hell yes!" Belle exclaimed, making a few people laugh, and even drawing a small smile from me. "Congrats!"

I nodded in thanks, and my hearts filled with affection for her, while a few other people in the room also extended their congratulations.

"That's wonderful news, Krogal!" Feidin said, reclaiming my attention. "This should be a time for celebration and unification. Am I to understand that your mother withholds her consent?"

"No! I was ready to give him a proper bonding ceremony, but he refuses to fight a grummoll to prove himself worthy of her, like a coward!" Mother exclaimed.

"That's enough out of you!" Feidin shouted, jumping to her feet, her anger palpable. "You should be ashamed to speak in such a way about your own firstborn son. Anyone with a brain knows that Krogal is no coward. Frankly, I'm more disturbed that, as the woman who raised him, you would be shocked that he wouldn't want to observe this ritual. He is a veterinarian, and an excellent one at that. Everyone knew he would balk at slaughtering a beast as part of the bonding. How did you not?"

"It is our tradition!" Mother exclaimed as if it was self-evident. "So what if he's not fond of that practice? Surely, he can cast aside his preferences for one day?!"

She glanced around the room for support, and further blanched when she found none.

"Why should he?" Fcidin asked, sounding genuinely confused. "Is it not *his* wedding?"

"And these are *our* customs!" Mother countered. "Are we now going to live in a clan where everyone switches things up on a whim just because? It is our duty as females to ensure the protection of our ways and traditions."

Feidin nodded slowly. "You are correct in saying that traditions are important."

"But so are moral values and identity," I interjected. "While I never agreed with the bonding ritual, I've respected it and stood by my clanmates for each of their ceremonies. And today, I expect to receive the same respect. More importantly, my female survived serious trauma. She will require time and care to heal. Barbaric displays are the last thing she needs right now. No offense to anyone, but as much as I like to fight—and you know I can trample any of you with little effort—I will not take part in this ritual slaughter. Above all, I won't have my mate offered as a sacrifice when she is still this fragile."

"That is fair," Ugrul said, his approval resonating loudly in his voice. "As your house's protector, it is your duty to act in the best interest of your mate's welfare."

"If she's too weak to face our customs—" Mother said.

"Enough!" Feidin snapped, interrupting her sister again. "Are you so oblivious not to see that you are further alienating a son ready to sever his bond with you? Clearly, serious mediation is needed."

"No, Matriarch," I said in a respectful but firm tone that brooked no argument. "Like I said, we are past that. You've always been more of a mother to me than she has been. I have nothing but the utmost respect and admiration for you, and I acknowledge your good intentions. However, this is done. I will not have my mate subjected to Talinsaya's authority. I came here to request you sever the bond with my mother. Should it be refused, and although this is my home, I will chop my braid off and leave if I must."

"Krogal!" Feidin exclaimed in a shocked whisper, as many other gasps and disbelieving mutterings rose from the crowd. "You would become a pariah! You can't make yourself homeless, and especially not with your mate's imminent arrival!"

I shook my head. "I have already spoken with the Azamphir Clan Leader. Should it come to that, Tomu will welcome me, with or without my braid."

Feidin waved a dismissive hand, her displeasure visible on her beautiful face. "That's unnecessary. You are beloved among our people. You are of *this* clan and of *my* bloodline. Azamphir Clan can set their sights elsewhere. This is your home, and here you will stay. As your differences are clearly irreconcilable in the short term, I will grant you your wish. From this moment forth, I sever your bound to Talinsaya Skortheatis and take you into my home, as my son."

"Thank you, Matriarch," I said.

"You cannot do this!" Mother hissed. "You cannot take my firstborn from me! How can you humiliate me like this, your own sister, over his folly?"

Feidin shook her head, her disappointed expression reflecting the emotions coursing through me. "You silly female. Even now, you think of your pride instead of the pain you're inflicting on your son. I warned you this day would come if you didn't change your ways. Just be grateful he agrees to stay with us. I strongly suggest you take the next few weeks and months working on yourself and on earning back his affection before you permanently lose him."

I couldn't tell if sorrow or humiliation prompted the tears welling in my mother's eyes. Whatever the cause, it broke my hearts to see her storming out of the room. The gentle rustling sound of Feidin's long white skirt reclaimed my attention. I watched her gracefully walk down the few steps of the dais to come stand before me. I blinked to staunch the tears pricking my own eyes and swallowed past the lump in my throat.

Squaring my shoulders, I took a deep breath before extending my braid to my aunt. It felt odd, almost sacrilegious to see her take it and run her palm over it in a gentle caress. The compassion in her yellow eyes almost wrecked me.

"For what it's worth, Talin loves you in her own clumsy way," Feidin said in a soothing voice.

"I know," I said sincerely in a tired voice. "So do I."

Her face softened with approval. "Good. Then things can be mended in due time, as they should be. As painful as this has been for both of you, I believe it was needed to open her eyes. Trust that she will fight for you. It will be a long journey for her, but she *will* reclaim you."

"Thank you, Matriarch," I said, my voice thick with emotion.

"You're welcome, son," she replied affectionately. "Now, tell me what you need to properly receive your mate."

I smiled at my aunt, my hearts filling with love.

# CHAPTER 4
## FARAH

I took a couple of deep breaths, willing my heart to stop trying to beat its way out of my chest as I disembarked the fancy cruise ship Kayog and I had traveled in. As much as I loved the comfort my soon-to-be-husband provided for my journey to his homeworld, it also gave me a distressing sense of déjà vu.

Liam, too, had always been generous when it came to having me travel in first class and dressing me in nothing but the finest designer clothes.

We descended the ramp, my eyes flicking this way and that as I took in the immense docking bay. People chattered excitedly as they hurried to whatever business called them, while others loitered, casually waiting for who knew what. While a variety of off-worlders mingled freely with the locals, the Zamorians retained my attention.

They were an impressive species, especially their massive males, with four muscular arms and just as many eyes that seemed to see all the way down into the depths of your soul. Their females also didn't lack in the height department. And although slender and very feminine, they had the fit and muscular bodies of female athletes.

I hastened after Kayog as he made his way to the private meeting room Krogal had booked for us to finalize our contractual union. Unfortunately, the Temern was urgently needed elsewhere and couldn't stay very long. In truth, he had made many sacrifices to accompany me here, knowing how stressed I was at the thought of meeting my supposed soulmate by myself. No words could express my gratitude for the paternal way in which he quite literally took me under his wing. But then, as an empath, he knew how I felt.

To my chagrin, instead of us wandering through countless corridors to reach our destination—which would have given me a bit more time to compose myself—the series of meeting rooms were located right outside the main exit of the docking bay. It made sense so that people only here to finalize some quick business deals could be in and out in the time it took their ship to refuel and restock.

*And of course, ours is the third door.*

My mouth suddenly felt dry, and my pulse went into a frenzy when Kayog waved his feathery hand in front of the door's control panel, and it swished open before him. My knees felt wobbly as I forced myself to follow him inside.

I no sooner stepped in than my jaw dropped in shock. I'd read Krogal's description and seen his 3D hologram. In fact, I studied the latter over and over again as I tried to convince myself to proceed with this. But now that he was standing before me, I couldn't help but think this had been a mistake.

Saying he was tall and big couldn't even begin to describe the mountain of a man standing at the other end of the small room. Granted, his profile clearly stated he was eight feet tall. But how my mind had translated that versus the reality now towering before me couldn't have been farther from each other.

*How can he possibly be my soulmate?*

Like with most women, men taller and bigger than me held an undeniable appeal. But this was ridiculous. He might as well be the Hulk and me the Black Widow. Krogal was just too much. With his size—and undoubtedly matching strength—if he ever lost his shit and decided to go berserk on me, he could break me with a single flick of his hand.

For all that, he wasn't unattractive, quite the opposite. Although his four eyes made me a bit dizzy, his body was nicely proportional, his muscles impressively defined, and his features very pleasant.

*Why couldn't all of that be in a much smaller package?*

To my shock, the expression on his face couldn't have been more different than anything I expected. He looked… shy. The way he clasped his lower hands before him, and how his right primary hand ran over his long black braid screamed nervousness.

For some silly reason, that instantly dampened some of my unease.

"There you are!" he said in a surprisingly gentle voice for how deep and rumbly it was. "Come in! Come in! I hope you had a good trip?"

His hesitant smile had something incredibly endearing about it. But it was the wonder in his black eyes, and especially the way he kept averting them as if trying to keep himself from staring at me that made him even more adorable.

*Adorable? Did the word adorable seriously pop up in my mind regarding this behemoth?*

Yep, it certainly did.

"Yes, thank you," I surprised myself by answering. "The ship was fantastic, and the accommodations were first class. Thank you for that."

His broad shoulders slightly relaxed as a huge smile settled on his face. As intimidating as he was, it softened him even more. In that instant, I believed I was getting a glimpse of the teddy bear Kayog had alluded to multiple times.

*Maybe this won't be so bad, after all.*

"My dear friend, it is good to see you," Kayog said with his usual cheerful disposition. "Farah, this is your soulmate, Krogal. Krogal, meet Farah, the elusive gem I was determined to find for you."

"It's a tremendous honor to meet you at last, Farah," he said with such sincerity it almost felt like a warm blanket wrapping around me.

"It's a pleasure to meet you as well, Krogal," I said, relieved that my voice hid my own nervousness.

"Unfortunately, I'm in a hurry. As my next flight departs in less than thirty minutes, we must make haste."

"Of course," Krogal said. He waved at the chairs around the rectangular table big enough for eight people. "Please, have a seat."

I swallowed hard. The blossoming panic, which had somewhat receded upon seeing the Zamorian's apparent timidity, came back with a vengeance at the thought I would soon be left alone with him.

To my surprise, a serious but very gentle expression settled on Krogal's face while he watched me take a seat across the table from him and next to Kayog.

"Farah, I can see that the prospect of Kayog leaving you with me scares you," he said in a soft voice, as if speaking to a frightened child. "There's no need for that. On my honor, I will never harm you. Kayog is always right. If he brought you to me, it's because you and I are destined. Remember that there is no rush. This is merely a formality, a contractual wedding to grant you every protection enjoyed by the citizens of Xoccoris."

I nodded, a little mortified that my fear was so obvious. I should do a better job of controlling my emotions.

"Yes, Kayog detailed the terms you agreed to. I truly appreciate your patience and understanding," I said sheepishly.

"Of course. In practice, we'll simply be two people getting to know each other, and me trying really hard not to make a mess of courting you," he added with a bit of self-derision.

To my surprise, I caught myself chuckling and then returning the gently teasing smile he was addressing me.

"Have no fear. I have no expectations from you. As agreed, you will have your own room. I also made arrangements so that you can have your own apartment, if you prefer," he continued.

My jaw dropped upon hearing those words. His smile broadened with a hint of smugness at my reaction.

"It's my duty to see to your needs and to make you feel safe, whatever it takes. We're not ruled by the PMA," he reminded me. "There's no deadline for us, no pressure. I've waited my whole life to meet you. A few more weeks or months to reassure you are nothing at all."

Once again, I caught myself smiling as a bit more of the tension that plagued me for the past few weeks faded. The sincerity in his voice, and the way he was holding my gaze unwaveringly as he spoke truly did wonders for me.

I also did my homework prior to accepting this mating offer. From all accounts, few worlds could boast about treating their females with as much consideration as they did here on Xoccoris. It didn't hurt that their society was a matriarchy. Although their males had an iffy reputation on the intergalactic scene, mostly where competing was involved, things had significantly turned around over the past six years. This was in large part due to his very own cousin, Bayron Skortheatis, who also happened to have married a human thanks to Kayog.

As if prompted by that thought, the Temern discreetly cleared his throat.

"Right, sorry," I said sheepishly. "So what happens now? What must I do?"

"You simply have to sign this marital contract," Krogal said, while tapping a few instructions on the discreet interface at the edge of the table.

A seamless panel parted in the center of the table, and a narrow device jutted out of the opening. It appeared to have two rotating heads. One aimed straight upward, projecting a holographic screen, and the bottom one aimed at me. It took me half a second to realize it was a biometric scanner.

Although I remained still while the blue light scanned my eye, a sense of unease wormed its way back into the pit of my stomach. This was standard procedure to identify the parties. However, with Liam still out there, I tried as hard as possible to stay under the radar. At least, this data would be kept within the Zamorian Hall of Records and had little to no chance of landing in my ex's lap.

As soon as it was done, the scanner rotated towards Krogal and repeated the process. Interestingly, where it had only scanned my right eye, it scanned both of his right eyes. The holographic screen immediately displayed the marital contract with our information already filled in.

"This is the exact contract I previously forwarded to you and Kayog," Krogal explained. "Feel free to read through it to confirm all is as it should be. And when you're done, simply press your thumb in the signature box at the bottom right."

A part of me wanted to drag this on to delay a little further. But Kayog needed to leave, even though nothing on his face expressed his impatience to do so. I merely skimmed through a few paragraphs of the contract before signing it. I had no reason to doubt its content, and Kayog would have felt any deception for my new husband had he tampered with it.

Right after me, Krogal also pressed his thumb in his signature box on the mirrored holographic display. The screen took on an orange hue, indicating that the form was ready to be filed, at which point it would become binding.

"Farah Toussaint, do you wish to have this marriage contract to Krogal Skortheatis legally filed with the Zamorian Hall of Records?" a synthetic female voice asked.

"Yes, I do," I replied with surprising assurance.

She repeated the question to Krogal.

"Yes, I do," he replied, a thrill in his voice.

"You are now legally married in accordance with Zamorian law," the synthetic voice said. "The contract has been submitted and filed. Have a good day."

With these last words, the holographic screen collapsed, and both the scanner and projector retracted into the table, the secret panel once again closing seamlessly.

"Congratulations to the both of you," Kayog said warmly while standing up. "It is not the most romantic union, and I hate to leave you so abruptly. But seeing you together only confirms what I already knew. You truly are soulmates, and I have no doubt you will be extremely happy together."

"From the bottom of my hearts, thank you," Krogal said, also rising to his feet.

The powerful emotion on his face and in his voice messed with my head. This man was truly happy to be married to me, even though he didn't know me yet. I still didn't understand how this behemoth and I were a perfect match, but like he said, the Temern was always right.

"Yes, thank you for everything, Kayog," I said with sincere gratitude.

"It was my pleasure. Take good care of each other and stay in touch," he said warmly before taking his leave.

Standing next to my chair, I watched the door close behind him, apprehension and nervousness rearing their ugly heads again as I turned back to glance at Krogal. The soft, almost mesmerized way he was looking at me did funny things to me.

"Unless there's something else you need to do here on the space station, we should be on our way," Krogal said in a gentle tone. "The crew from your vessel should have already transferred your belongings to my shuttle. I understand you have few bags?"

I nodded, embarrassed by what little I actually possessed. It shamed me to be this helpless and to bring so little to this marriage. Liam made certain to keep me dependent on him for everything, specifically to make it difficult—if not impossible—for me to ever consider leaving.

"There are only a few bags, and I don't need to do anything else here. We can go," I said nervously.

"This way then," he replied, gesturing at the door before circling around the table to walk towards it.

To my surprise, he frowned when I waved my hand in front of the door's control panel and exited first. I immediately tensed, wondering how I had already messed up.

"What is it?" I asked warily. "Did I do something wrong?"

He smiled in a reassuring fashion although he slightly hesitated, as if choosing his words carefully. "Technically, you didn't do anything wrong."

"But?" I insisted.

"You will discover that our people have many little quirks about specific things," he explained. "One of them is how protective we are as a people. It's the duty of the strongest to look after the others in their group. Between the two of us, I'm physically stronger. Therefore, I should always lead the way to assess any potential danger to you."

My eyes widened in understanding. "So you should have exited the room first?"

"Correct. Inside the room, we know what threats may or may not exist. But once we exit, it becomes a new environment where much could have changed negatively while we were inside," he said in a gentle tone.

"I see. Sorry about that."

He chuckled and gestured for me to follow as he headed towards the shuttle hangar. "It's okay. You didn't know. For what it's worth, it can make for amusing—and sometimes ridiculous—situations."

"Oh? How so," I asked, genuinely intrigued.

"Most Zamorian males are major braggarts," Krogal said with derision. "Each one wants to one up the other and prove they're the most intimidating one."

I snorted, a clear visual flashing before my eyes. "Oh, God! They fight over who gets to go first?"

He nodded with a grin. "My people can be quite absurd at times. But just so you know, it also applies to females. So far, my cousin's human wife has had no issue with any of this as Zamorian females are naturally stronger than humans. Once the two of you go out together, I'm quite curious to see which one will deem herself the protector."

I gave him a horrified look, and instinctively shook my head in denial. "I'm more than happy to be deemed the weakest."

He burst out laughing, a mischievous glimmer sparkling in his obsidian eyes. "If you say so."

I liked the sound of his laughter. It was powerful and full-throated, with a deep, masculine edge that I found quite sexy. More importantly, I loved how relaxed and jovial it made him look.

We entered the shuttle hangar, which was adjacent to the docking bay. Here, too, countless people milled about, all of them Zamorian. Although a few of them stole discreetly curious glances my way, they kept going about their business.

"This is my Stinger," Krogal said, pointing at a sleek-looking personal shuttle.

All black, with a huge shield, it vaguely reminded me of an apostrophe lying horizontally. It only had two seats and space in the back for some small cargo. A single look sufficed to know it wasn't a cheap model. That once more reminded me that I was partnered with a wealthy man. I could only hope he wouldn't also try to keep me entirely dependent on him. I learned the hard way that it was a bad idea to be fully at someone else's mercy.

Despite the short steps that were deployed to allow me to

climb inside the small vessel, Krogal extended his primary hand to help me up. I took it on instinct. His massive fingers closed around my hand, swallowing it whole. With the slightest squeeze, he could easily squish it into a pulp. But the infinite care with which he held it instantly put me at ease. His palm was as rough and calloused as his touch was gentle.

Veterinarian though he was, his hands revealed they'd been well used, likely in combat and wielding deadly weapons. I peered at the back of the shuttle, both relieved to find my belongings there and mortified by their meager amount.

But as soon as the shuttle took off, all such petty thoughts vanished. The unencumbered view that the large windshield gave me of my new homeworld mesmerized me. Despite belonging to a highly advanced species, the Zamorians' planet could easily fool you into thinking it was still a developing world. It had extensive amounts of untamed wilderness, immense bodies of the clearest water, majestic mountains, and endless forests. The only marks of civilization were the gigantic compounds that served as a city for the different clans.

Krogal took the time to point out a few landmarks to me on our way home, some of which I recognized from having read or heard about them.

From my studies, while preparing for my arrival here, each clan had its own fortified city. And within that city, the various bloodlines possessed their own fortresses, which acted almost like a massive apartment complex with its own gathering hall where the multiple families of that bloodline each had their individual dwelling.

I had mixed feelings about that. Having so many relatives as your neighbors could be fairly invasive at times. But in the same token, it also guaranteed an amazing support system within reach.

As we began our descent towards the city, my eyes flicked this way and that, greedily taking in our surroundings. Beyond the fact that the entire place was drowning in an excess of brown, from the exposed dark wood and dark metal beams to the brown stones and bricks of the buildings, it was the architecture itself that kept me fascinated. I wouldn't quite call it industrial style, but everything had clean, sharp lines, and the streets were wide and perfectly perpendicular to each other, making it easy to know which direction you were headed. I'd visited my fair share of cities with circular or winding roads. When you thought you were heading south, you ended up realizing you'd been going east instead because it curved and swerved so many times.

For all that, plenty of greenery, gardens, parks, and fountains kept the place feeling warm and inviting rather than cold and sterile.

To my shock, instead of heading for a ship hangar, Krogal flew us directly towards a huge balcony on the upper levels of what appeared to be the main fortress within the compound. It shouldn't have surprised me. After all, Krogal was the nephew of this clan's Matriarch.

He skillfully set the shuttle down on the far-left corner of the terrace. The wimpy part of me rejoiced at not having to confront his clanmates and family just yet. But my paranoid half wondered if he was deliberately hiding me. I gave me no reason to think so. From the way he looked at me, Krogal seemed quite pleased with my appearance.

Him hurrying around the shuttle to help me down put an end to my ridiculous musings. The beak-like back of the shuttle opened up like the trunk of a car, giving us access to my bags. Before I could reach for one of them, Krogal grabbed them all, two in each of his primary hands, and one in his secondary ones. Looking at him, you'd think they weighed no more than a cloud.

"Okay, all those arms are seriously practical. You can color me impressed," I said sincerely.

He puffed out his chest, the slight coloring of his pointy elf ears betraying his embarrassment and pleasure at the compliment. That the males all had the sides of their heads shaved, only made his ears stand out more. He was truly adorable. I caught myself smiling, surprised by my sudden urge to give him a hug.

I'd always been the cuddling type. When Kayog described Krogal as being the same, it piqued my interest. Liam had been many things, but a snuggle bunny never featured on that list. He loved flaunting me like a trophy but never wanted to share those simple moments of tenderness that defined a true couple for me.

"It's extremely practical, especially when cooking or caring for pets," Krogal said enthusiastically, oblivious to my inner turmoil. "Some animals wiggle so much when you try to feed, bathe, or administer medicine to them that with only two hands it would be impossible."

"I can only imagine," I said with a chuckle.

As Krogal led the way inside the huge apartment through the floor to ceiling patio doors, I stole a few discreet glances at him. This man was crazy intimidating. But the thought of being cocooned in the gentle embrace of those massive arms of his had my stomach instantly fluttering.

*Yeah, I can see myself snuggling with him.*

Like with the city outside, browns and dark grays dominated inside the apartment. However, the off-white walls and immense windows all around kept the place from feeling gloomy or suffocating. In the upcoming weeks, I hoped he would allow me to add a touch of color here and there. Aside from that, I really loved the decor. It had just the right level of casual chic that screamed luxury, but that you could actually also indulge in. In the stuck-up circles Liam had evolved in, I'd far too often found myself sitting at the edge of a couch, not daring to get too comfortable or to touch anything because it looked like it belonged in a museum far more than inside someone's living room.

He gave me a quick tour as we headed for the room he reserved for me. The place was gigantic. It easily measured four or five thousand square feet. The living room possessed three distinct sections including the seating area with a giant vidscreen, a reading and music corner, and a play area perfect for board or card games while sipping on some fancy drinks from the mini bar right next to the extensible round table.

We walked past a huge office, which he claimed to very rarely use, and two guest rooms—which he hoped would one day be occupied by our children—before reaching my bedroom. There again, my jaw dropped. In major cities on Earth, that room alone would be deemed a fancy studio apartment.

Despite also featuring a dominance of brown, the colors were a lot softer. Like the living room, my bedroom possessed its own balcony, although significantly smaller than the one we landed on. Aside from the humongous bed, which barely used a fifth of the space, it had its own little seating area, a work desk, a break-fast table by the floor to ceiling windows looking out onto the terrace, a ridiculous walk-in closet large enough to serve as a coat check in a club, and its own hygiene room, complete with a standalone Roman shower and sunken jacuzzi tub that could accommodate three or four adults.

I turned back to gape at Krogal in disbelief after taking in the space. The nervous look on his face once more messed with my head. Did he truly think I could find anything to complain about regarding this room?

"This is amazing!" I whispered with awe.

My chest filled with warmth seeing the way his shoulders relaxed and the biggest smile settled on his face. He reminded me of a kid who just received the present he'd been dreaming of on Christmas.

"I'm glad you like it, Farah," he said, a smile in his voice. "If there's anything missing, or should you wish to make any changes—from the colors to the furniture—you only have to say the word."

"It's perfect," I reassured him.

He beamed at me and brought my bags inside the walk-in closet. When he came back out, he pointed at the mechanism I hadn't previously noticed on the door.

"This door is made of reinforced steel, is fireproof, and can only be locked from the inside. Do not hesitate to use it," he said in a gentle tone.

"Oh, I'm sure that won't be necessary," I said, my cheeks heating.

"It won't be," he concurred with confidence. "But it is there for you. Nothing matters more to me than you feeling safe. If you get the urge to use it, don't hesitate. It won't offend me. I cannot begin to imagine how stressful it must be for you to uproot yourself and come settle here on a foreign planet and with a complete stranger. Whatever you need to make things easier for you to adapt to your new home, just ask, and it will be yours."

"You're really sweet," I breathed out, my chest warming up some more for my behemoth.

He scrunched his face in that adorable way I was starting to believe expressed embarrassment for him, and he ran a hand over his braid.

"Thanks," he grumbled, the tips of his cute elven ears darkening again. "But try not to call me that in front of my clanmates."

I immediately burst out laughing. From all accounts, Zamorian males loved to boast about their virility, fierceness, and toughness. Being labeled sweet, cute, or any other fluffy title would definitely not sit well with them.

"Sorry," I said with mischief. "I promise to try not to do it."

He grinned with a happiness laced with what I could only interpret as pride and possessiveness. Not only did it not freak me out, it made me smile further. I didn't know how he was pulling it off, but Krogal was genuinely putting me at ease.

"Come on, let me quickly finish giving you the—"

I yelped in surprise when a chiming sound resonated through the apartment, interrupting him.

"It's okay, Farah," he said in a reassuring tone. "It must be our Matriarch. I expected her but thought we would have time to finish the tour. Come, all is well. She's here to make your status official among our clan."

Feeling stupid for being so jumpy, I followed him as he headed for a pair of large, ornate wooden doors on the left side of the living area. He opened them, revealing an antechamber to another set of heavy doors with a locking mechanism, identifying them as the front entrance.

Krogal opened the right door behind which stood a stunning Zamorian female who could have given Amazonian women a run for their money. At least 6'4, slender but with that firm and toned body of a triathlete, she had golden-yellow eyes, long midnight-blue hair loosely cascading down to her lower back, and a beautiful face that even the strangeness of her four eyes couldn't distract from. There was something noble and regal in the way she carried herself—fitting for the clan's Matriarch.

It baffled me that she came to us instead of us going to her in her throne room or whatever chamber she ruled from. It surprised me even more to see the warm way in which she greeted both Krogal and me. Despite having no reason for it, I expected her to have a snobbish or superior demeanor when addressing us.

"Matriarch, please come in," Krogal said in a voice that I could only qualify as affectionate. "And thank you for coming so promptly."

Then again, considering she was his aunt, it made sense.

"Don't mention it," she said in a friendly tone, although her eyes remained glued to me.

I smiled timidly and took a few steps back inside the living room to let her in, not like there wasn't plenty of space with both inner doors wide open.

"So this is your human soulmate," she said in a warm tone.

The sliver of approval in her eyes took me aback. Again, for an irrational reason, I expected his people to find me lacking or a disappointing choice for him.

"She is," Krogal said with a possessive pride that had my stomach fluttering. "Matriarch, please meet Farah Toussaint. Farah, please meet our Matriarch—and my beloved aunt—Feidinsaya Skortheatis."

"Hello, Matriarch," I said in a polite voice, laced with shyness. "It's an honor to meet you."

"I'm the one delighted to meet you, my dear," she said in an almost maternal fashion. "And you can simply call me Feidin. It looks like Kayog has once again outdone himself. Such a pretty and delicate little thing. You are stunning, child. Expect a lot of grumbling, my poor Krogal."

He burst out laughing even as he smugly squared his shoulders in response to the deluge of compliments the Matriarch was showering me with.

"Grumbling?" I echoed both with curiosity and to hide my embarrassment at so many kind words.

"Other males will want to challenge me for you," Krogal said with a slightly annoyed expression.

"Excuse me?!" I exclaimed, worried.

"It is common practice for our males to try to prove to a desirable female that he would make a better partner for her than whoever is currently courting her or engaged to her," Feidin explained.

"Try to prove it how?" I asked, baffled.

"By terrifying her, of course," she deadpanned.

"WHAT?!"

It was her turn to burst out laughing. Krogal gave her a playfully chastising look before turning back to me.

"My cousin's wife, Belle, was not amused when we challenged Bayron for her. She thought we wanted to kill her, which obviously couldn't have been farther from the truth," he said with a wistful smile. "Human women are quite small and fragile compared to our females. It stirs our protective instincts."

"It does," Feidin concurred. "Even I feel a strong urge to protect you, just like with Belle when my son brought her to me."

"I'm sorry but terrifying her seems to contradict that urge, no?" I countered, failing to see the logic in their approach.

Krogal gave me an indulgent smile. "Because here, the more terrifying a male is, the better a protector this makes him. But fear not, Belle sternly warned us against doing that to you."

"And Krogal promised major pain to anyone who traumatizes you that way," Feidin added with a mischievous glimmer in her golden eyes.

I made no effort to hide my relief. "Thanks for that," I told Krogal with genuine gratitude. "Fear and I don't mix too well."

"It is my pleasure and my duty to see to your welfare in all the ways that matter," he said, smugly.

Once again, he looked so cute I wanted to hug him.

"You've got yourself a wonderful male," Feidin said, her face suddenly taking on a serious expression. "I prayed to the gods that Krogal would find himself a good female. Too few can fully appreciate the greatness of his hearts, which are both gentle and fearless."

The powerful emotion that settled on Krogal's face turned me upside down. The love in his eyes as he gazed upon his Matriarch was akin to that of a son for his mother. With a certainty I couldn't explain, I felt at a visceral level that something much deeper had prompted this reaction. In time, I hoped to find out what it was.

She extended a hand towards him. To my surprise, Krogal took his braid and placed it in her open palm. She looked at him with that same motherly affection as she ran her hand over the length of his braid then slowly unplaited it. Once done, she combed her fingers through the shiny obsidian strands.

"Krogal Skortheatis, I did not give you birth, but as your aunt and Matriarch, I love you like the son of my own body. I took you into my house when you left yours. And today, I release you."

Feidin then turned to me. Just like she had done with him, she extended one of her free hands towards me. I hesitated, wondering if she was expecting me to also give her one or both of the long braids I had plaited my hair into. But before I could fully process these thoughts, I instinctively took her hand. To my utter relief, it appeared to be the right choice.

It was a good thing, too, because my own braids were nowhere near as long as Krogal's.

To my shock, she placed Krogal's now loose hair in my open hand. I instinctively took it, my mind vaguely registering how soft it felt against my skin.

"Farah Toussaint, I give you my nephew," Feidin said, releasing his hair. "From this day forth, no female but you shall touch his braid or have any claim over him. Plait it while repeating after me."

I gave her a stiff nod, licked my lips nervously, and proceeded to plait his long hair into a single braid. I couldn't look at Krogal. The powerful emotion on his face—mostly pure happiness—was messing with my head.

"Krogalsenyiek Skortheatis, I bind you to me, hearts, body, and soul," the Matriarch said.

I repeated her words, patting myself on the back for having practiced saying his full name before arriving here.

"I bind you as my protector and as the protector of our home and of any offspring we may be blessed with," Feidin continued, which I once more repeated. "I bind you as my life mate, as my best friend, and as my lover. For as long as you draw breath, you are mine. And for as long as I draw breath, I pledge to love and honor you, to nurture our bond, and to be your safe haven."

As I finished braiding his hair moments before repeating the last two sentences, I caught myself looking up at Krogal. Something no words could describe passed between us, and I drowned in the inky depths of his eyes.

I couldn't tell if seconds or minutes had ticked by, but Feidin's soft hand on my shoulder snapped me back to reality. For the briefest instant, I feared I had missed more words of the pledge I should have repeated. Thankfully, Feidin merely looked at both of us with sincere happiness.

"Take good care of each other," she said in a maternal fashion. "This is only half of the bond. The day you are ready to permanently bind your faith to ours, Farah, we will complete the bond with a proper wedding ceremony. For the time being, welcome to your new home. This clan, this entire city is your family now. Whatever you need, just ask."

"Thank you, Feidin," I said, my throat constricted with emotion.

"Yes, thank you," Krogal echoed.

She smiled, caressed Krogal's right cheek, and pressed an unexpected kiss on my forehead before turning on her heel and leaving our apartment. In that instant, whatever lingering doubts I had about listening to Kayog faded.

I was home.

# CHAPTER 5
## KROGAL

I felt almost like I was walking on a cloud as I finished giving the house tour to Farah. Since our departure from the space station, she had increasingly relaxed around me. Granted, it would take a while before she fully trusted me, but things were heading in the right direction. She declined moving into the separate apartment I offered her, if sharing my dwelling made her too uncomfortable. It further confirmed that she believed I wouldn't harm her. More importantly, it told me that she genuinely wanted to give our relationship a fair chance.

Even now, as I led her into the kitchen, a wave of love swelled in my hearts for our Matriarch. Feidin greeted her with the warmth I dreamt she'd receive from my birth mother. That welcome went a long way to making my mate feel even safer here. By the time Feidin finished binding our fates, something had visibly shifted in my Farah. Something magical had taken root, a silent communication that heralded the amazing future I didn't doubt awaited us.

"And this is the kitchen," I said proudly, waving at the spacious area.

Belle had told me how much an amazing kitchen was a big

selling point with humans, both males and females. As I enjoyed cooking, I invested quite a bit in setting it up. The large island had its own grill as I loved a huge, juicy steak. It also boasted every top-of-the-line appliance one could dream of, including two ovens, an eight-burner stove top, and a massive cooling unit, to name a few. The pantry itself was large enough to get lost in.

"Holy cow! This kitchen is a chef's paradise!" Farah exclaimed, her dark-brown eyes sparkling with wonder.

"It absolutely is!" I said proudly. "Are you hungry?"

She smiled at the hopefulness clearly audible in my voice.

"I'm not starving, but I wouldn't mind a bite."

"Perfect!" I exclaimed before waving at one of the tall stools in front of the island. "Have a seat. I will prepare a light local delicacy for you."

Farah complied. Her delighted expression hinted that she liked being taken care of—or at least so I hoped. I fully intended to excessively dote on her.

I took out the meat, vegetables, spices, and dry bread necessary for the recipe. I usually made fun of my male clanmates' propensity to show off. But this time, it was my turn to go all out flaunting my cooking skills to my woman. My cousin Bayron told me how impressed Belle was with his ability to multitask in the kitchen with his four hands. I wouldn't miss out on this opportunity to score a few points with my mate.

While my left hands washed the vegetables in the sink, my right ones tenderized the meat. The way her eyes widened, and her jaw dropped not only filled me with pride, but also had me making an even bigger show of it.

"Jeepers! You are insanely skilled!" she exclaimed with genuine awe.

"Thank you, my Farah," I said, my ears heating with pleasure instead of embarrassment. "I love cooking and hope you will enjoy my food. Zamorian cuisine is amazing, and I intend to make you sample all of it."

"I have no doubt I will," Farah said enthusiastically. "But I intend to return the favor. Haitian cuisine is also absolutely fantastic. You will be licking your plate once you've tried some of my recipes."

I froze halfway through peeling the equivalent of what humans would call onions. I couldn't say what expression sat on my face, but Farah's smile instantly faded, and she eyed me warily.

"What... what's wrong?"

"Females do not cook," I said cautiously. "It's at male's duty to provide sustenance for his mate and offspring."

"Oh," she said, her shoulders slouching.

She opened and closed her mouth a couple of times before giving me a stiff nod. My stomach immediately twisted. I didn't need to be a psychologist to recognize conflict avoidance. Farah wanted to argue but kept silent to prevent a confrontation or potentially upsetting me. This wouldn't do.

"My words upset you," I said in a gentle tone.

She gave me an overly bright smile and shook her head.

I bit back the urge to tell her not to lie. The last thing she needed was for me to use aggressive terms, even if spoken softly and without anger. Although we'd only met a few hours ago, I could already read her body language enough to see the tension creeping in her back, and that she was shrinking on herself, bracing for what I would say next.

I put down my utensils and leaned on my elbows on the top of the island to make myself smaller.

"Farah, marriage is an equal partnership," I said in a soothing voice. "If you don't like something I do or say, it's important that you call it out. Sadly, I do not have Kayog's amazing empathic abilities. The last thing I want to do is upset you. But on the hopefully extremely rare occasions I will, chances are I won't be aware of it unless you tell me. Once I know, we can discuss it and either resolve it or find a compromise we can both be happy with."

She smiled and nodded again. It was still contrived, and I could see her wheels spinning as she searched for a response she believed would placate me.

"Is it my cooking? Are you afraid I will over spice it and set your mouth on fire? Or that I'll undercook it and make you sick?" I asked teasingly to try and relax the atmosphere.

This time, her smile was a bit more genuine as she shook her head. "I'm Haitian. I can handle spices. Not so much under-cooked, though."

"So it's the fact that women don't cook on Xoccoris?" I asked in the same gentle fashion.

She licked her lips nervously then nodded while peering at me warily. "I actually like cooking, a lot," she replied timidly. "And this kitchen is so amazing, I would have a blast cooking up a storm here. But I understand if it's not allowed."

I frowned and shook my head. "It is not a law, but merely tradition," I corrected. "Our male's hunt and cook to feed their families. We take great pride in it. However, this is *our* marriage. We will run it according to *our* rules. If you enjoy cooking, then I will not deprive you of something that gives you joy. My duty is to bring you happiness, not take it away. Believe me, Farah, I understand all too well what it's like when people try to force you to fit into their mold, regardless of your own wishes and desires. I will never do that to you."

Seeing her relax a bit more with each of my words and the air of gratitude and hope that settled on her beautiful face made me melt from the inside out. My fingers twitched with a powerful urge to draw her into my embrace, hug her, and tell her that everything would be okay.

"Thank you," she said with that same shyness. "I promise not to break anything."

I waved a dismissive hand as I straightened from my leaning

position. "Don't worry about that. In fact, feel free to do so. It will give me an excuse to buy the latest upgraded versions of these appliances."

She burst out laughing. Kromor's teeth! My mate was beautiful. The way happiness lit up her entire face mesmerized me. I would do everything in my power to always keep her this joyous… and more.

"But I still get to provide the meat that we eat," I said with false severity as I wagged a warning finger at her.

Farah snorted. "I'm the biggest wimp. Hunting is definitely not my thing. That duty is all yours. I even get squeamish cleaning up anything that still has fur or scales on it," she said with an exaggerated shudder.

I grinned while resuming to prepare our meal. "Good, I will gladly take care of that part."

She beamed at me as I started spicing the food and heating the oil in the pan.

"You know, I don't mean to hog all the cooking," she said in a soft voice. "I'm more than happy for us to take turns. So long as I get to cook from time to time, then it's all good."

Shamelessly seizing on this opportunity, my mouth ran away with me. "Perfect! Then I will cook on the odd days of the week, and you cook on the even ones."

Not fooled in the least, Farah narrowed her eyes at me. "So you do four days, and I get the other three?"

"Yes," I said with an unrepentant expression as I dropped the meat in the pan.

Once again, she laughed while shaking her head at me as if I was a hopeless case—which I was in this instance.

"Fine. That's fair," she said graciously.

"See?" I asked in a gentle voice. "You and I can discuss anything and reach a compromise. Never fear to speak your mind, my mate. I know you had a difficult past, and I won't pressure you for details. When you're ready, you can open up to me about it. And if that day never comes, that's also okay."

"Thank you, Krogal. It really means a lot to me," she said, her voice filling with emotion as that same hopeful expression lit up her stunning features.

I winked at her and quickly finished preparing the meal, describing the different ingredients and spices I was using and how they compared to human produce. The smart questions she asked about them, from preparation techniques, cooking times, and preferred pairings, my Farah sounded like she was truly well-versed in the culinary arts. That made me quite curious to sample what she would prepare for us in the future.

"I especially cannot wait to make soup joumou for you," Farah said with a grin.

Despite my inner flinch, I plastered a neutral but politely inquisitive expression on my face. "A soup? How do you call it?"

"Soup joumou," she replied.

By the look on her face, I hadn't fooled her in the least in my efforts to hide my lack of enthusiasm. Soup was for teething younglings and sick people, not for seasoned warriors like me.

"It's a hearty, thick squash soup with lots of meat, vegetables, and noodles," Farah said proudly. "On top of being delicious, it's also of great importance to my people."

"Oh?" I asked, this time genuinely intrigued.

She nodded. "Centuries ago, back when humans clashed over ethnicity, my people were enslaved. During that time, they would prepare that soup for their masters, but were forbidden to eat it themselves. It was a delicacy 'too good' for slaves."

"Ouch," I said with a frown.

She smiled. "Ouch, indeed. Eventually, the slaves fought and regained their freedom on January 1, 1804. As part of the celebration, they all ate soup joumou. It has since become tradition, which endures all these centuries later, for Haitian people to eat soup joumou on the first of January to celebrate our Independence Day."

"That's wonderful! So you will make it for me on that day?"

"Yes, but you will also get to sample it before then," Farah said smugly. "We're not restricted to eating it just on that day. I just need to see if I can find all the ingredients locally or their equivalent."

"I'll make sure you do," I replied with a smile.

By the time I finished, the hungry look on her face made me both nervous and exhilarated at the thought of her eating my food.

I directed her to take a seat at the dining table in the kitchen. There was an adjoining formal dining room. But in these early days, I wanted us to get to know each other in a casual setting more conducive to a relaxed atmosphere. To my delight, she continued smiling at me excitedly as I brought the dishes and then settled at the head of the table next to her.

Too impatient for my own good, I started putting small portions of everything on her plate. Thankfully, she chuckled and seemed genuinely amused. It might have annoyed some people.

I held my breath as she went straight for a piece of meat. No sooner did it enter her mouth than her eyes widened. She stared at me with pure awe and began chewing with an air of wonder that had me tingling with pleasure. But the voluptuous moan that escaped her nearly undid me. I didn't want to have inappropriate thoughts about my mate right now, knowing there would be no naughty play anytime soon between us. And yet, that sound resonated straight in my groin.

"Oh, my God, Krogal! That's fantastic!" Farah said as she greedily stuck her fork in another piece of meat.

I just sat there with a stupid grin on my face, marveling at her while she wolfed down three more pieces. Noticing me staring, she slowed down and gave me an embarrassed look.

"Sorry, I didn't mean to stare," I mumbled before lowering my head to eat some of my own food.

She smiled and gave each of the sides a try before refocusing her attention on the meat. As a proud meat lover myself, it pleased me to no end to see that we had that in common.

"You know, if every meal you cook is this tasty, I may end up letting you have even more of my days to cook instead," Farrah said only half teasingly between two bites.

"I'm more than happy to take them," I said shamelessly, making her chuckle again.

By Khivolt! Who would have thought such simple interaction with my soulmate could bring me this much joy? How much better would things be between us once we knew each other better?

"Kayog said you were looking forward to pursuing some studies and getting a degree," I said casually.

Farah's eyes flicked towards me, the now familiar sliver of worry seeping into them. She swallowed her mouthful, wiped her mouth with a napkin, and slowly nodded.

"Yes. I was studying office administration while at the Khendis refuge," she said carefully.

"Is that the field you want to work in?" I asked in the same relaxed tone, pretending not to see her tension so that she could realize it was just a normal conversation.

She shifted in her chair and nervously licked her lips. For a split second, I believed she considered saying yes—which I didn't doubt would have been a lie. To my delight, a determined glimmer shone in her eyes moments before she shook her head.

"In truth, not really," Farah conceded. "There were very few curricular options at the shelter for someone with my limited background. It was also the fastest program that I could go through in the hopes of landing a decent job so that I could take care of myself."

"Well, here on Xoccoris, any field you're interested in is

available. And now, there is no deadline or time pressure. So you can pick whatever you like," I said gently. "The next semester won't start for another three months. This gives you plenty of time to look at the various programs and talk with counselors to see what will be best for you."

"That's awesome to hear," she said with a thrill in her voice. "But I only graduated high school before pursuing a music career. I will have a lot of prerequisites to catch up on before I can pursue certain programs."

The embarrassed way in which she spoke those last words clawed at my hearts. I hated that she seemed to think little of herself. The number of degrees one possessed did not define them or their worth.

"That's not a problem. Once you've assessed what you want to do and that you have the list of prerequisites, we'll just hire a private tutor to get you up to speed," I replied, matter-of-factly. "Like I said, you have all the time in the world to achieve your dreams."

"Oh, wow!" she said, seeming unsure whether she wanted to give in to happiness or to wariness. "That's extremely kind of you, but won't that be very expensive?"

I snorted. "Not at all. Education is very affordable on Xoccoris. And even if it wasn't, money is not an issue. I have too many credits collecting dust and feeling highly neglected."

She smiled at the overly dramatic way in which I spoke those last words. "That's great but…"

"But?" I insisted when her voice faded out.

"I don't want to take advantage or for you to think I'm some kind of gold digger," she replied sheepishly.

I huffed and waved a dismissive hand. "Farah, I've waited my whole life for a mate and offspring to spoil. Allowing me to take care of you and to provide for your needs is not being a gold digger. In truth, I can't promise to be able to rein myself in when it comes down to not spoiling you. If that prospect truly displeases you, I will *try* to keep it to a minimum. But don't be surprised if I fail."

She scrunched her face at me, seeming unsure how she wanted to respond to that, while also looking amused.

"For what it's worth, I know you won't try to take advantage," I added in a more serious tone.

She raised a stunned eyebrow and eyed me with curiosity. "How can you *know* that?"

"Because you're my soulmate," I said, as if it was self-evident. "That means you are perfect for me just the way you are."

Her face dissolved into a soft expression that warmed me to the bone. Fuck, I wanted her to always look at me like this.

Seeming a little shy, Farah averted her eyes and started fiddling with her food. "So, you're a veterinarian?"

I nodded, allowing her to shift the topic away from herself. "I love animals."

"Let me guess, the giant and terrifying beasts that make regular people pee themselves?" she asked teasingly.

I burst out laughing. "Sometimes. Even the feral ones deserve care. But I prefer the tiny, fragile, and helpless ones," I admitted, the usual old worry rearing its ugly head at the thought she might find it not virile enough.

"Really?" she asked with genuine curiosity devoid of any disdain or disappointment.

I nodded again. "Those are the creatures who need me the most. And truth be told, I like feeling needed."

She gave me a gentle smile. "Yeah, it is a great feeling. But do they even know what you do for them?"

"Absolutely!" I exclaimed. "Once you're all settled in—and only if you want—I will show you my clinic."

"I would love that!" Farah replied with genuine enthusiasm. "I love animals, too… Well, the cute and cuddly ones."

I chuckled, trying to picture her face if she ever ran into Ferach, Belle and Bayron's stone wolf.

"I understand your cousin married the other human who lives here?" she asked, as if she'd read my thoughts,

"Yes. You will absolutely love Belle," I said with conviction. "She'll help you adapt to your new home. She travels often with her husband, who is a professional hunter. But with their twins still so young, she's spending a lot more time here at home. She cannot wait to meet you."

"I cannot wait to meet her, as well," my mate said with a sheepish expression that took me aback. "I've heard of her and her art. But I mainly discovered her thanks to the awesome adorned braid trend that she started. In fact, I've freely reinterpreted some of the styles she did for her husband's braid to do my own hair."

"That's wonderful!" I exclaimed with genuine excitement. "You are aware that Zamorian wives are expected to adorn their husband's hair, right?"

She nodded, her eyes flicking towards my braid.

"I am. Before seeing the Matriarch earlier, I didn't realize there were strict restrictions as to who could touch your braid. It's kind of cool. But when am I supposed to start doing that for you?" she asked.

"Technically, as of today, since we are married," I said gently. "However, as you are an off-worlder, no one will balk if you want to take a few days to learn our ways before taking on that duty."

"Oh, as you can see, I'm used to braiding hair," Farah said, pointing at the quite beautiful way she had plaited her own with three large braids, and four smaller ones framing her pretty face. "I already have plenty of ideas. So as of tomorrow morning, I'm ready to roll."

Another silly grin settled on my face as I stared at my woman. "I am truly looking forward to it, my mate."

# CHAPTER 6
## FARAH

Later that day, excitement bubbled within me as we traipsed around the city. Krogal was a fantastic tour guide, showing me various landmarks, the best shops, his favorite cafes and restaurants—including dish recommendations—and the must-see hangout places. The warm sun and fantastic weather made it an all-the-more agreeable experience. It was the perfect blend of warmth, soft breeze, and total absence of humidity that made you want to stay outside forever.

Although bustling with activity, the streets didn't feel overwhelming or overcrowded. People were courteous and the vehicles driving down the streets showed proper restraint and deference to pedestrians.

"This is the museum," Krogal said as we walked past a massive building, with the same symmetrical and simplistic lines as everything else in this city. "An entire section is now dedicated to Belle. Many of her pieces feature my cousin in various combat situations, including the famous painting of him comforting the Atreall Queen after he rescued her from the monster trying to eat her. As you can imagine, that has Bayron showing off even more than before."

The false air of despair with which he spoke that last sentence made me laugh.

"Your cousin sounds like quite the braggart," I said teasingly.

He chuckled. "Bayron most certainly is, but it's warranted," he replied, his voice dripping with affection. "In truth, he's more of a brother to me than my own."

"You have many siblings?" I asked with genuine curiosity as we kept walking past the entrance of the museum, which stood next to one of the city's three art academies.

"I only have one younger brother," he replied, a sliver of tension creeping onto his handsome face. "Zamorian families rarely have more than two or three offspring. You'll meet my family soon enough."

"Hmm, it sounds like there are some tensions there," I said carefully.

He heaved a sigh. "That's sadly an accurate assessment. Do you remember when I told you that I understand what it feels like when people try to keep you from following your dreams?"

I nodded, struggling to admit this conversation was headed where I thought it was.

"I was referring to my parents, and especially my mother," Krogal said dejectedly. "She has very definite ideas as to the type of life and ambitions her sons should have. My brother Demar is more than happy to snugly fit in the mold she has set for him. Me, not so much."

My mind reeled at that revelation. "I don't get it. How are you lacking? What more could your parents possibly expect from you? You're a freaking veterinarian!"

"Exactly," he replied, bitterness oozing out of his voice. "According to my mother, it's not a virile enough career, especially for a male my size and with my strength."

"Fuck that!" I exclaimed, feeling outraged on his behalf. "I *love* that you're a vet. In fact, *that* made me want to further listen to what Kayog had to say when he first brought up a potential match between us. I was not in the mood for romance *at all*. But it takes a certain type of person with a very big heart—like first responders and firefighters—to take on this career. Someone who would devote his life to care for the helpless creatures without a voice to express their pain and distress could only be a good man. And you've got two hearts. That makes you extra devoted," I added teasingly.

My throat tightened seeing the powerful emotion settling over his face. In that instant, I realized how much his parents' disapproval had been eating him inside. Had he expected me to share their views? By the way he shifted his arms and rolled his shoulders, I strongly suspected he wanted to hug me. I almost did it for him, but a stupid shyness took me over. The fact that we were standing outside, with so many passersby casting discreet glances our way made me even more self-conscious.

Instead, I found myself grabbing his primary right hand. He slightly stiffened with surprise, his four eyes widening before filling with an air of pure adoration that had my stomach doing a series of backflips. Never in a million years would I have expected such a beast of a man to be so hungry for such simple displays of affection.

Something wonderful settled in my chest. While I never would have even considered dating a guy like him, getting a glimpse of the snuggly teddy bear behind that intimidating façade had me starting to believe he was indeed my perfect match.

I almost opened up about my own strained relationship with my mother. Sadly, she had passed away in the third year of my involvement with Liam. A hit and run had taken her away from me before we could patch things up—not that my ex would have ever allowed it. To think the very relationship she never condoned caused that rift... I should have listened to her, focused on my education, and not allowed myself to be lured by the glamour of being the girlfriend of a rich, handsome, and powerful guy.

There would be plenty of time for us to go over my less-than-brilliant past, riddled with stupid decisions. But today, it was all about discovering my new home and getting to know my new man.

*Correction, my forever man.*

Walking hand in hand, we entered the town square. The place was immense with various sitting spots with exotic flower beds and vegetation. Clusters of people hung out in the multiple open areas, one of which had many impressive women performing what I could only interpret as the Zamorian version of tai chi. It was even more mesmerizing watching the graceful movement of their four arms.

After one year of being single, it felt wonderful to get back in the saddle with someone so gentle and patient. I had dreaded what it would be like, constantly casting out any such considerations. But this romantic stroll, no pressure, no expectations, in this fantastic new world was exactly what I needed. I almost felt like a teenager on her first date when he led me to an ice cream stand on the east side of the square.

That fuzzy feeling quickly faded when I spotted a trio of young women—likely in their late teens or early twenties—standing near the stand and chatting away. The way they ogled Krogal with appreciative smiles instantly had my hackles up. I felt disrespected as they could clearly see we were a couple. By all accounts, they'd likely also heard about their Matriarch's nephew—and temporarily adopted son—finding himself a human mate.

I couldn't tell whether Krogal was ignoring them or simply oblivious, but his focus remained on me. Refusing to feed the trolls, I decided to do the same and ignore the obnoxious females. He walked up to the ice cream cart with a boyish grin.

"I'm going to get you a sampler bowl," he said with enthusiasm. "Topi makes the best frozen treats on all of Xoccoris. This will allow you to taste the most popular flavors. I'm curious to see which one will be your favorite."

"I'm eager and willing to try it all," I replied.

The merchant called Topi—an older male likely in his seventies or eighties—beamed proudly at me. I returned his grin then let my eyes flick greedily over the colorful crates filled with a variety of ice creams, some of them smooth, and others overflowing with goodies. I was a sucker for anything that had some kind of crunchiness and sweetness. Fruits and nuts, crushed chocolate bars, and other such mixes were always a huge success with me.

Topi filled an edible, waffle-looking bowl with nine different scoops, each one generous enough to be a portion in and of itself. He handed me a little spoon, the handle wrapped in paper. Only then did I realize that it, too, was edible. Krogal got one for himself as well and paid the vendor.

Just as I was about to bring the first spoon full to my lips, a frightened shout escaped me at the sound of a savage roar behind us. In my fright, I dropped the bowl. With dizzying speed for a male this big and muscular, Krogal caught it with his primary left hand and gently wrapped his secondary left arm around my waist in a protective fashion.

I jerked my head to the right to see what had scared the living daylights out of me. To my shock, a large male was roaring at the cutest brown-haired Zamorian female who had been apparently coming to get some ice cream as well. An older version of herself—who I presumed to be her mother—was standing by her side, giving the roaring male an assessing once-over.

To my dismay, the male just carried on shouting, slapping his chest and making threatening moves in front of the two females. My innards twisted, and I nearly felt nauseous at the thought he was going to strike them. On instinct, I pressed myself against

Krogal, even as my brain demanded that he should intervene and protect them. Although maybe only a few seconds had lapsed, it felt like an eternity had gone by before I finally caught on.

No one was intervening, most people even looking amused if not downright impressed. He wasn't actually threatening those females.

"Oh my God! Is he flirting?" I asked, horrified.

Krogal chuckled, his arm tightening around my waist while he handed me my sampler bowl back. "Yes, he is. And doing a rather impressive job of it for someone only seventeen."

"That's terrifying!" I said with a shudder.

"That's the whole point," he replied, sounding amused.

As much as it freaked me out, I remained glued there, observing the whole thing with morbid fascination. The poor girl looked genuinely scared. I wanted to go over there, hug her, and chastise her mother for allowing this to go on. But to my shock, the cutie brown-haired girl suddenly ran her fingers over her locks and cast an appreciative look his way. She then tapped something on her bracer.

With a victorious roar, the male slapped both his palms on his broad chest, and also tapped something on his bracer. Once done, he grinned at her then politely bowed his head at her mother. To my surprise, she gave him a slight nod, as if to grant him her blessing to woo her daughter. The women then continued on their way, not stopping at the ice cream cart as I first thought had been their destination.

Pushing out his chest and strutting like a peacock, her suitor left the square in a different direction under the cheers of the crowd and interested glances of the bitchy trio that had been ogling my man.

"What just happened?" I asked, bewildered.

"She likes him, and her mother approves. Therefore, she gave him her contact information," Krogal said with a chuckle.

"Wow! So all he had to do was to act like a rabid gorilla?"

He snorted. "Yes, pretty much."

"And that's what you guys did to Belle?" I exclaimed.

He laughed. "Yes, at least seven or eight of us back-to-back."

"And she didn't pass out?!"

"Not quite, but almost. Bayron was not amused," he said with a shit-eating grin. "But fear not. Like Feidin said, it won't happen to you. I've already warned everyone that I will crack their skulls if they frighten you like that."

"Thank God!" I said with genuine relief. "But I'm still baffled that this was all it took for him to win her over."

Krogal shook his head. "He didn't win her. She just gave him permission to court her. In her stead, I would beware if she's truly interested."

"Why do you say that?" I asked with curiosity.

"She didn't lay claim to him or agree to be his," he explained. "By the number of females impressed by his performance, one of them could make a move soon. To lay claim, the girl should have given him some sort of commitment token, like a band or a ribbon from her hair to put in his own. A male without any form of adornment in his hair indicates that he is single or available. The exception is if he has his mate's brand on his chest."

"Like your tattoo?" I asked.

He shook his head. "That's merely decorative. The day you and I formally bond, you will choose a symbol that represents you and permanently mark it on me. If you look around at the males without shirts, you will see all the married ones have a unique symbol over their left heart."

I glanced around us and indeed noticed all the men with adorned braids also had a symbol on their chests. A frown creased my forehead as I glanced back at my man. As I had not yet done anything for his hair, and he obviously was not bearing my mark, no wonder that little trio was looking at him the way they did.

"So those chicks think you're available?" I asked in a clipped tone while casting a less-than-subtle look in their direction.

Krogal followed my gaze before huffing. "Technically, yes, they could assume that."

Without thinking, I removed one of the golden rings from my right braid and clipped it around Krogal's, Just below his shoulder. It matched perfectly with the golden earring in his left ear. As soon as I finished, I turned back to glare at the white-haired chick that seemed to be the leader of the little trio. She scrunched her face at me then turned around with her little clique and walked away.

As good as that had felt, my stomach knotted at the thought Krogal might not approve of that course of action. I cast a nervous glance his way only to find him beaming at me. He pulled his braid in front of his chest as if to make it even more obvious to everyone he was officially claimed.

That had my stomach doing a couple of very pleasant backflips. His arm still possessively wrapped around my waist, Krogal led me across the massive plaza as we both devoured our respective sampler bowls and casually chatted. He showed me the parts of the square where street performers and occasional events entertained the crowds. It eventually took us to the equivalent of their downtown area. I finished eating my ice cream—my stomach feeling on the verge of bursting—just as we were walking past a series of shops and cafes.

A few moments later, we entered what I believed to be a bank. He took us straight to some sort of automated banking machine. I meant to step away to grant him some privacy, but he held my hand before leaning forward to get both of his right eyes scanned by the biometric scanner. He tapped a few instructions on the interface then tugged on my hand to make me stand in front of the machine.

Although I instinctively complied, I glanced at him questioningly. "What are you doing?"

"Setting up your bank access," he replied, matter-of-factly.

"Oh!" I said, unsure how I felt about it.

This reminded me of far too many bad memories of how Liam had taken control of my finances, making certain he could oversee all the ways in which I spent money. That also allowed him to block access to my funds the day I ran.

After the device finished scanning my right eye, Krogal tapped a few more instructions. Then an A.I. voice resonated, startling me.

"Please confirm full account ownership transfer from Krogalsenyiek Skortheatis to Farah Toussaint," the voice said.

"I confirm," Krogal replied firmly, before getting his right eyes scanned again.

"Ownership transfer complete," the A.I. said.

My brain froze as I tried to process what I just heard.

Krogal turned to look at me with a gentle expression. "This is now your bank account. Press your thumb here to enable your signature."

Heart pounding, I once again complied.

"Signature for Farah Toussaint enabled," the A.I. said.

Seconds later, the screen displayed the account information. My jaw dropped, and my knees wobbled when I stared at the balance of fifty thousand credits. I jerked my head towards Krogal and gaped at him in disbelief.

"This is your account alone, my Farah," he said in a soft voice. "I no longer have access to it or any control over it. I cannot check its balance or how you spend the funds. It is yours, and only yours."

My lips quivered, and tears pricked my eyes. Less than two weeks ago, I was on the verge of getting evicted from the shelter with no hope and nowhere to go. And now, all this—beyond any dream I could have hoped for—was sweeping me away.

"Every month, I will deposit an additional allowance for you until you finish whatever studies you settle on and find a job with a salary that will match or exceed that allowance," he continued before taking on a sheepish expression. "In truth, I'll likely continue regardless of whatever wages you end up earning."

"That's too much!" I whispered, still too shocked to fully process what was happening.

"No, Farah, it is not," he said firmly but gently. "It's just enough so that you will never feel stranded or trapped. I want you to stay here with me because that is your desire, not because you feel like you have no other choice."

"I don't know what I did to deserve you, but I thank God that Kayog led me to you," I said in a shaky voice before throwing myself into his arms.

He returned my embrace with a gentleness that wrecked me inside. By giving me the means and option to leave if I wished, Krogal confirmed there was nowhere else I would rather be. We may not be in love with each other just yet, and it would probably take a while for us to get there, but I didn't doubt we would.

I was home, and he was my soulmate.

# CHAPTER 7
## KROGAL

In my thirty-five years of existence, I'd never felt so restless, impatient, and frantic. Every fiber of my being thrummed with excitement at the thought of the living, breathing perfection who slept in my guest room.

Farah exceeded my wildest dreams. Beyond the fact that she was breathtakingly gorgeous, funny, and of delightful company, she was proving more open to this relationship than I dared hope for. Considering her past, I'd braced for a very steep hill to climb to get her to relax around me. Granted, she hadn't endured any physical abuse, but the fallout of mental violence was insidious and could be even more damaging as it was harder to detect and treat than an obvious bruise.

I didn't know the details of my mate's ordeal, only what little information was available from the public records surrounding her case. Although her domestic abuse claims against Liam Manning had been dismissed for lack of evidence, a judge had granted her restraining order request. With her escaping more than a year ago, I could only assume she benefitted from a certain amount of therapy, which helped her heal, if only in part.

Soon, I hoped, she'd feel comfortable enough to open up to me about it. But I wouldn't pressure her.

Either way, seeing my Farah so open to getting to know me better had me over the moon. My fingers twitched from the lingering wondrous feel of her delicate hand in mine. Kromor's teeth, my head still spun thinking of how she had publicly claimed me! I considered myself a rather confident male, but yesterday made me realize just how badly I longed to be wanted, wholly and proudly, just as I was.

I strained my ear again, trying to catch any sound of my woman stirring. After a long battle to stay awake as late as possible, Farah had finally given up at 8:30 PM. The significant time zone difference had gotten the best of her. She hoped that by going to bed closer to a normal hour here, she would adjust faster to local time.

And here I was pacing around, dying to see her pretty face again and to hear her voice. I'd already prepared everything for a generous breakfast. Despite her slender figure, my woman seemed to have a very healthy appetite, which I intended to keep satisfied at every opportunity.

My hearts leapt in my chest when the long-awaited sound of my Farah waking up finally reached me, muffled though it was. The silly grin that stretched my lips made me feel stupid. And yet, there was no wiping it off. I immediately burst into action, preparing a variety of traditional Zamorian breakfast dishes, from sweet to savory, including fresh fruits, yogurts, and cereals in case she preferred something lighter to start off the day.

I paced myself so that everything would be freshly off the stove by the time she finished showering and dressing. After what felt like an eternity, she came out of her room. My brain went blank, and I nearly swallowed my tongue upon seeing her ethereal beauty.

Once again, Farah had plaited her hair, but this time in two long braids on each side of her head. Golden rings of various sizes adorned their length. At the center of her head, right above her forehead where she split her hair in two halves, she placed a lovely golden clip with some kind of symbol I could not identify embossed on it. She wore a sleeveless black dress with some embroidered golden patterns that matched the decorations in her hair. The short skirt hid nothing of her endless, perfectly sculpted legs. Her adorable toes with painted nails peeked at the front of delicate open sandals with medium heels.

"Good morning, my mate," I breathed out, stunned that I managed to speak any word. "You look breathtaking."

She smiled and demurely lowered her eyes, looking both flattered and shy. By Khivolt, she was unbearably adorable. Everything in me ached to just squish her in a big hug.

"You don't look too shabby yourself," she said as she approached the island where I was starting to plate our food.

I snorted with derision as I glanced down at myself before peering back up at her. "I'm bare-chest with black pants," I replied teasingly. "That hardly qualifies as high fashion."

"No one talked about fashion. I was merely stating how much I appreciated the view," she replied in a similar tone.

My jaw dropped, and she chuckled with a mix of amusement and embarrassment, apparently not having expected herself to speak so boldly. Zamorian males often traipsed around bare-chested. While we had shirts, and occasionally wore them, topless was usually more comfortable with our four arms. Knowing that my woman liked what she saw had my stomach fluttering some more.

"I'm glad you approved then," I said with yet another silly grin.

Kromor's teeth, at this rate, she would think me the village idiot if I kept displaying these kinds of stupid expressions every time something she did or said made me happy.

"I do," she said, her air of timidity creeping back in. "Sorry for sleeping in. But waking up to this wonderful aroma is definitely something I could get used to."

I puffed out my chest as she greedily looked at the food I had prepared. "No need to apologize. I'm glad you were able to get some rest after the long journey here. I hope your bed was comfortable."

"Are you kidding? That bed is freaking amazing! It truly felt like sleeping on a cloud. If not for my stomach clamoring for food, I probably could have slept for a few more days, it was so comfy."

I chuckled and gestured at all the food on the counter before me. "I'm glad to hear it, on both fronts! While I can eat an obscene amount of food, I'm glad you will help me polish this off."

"If it tastes even a tenth as good as it smells, you'll be lucky if I leave any for you," Farah replied teasingly.

She helped me bring the plates to the table, and we settled down to eat. Once again, watching my woman heartily devour the meal I prepared for her filled me with more joy than I could ever put into words. My throat tightened with emotion as I realized this was indeed the beginning of the rest of our lives. And I intended to make each day even better than the previous one.

"I reduced my hours this week at the clinic so that I can be available for you as you settle in and familiarize yourself with your new home," I said after washing down my last mouthful with a sip of tea. "Unfortunately, I have to go to the clinic this morning for an important surgery."

"Oh, that's entirely fine. There'll be plenty of time later for you to show me around," Farah said with understanding.

"It's not for another two hours," I told her reassuringly. "That will give me the time to show you around the clinic. And then Belle will take you shopping for everything you need. I have a tab in most of those stores. So just have your purchases added to my account."

Farah recoiled upon hearing those words and frowned at me. "Why would I charge it to your account? You gave me tons of credits!"

I nodded. "You're correct. However, those credits are for you to use on yourself for personal stuff. Like if you want to go to a cafe, a spa, purchase gifts, or anything else of that nature. It is *my* duty to provide for all your necessities. That includes groceries, clothes, furniture, and anything else of the sort."

"But... shouldn't I also provide for the household?" she asked.

I gave her a mischievous smile. "Belle says my house is drab and boring. It needs a little bit of spice and color. If you spend your own credits buying decorations for it, I won't be able to return them because I think it's too colorful."

She scrunched her face at me. "If that's a dare, you know I will go all out buying decorations, right?"

"This is your new home, my mate. Do with it as you please," I replied tauntingly. "But just so you know, most stores are automatically set to debit the husband's account, as it is standard here. Be prepared to explain to the merchants why you deem me unworthy to provide for our household."

She gasped. "Oh, my God! I never said that!"

"You didn't, but that's what they'll assume," I deadpanned.

Farah glared at me, not fooled in the least by my overly innocent expression. "I can't believe you're 'bully spoiling' me," she grumbled.

I burst out laughing. "I am what?"

"You're forcefully spoiling me! That's bullying!" she said before taking another mouthful of food and chewing with pretend anger.

"I wish I could be sorry about that, but I'm not," I replied with an unrepentant grin. "In fact, I'm only getting warmed up."

She shook her head at me as if I was a hopeless case then put down her utensils on her now empty plate with a satisfied sigh.

"I can't even be mad at you because you're such an amazing cook," she said, making me feel all warm and fuzzy inside.

"I'm glad you enjoyed it. Ready to go?" I asked while taking the empty dishes to the sink.

"No, not yet," Farah replied, sounding surprised as she brought a few empty plates for me. "What about your hair?"

I froze, an impossible hope blossoming in my hearts. "My hair?" I echoed.

"Yes," she replied as if I should know exactly what she meant. "Am I not supposed to adorn it for you?"

That stupid grin came back on my face with a vengeance. "You want to?"

"Of course! And last night, I said I would," she replied in a self-evident manner.

"Great! Let me load this up in the dishwasher, and then I'm all yours," I said with a thrill in my voice.

Judging by her expression and the way she giggled, I had to look extremely silly right now. But I couldn't have cared less. My mate was going to adorn my hair!

"Perfect. Let me go get my things," she said.

The excitement in her own voice did the most wondrous thing to me. My Farah wasn't just doing it out of duty, but because she wanted to. I made quick work of rinsing the dishes and stuffing them into the machine before turning back to my woman who had returned with a medium-sized wooden box.

"Where do you want me?" I asked, feeling beyond restless.

She pursed her lips, her beautiful dark-brown eyes flicking between the stools by the island and the chairs by the table.

"Seeing how impossibly tall you are, a chair would be best."

I nodded and immediately complied. My breath caught in my throat when her dainty fingers gently brushed against my naked back when she grabbed my braid. It felt incredibly odd having someone else touch my braid. But it didn't trigger the more submissive behavior expected when my mother would touch it, or the uneasy feeling and semi sense of betrayal it stirred in me when Feidin did so after taking me into her house. This felt right. An incredible sense of peace and of belonging washed over me. It was as intimate a touch as exchanging sensual caresses with our beloved.

"Wow, your hair is really soft," Farah said behind me in a voice filled with awe as she started unbraiding it.

"Thank you, my mate," I said, my voice involuntarily dipping down an octave.

By Khivolt, I could see myself quickly getting addicted to having her playing with my hair. She finished that first task too quickly. I almost whimpered when she let go of it for a brief second. Moments after, the teeth of a comb gently scraped my scalp from the top of my head in a downward movement as Farah detangled my hair.

The loud and powerful purr that tumbled out of my throat and vibrated through my chest startled even me. My mate froze for a split second before bursting out laughing. I couldn't decide if I felt more mortified for making such a spectacle of myself, or more eager for her to do that again. As if she'd heard my silent plea, Farah resumed combing through the long strands, making sure to scrape my scalp with each stroke.

At that point, I didn't even try to rein in the sounds emanating from me. Eyes closed, I almost felt drunk with bliss and the most delightful sense of well-being. Behind me, my female sounded on the verge of choking with laughter.

"Good God, someone sure loves getting their head scratched," she said between two chuckles.

Too busy purring, I merely responded with a grunt. Putting the comb down, my mate sank her fingers through my hair at the top of my head and started massaging both my crown and the clean-shaven sides. This time, I all but went feral.

"Oh, my God! What's happening to you? Are you going to shapeshift into a wild beast?" she asked, still laughing.

I shook my head and replied with another grunt.

"You are so insanely cute! Now I know your weakness. Expect me to shamelessly exploit it in the future," she warned teasingly.

If I weren't so busy flying high, I would have told her to go right ahead and exploit all she liked. For all I cared, she could ask me for the moon in exchange for a head scratch, and I'd fly right up there, pluck it out from the stars, and hand it over to her.

Although she spent a good amount of time scratching and massaging my scalp, it felt way too soon when she finally started plaiting my hair. From time to time, she would pause and rummage in the box she had placed on the table. Curiosity burned in my gut.

A few times too many, I involuntarily caught myself trying to turn my head to get a glimpse. She would systematically turn my head back to the front and sternly tell me to stay put. I tried to comply, but I was just too impatient. Not for the first time since she began taking care of my hair, I berated myself for not encouraging her to do it somewhere with a mirror so that I wouldn't be left in the dark.

On the seventh or eighth time, she flicked the pointy tip of my left ear.

"Ow!" I exclaimed with an exaggerated air of outrage.

It hadn't hurt, but I was in complete bratty kid mode.

"Stop moving your head!" Farah said sternly. "Next time you make me repeat I'll bite your ear off."

"But I want to see!" I said in an overly whiny tone that made her laugh.

Kromor's teeth, how I loved the way she laughed.

"You'll see when it's done. If you didn't fidget so much, I'd be done by now."

"Fine," I grumbled. "And you call *me* the bully."

She snorted. "You big baby! Just hold a couple more seconds, I'm almost done."

I grunted in a pouty way. While I was truly pouting a little, I was mostly playing to amuse her. I loved her playfulness, which seemed to match my own.

"There!" she said as she ran her palm over my braid. "All done!"

Before I could reach for it, Farah circled around the chair while still holding my braid. She brought it over my shoulder so that I could admire her work. Despite the smug expression on her face, I didn't miss the sliver of tension and apprehension that she felt at how I would respond to her work.

My eyes widened, and a maelstrom of emotions engulfed me as I looked at the elegant but simple design. Just like she did with her own braids, Farah clasped evenly spaced-out golden rings in mine. The width of each band gradually narrowed the lower its position along the length of my braid. The color perfectly matched not only the golden hoop of my earring, but also the adornments in her hair. A single thin golden wire woven into the pattern of the braid gave it a magical edge.

"My mate!" I whispered with awe. "This is beautiful, and it matches yours!"

She puffed out her chest and beamed at me proudly, all tension evaporating from her. "Yes! I figured it would be nice if we coordinated."

"Great choice! I absolutely love it!" I said in all sincerity.

With a will of their own, my primary hands reached for her. I barely caught myself, stopping before I pulled her into an embrace she had not consented to. By the look on her face, she realized what I had almost done. To my utter relief, I didn't perceive any fear or outrage from her. However, I also couldn't tell whether she would have welcomed it. Her expression was too unreadable.

I rose to my feet, and she took a couple of steps back to make room for me. But she did not move away. Was that her way of telling me it would be fine for me to hug her?

*She let me hold her hand yesterday.*

Did I dare push my luck? Would my eagerness bear fruit or damage the progress we had done so far? When she continued to stare at me with an expectant expression, I decided to go for it. The worst thing that could happen is that she would turn me down. But at least, it would also let her know that I wouldn't initiate physical contact with her without making sure it was consensual.

I cleared my throat. "Would it be acceptable for me to hug you as a thank you?" I asked, annoyed by the nervousness in my voice.

Her unreadable expression shifted into the most adorable timidity. She gave me a small smile and nodded. My hearts leapt in my chest, and my fingers twitched with impatience as I returned her smile. Moving slowly, I carefully placed my primary hands on her hips and gently drew her to me, giving her every opportunity to pull away had she changed her mind.

Thankfully, my mate came willingly into my embrace. I nearly died with bliss when her fragile and delicate body aligned perfectly against mine. She pressed her cheek to my chest and wrapped her slender arms around me. I closed both of my sets of arms around her, cocooning all of her, while making sure not to smother her.

Khivolt take me! I never wanted to let go.

She felt so good, so warm, so perfect right there. This woman was truly made for me. Naturally, that stupid inner part of me had to break the magic of the moment with a growling purr of content. Farah chuckled. To my delight, she didn't pull away, but appeared to tighten her hold around me instead. Obviously, I reciprocated and rested my cheek on top of her head.

I couldn't say how long we remained like that. It could have been seconds or minutes. Either way, it was nowhere near enough. But as I didn't want to abuse this first permission to hug her, I prepared myself to let go. Just as I was about to do it, Farah emitted the most piteous and hilarious wannabe beastly growls I ever heard.

Throwing my head back, I burst out laughing. She lifted her head to peer at me with a mischievous glimmer in her beautiful dark-brown eyes and a broad grin.

"I do not sound like that when I purr," I growled in a falsely outraged tone.

"You totally do! You sound like a grummoll!" she teased before emitting that hilariously high-pitched, failed attempt at a vicious growl.

I laughed some more while playfully glaring at her. "I do not, you evil woman. I sound like a cute pup."

She shook her head vigorously. "More like a rabid dragon."

"I'll take dragon, but not rabid," I countered in a stubborn tone. "I'm cuddly."

Farah snorted. "Okay, fine. I'll grant you cuddly dragon," she said as if making a huge concession.

We both chuckled, eyes locked, and our arms still wrapped around each other. I gave her one last gentle squeeze then released her with much reluctance.

"Come, my mate. I have a tour to give you and a braid to flaunt," I said smugly.

She laughed and cast a proud and possessive look over my braid. No word could express how wonderful that made me feel. To my great chagrin, I led her to our personal shuttle on the main terrace. Her slight frown didn't go unnoticed when I helped her inside the vessel.

"I want nothing more than to strut outside with you," I explained after I settled in the pilot's seat. "I had not expected to be blessed with my hair getting braided. If we walk to the clinic,

I will be late for the surgery and won't have time to show you around before Belle arrives."

"Right, that makes sense," she said with a smile.

"But fear not, my mate," I said enthusiastically as I took flight. "I will be doing plenty of flaunting at the assembly later tonight."

# CHAPTER 8
## FARAH

K rogal landed our shuttle on the roof of the medical center of the fortified city in a reserved parking spot. Chivalrous as always, he rushed to my side of the small vessel to help me down the couple of steps. Obviously, I didn't need it. Still, his attentiveness to me truly warmed my heart. Then again, I believed he was seizing any opportunity to touch me without coming across as a creeper or pushing my boundaries.

It was becoming increasingly clear to me that my brand-new husband loved physical contact. I couldn't forget how his face lit up when I took his hand yesterday. None of the other Zamorians we encountered during our stroll displayed any form of affection in public, aside from the occasional wife touching or caressing her husband's braid. But Krogal seemed to crave it. And frankly, so did I.

Nowadays, people too quickly ended up in each other's beds, often on the very first night they met. Going through this old-fashioned and slow-paced courtship with Krogal was every shade of awesome. He was making me feel safe and respected. That he gave the best hugs in the universe certainly didn't hurt.

Even now, I couldn't stop thinking about how it felt being

surrounded by those massive arms of his. I could have stayed there forever. He was so big and strong that I felt tiny and fragile, and yet completely sheltered and protected, like a nuclear bomb could go off right next to us and I'd remain unscathed.

And he smelled so freaking good!

I wanted to rub my face all over his muscular chest. The softness of his skin, stretched over his firm and bulging muscles, had taken me by surprise. I had to invoke every ounce of my willpower not to run my palms all over his back. I didn't want to rush things between us or send him any misleading signals. But damn, my man was fine!

Noticing the uncertain glance he cast towards my hand, I reached out for his and held it. He immediately beamed at me, happy I guessed his unspoken wish.

Yep, my man was a snuggle bunny!

We took the lift down to the basement of the facility. The wide doors opened directly in front of the clinic's reception. A jovial Zamorian female in her early fifties greeted us with a warm smile that lit up her four light-brown eyes. Despite her blatant curiosity as she ogled me, I felt nothing but kindness emanating from her. Her friendly smile was intoxicating, and I immediately liked her.

"Dhalgal, this is my mate, Farah," Krogal said proudly as he introduced me to her. "Farah, this is Dhalgal, the queen and taskmaster of this clinic. She has us all terrified and has no qualms cracking her whip whenever we stray from the right path."

Dhalgal snorted and waved a dismissive hand. "Don't listen to him. I'm the sweetest person you'll ever meet. But I do have to crack my whip with this one," she added, designating Krogal with her chin while taking on an air of pure discouragement. "Bring in a cute little critter, and he will spend a ridiculous amount of time caring for it and neglecting his other duties. I have to kick him out sometimes or he would forget to eat or go home to sleep. He's a hopeless one!"

"Sounds like a dedicated one," I countered while casting an approving glance at Krogal.

"See?! She gets me!" Krogal replied smugly to his receptionist.

"I do, but she also has a point. You have to take care of yourself as well. And I'll help her make sure you do," I warned.

"Ha!" Dhalgal said mockingly at Krogal.

He scrunched his face at me as if I had committed the ultimate betrayal. But Dhalgal's next comment had him puffing out his chest again like a peacock.

"That is one magnificent braid you're boasting, Krogal!" she exclaimed. "I've never seen such a design before. Your cousin is going to be green with envy!"

"Him and everyone else!" he replied with a huge grin. "My mate is the best."

I felt both flattered and a little embarrassed. A mix of relief and worry swelled within me. Obviously, I hoped my design would be well-received. But I wasn't here to compete with anyone, especially not Belle who had become the queen of adorned braids throughout the galaxy. I just wanted to make sure my man would always be happy with what I did for him without feeling insane pressure to constantly try to outdo myself every day.

But there would be plenty of time to cross that bridge later.

After exchanging a few more pleasantries, Dhalgal shooed us off, reminding Krogal he had less than thirty minutes left to give me a quick tour before he had to go prep for surgery. Still holding my hand, he led me down the corridor on the left which gave access to a series of rooms.

The first one was his office complete with a massive couch that could be turned into a sofa bed for the occasions where he decided to sleep over to be close to a patient in critical condition.

The others included the staff's recreation room, a small board-room, three separate examination rooms, an operation theater, a massive storage room, and one holding area where they could keep a few pets overnight.

Like with everything else on Xoccoris, brown colors dominated. Here at least, most of the walls were the palest shade of beige, with the only dark browns stemming from the hardwood floors and exposed wooden beams. Photos of exotic pets on the walls with a short text below with clever tips and tricks regarding their care gave the place the splash of color it needed to make it inviting instead of drab and clinical.

But seeing a live version of a couple of those same animals in the holding area had me bubbling with excitement. About the size of an eight- or nine-month-old cat, the creature had the body of a squirrel, the face of a guinea pig with the chubby cheeks of a newborn baby, and a massive pair of wings that extended from behind its ears and down the length of its body. Tan fur with the occasional black spots covered its body, while the fluffiest, snowy-white fur puffed out around its chest and the upper part of its underbelly like a Maine Coon.

It peered at me with the most adorable big blue eyes and with undisguised curiosity.

"Oh, my God! He's the cutest thing ever!" I exclaimed while approaching the large cage it was held in.

"It's a she," Krogal corrected gently while opening the door of its cage. "Her name is Joree. She's a Nulia."

"Hi Joree," I said in that silly, high-pitched voice we instinctively took whenever addressing animals or young kids. "May I touch her?"

"You can pet her head and scratch her neck, but be gentle," he said, caressing her head first as if to show me how to do it.

The way Joree stretched her neck to increase contact with his hand screamed how much she craved being petted. My heart instantly melted when she welcomed my touch with the same eagerness. The loud purr steadily flowing out of her could have easily belonged to a cat. In between, she emitted brief, high-pitched little yips with the sharpness of a bark, but which struck me more as a pained or distressed whine.

"What's wrong with her?" I asked, my chest constricting with compassion.

"Joree is the runt of the litter," Krogal said with a sad expression. "She was too small and too weak, so her mother kicked her out of the nest. Considering the height it was located at, she fell and broke her front legs, and sustained a couple of fractures in her ribs and her right wing."

"Shit! That's terrible! But you can fix her, right?" I asked, hope filling my voice.

He hesitated before nodding. "I can mend her injuries and give her all the nutrients and supplements she needs to gain a normal weight and be healthy."

"But?" I insisted.

"The fact that her mother kicked her out is very problematic for her development," he said with a sigh. "Her owner is extremely unhappy about it. Nulias are worth a lot, especially when properly trained."

"Trained to do what?" I asked, genuinely intrigued as I scratched the fluffy fur under her chin.

I couldn't help but smile when she stretched her neck to give me better access, her eyes closed as the volume of her purring went up another notch. Joree's front paws, with the same type of padded mittens of a cat, kneaded the plush cushion she was lying on.

"Nulia's are service pets, like the humans' service dogs," Krogal explained. "They have empathic abilities that allow them to sense what their owner needs, from thirst and hunger to pain requiring medication, or simply help them overcome a bout of depression. They can also work as messengers, watch guards, and search and rescue pets. As they can easily reach places that are difficult to access, Nulias can greatly accelerate rescue efforts, on top of bringing emergency supplies to the victim, be it some water or medication."

"Holy cow! I never thought such a little cutie could be so amazing!" I exclaimed, impressed. "But what does her mother have to do with any of that?"

"Most of her empathic abilities require stimulation from her mother. Without it, that skill will be stunted. The window to get trained before those muscles atrophy is very narrow. A number of other interactions with her are required to help Joree fully develop. If we can't get her to a state where her mother will accept her within the next week, it will be too late," he said with a somber expression.

My chest constricted as I looked sadly at the adorable little female. "What does that mean for her?"

"If we fail to get her back with her pack by Friday, her owner, Cyric, will discard her."

"What do you mean by 'discard'?" I asked, my voice filled with tension. "You're not going to put her down, right?"

"Technically, that would be the expectation. But I won't do that," he added quickly when I opened my mouth with an air of outrage. "My goal will be to find her a forever home to settle in if things don't work out."

My shoulders instantly relaxed as I once more smiled at the little cutie. She made that yipping sound again and licked my fingers. The roughness of her tongue tickled. I looked back up at Krogal with my most shameless puppy eyes. Finding him frowning at me with a stern expression testified to the fact he was already anticipating the next words about to come out of my mouth.

"Don't even think about it, woman," he said preemptively in a tone that brooked no argument. "This is your first visit here, and you're already getting sucked in by an adorable little face? Do you know how many pets I would have at home if I allowed myself to become smitten by all my homeless patients?"

"But she's so cute!" I said in a pleading and somewhat whiny tone. "See? She likes me and needs a home!"

"Cyric might take her back," I countered.

"But if he doesn't—"

"*If* he doesn't, we will reassess at that time," Krogal said begrudgingly.

And yet, my gut said I had already won. To my shame, as much as I wanted little Joree to be reunited with her family and achieve her full potential, the selfish part of me was hoping Cyric would discard her so that I could take her home.

Leaning forward, I booped her snout, and she rewarded me with a lick on the tip of my nose.

"You like me, don't you? Yes you do, you little cutie pie," I said before pressing a soft kiss on her forehead.

Behind me, Krogal groaned in discouragement.

*Yeah, I have no shame.*

After petting Joree one last time with a gentleness that had me melting from the inside out, he closed the door of her cage and led me out of the room mumbling something about how we better get out before I tried to adopt another wounded creature.

We were walking towards his office when the elevator chimed, and a pretty blonde stepped out of it. I immediately recognized the now famous face of Annabelle Parker—AKA Belle. She waved enthusiastically at the receptionist then jerked her head to the left, having likely perceived movement at the edge of her vision. The way her face lit up when she spotted us put a smile on my face.

"Sorry, I'm late!" she exclaimed while walking hastily towards us. "The twins were being a pain. Oh my God, you're so pretty!"

I couldn't help but chuckle at the exuberant energy that

emanated from her. Clearly, Belle was the type of person that lit up a room and made you want to laugh.

"Thank you," I said with a grin. "You look lovely as well."

She huffed as if I'd said something silly and continued in the same upbeat tone. "I'm Belle. I married this big guy's cousin," she added, pointing at Krogal.

Before I could answer, she did a double take. Her jaw dropped, and her pretty blue eyes widened with awe.

"Oh wow! Your braid looks totally badass!" she exclaimed.

Krogal pushed back his shoulders proudly. "It most certainly does!"

Belle glanced back at me with a glimmer of approval on her pretty face. "I see I'm gonna have some competition. That's awesome. I never thought of an ancient Egyptian style like what you did or to even match my hair to my mate's. Don't be surprised if I start stealing ideas from you."

I snorted. "I've been taking inspiration from you since the day they posted that first painting you did of Bayron. In case you haven't guessed yet, I'm a huge fan."

She giggled. "Aww, thank you. You and I are going to be the biggest BFFs! I can feel it!"

I could feel it, too.

"Don't let her overwhelm you," Krogal warned me before giving Belle a stern look.

"We'll be fine," I said with a smile.

Belle playfully glared at him before glancing back at me with a sheepish expression. "When I get nervous or excited, I can be a little over the top. Never hesitate to tell me to rein myself in or to slap my wrist if I get fidgety. I'm the type who will tap my foot, tap my pen on a hard surface, or make all those obnoxious noises that drive people crazy without even realizing I'm doing it."

I burst out laughing. "No worries, I don't mind at all."

"Like I said, you and I are going to be BFFs!"

Dhalgal poked her head into the hallway where we were talking. She cleared her throat and gave Krogal a severe look, putting an end to our chatter.

"Right, I better go get ready before she cracks her whip at me," Krogal said with an exaggerated air of despair.

"And we are off shopping. We're going to spend all of your money, and I will spill all of your secrets," Belle added as she gave Krogal a mischievous look.

"Hey!" he exclaimed, glaring at her with pretend ire.

"Just kidding!" she said with a less-than-innocent expression before leaning towards me and whispering loudly, "not really."

"Be back in time for the assembly," Krogal grumbled.

"Will do!" she replied.

Belle waved goodbye to him then faced me, waiting for me to tell him goodbye as well. I glanced at him, and we stared at each other awkwardly, not knowing exactly what would be an appropriate manner for us to part ways. I wanted to get on my tippy toes to kiss his cheek. But we'd never exchanged any kiss before, even a chaste one on the cheek. Not wanting to let time stretch to where things would become truly embarrassing, I just wrapped my arms around him and gave him a hug. He happily returned it and rested his cheek on top of my head for a brief second before releasing me.

Feeling stupidly shy, I waved at him and flicked my braid over my shoulder before turning away. Belle's intense stare was making me incredibly self-conscious. But her happy smile reassured me that we were doing okay.

I followed in her wake, and we left the clinic.

# CHAPTER 9
## FARAH

As we headed towards one of the shopping malls in the commercial sector of the city, Belle and I chatted away happily. She was so incredibly easy to love, and at the opposite end of the spectrum from me exuberance-wise. While some people could find that type of personality overwhelming or irritating, I just found her endearing.

I could see myself becoming the BFF she was alluding to earlier. When Kayog first mentioned her, I instantly held the secret hope that we would hit it off so that I wouldn't feel so alone and isolated here. This first meeting exceeded all my expectations. Belle had become such a famous artist over the past six years that I feared she would be a major diva, with that obnoxious haughty attitude people developed when their egos grew out of proportion. She was sweet, laid back, and incredibly humble.

"I'm so happy Kayog found you for him," she suddenly blurted out. "Krogal is the best!"

I gave her an indulgent smile. It was quickly becoming apparent to me that she didn't have much of a filter. That, too, was fine with me. I hated hypocrites and backstabbers, having been surrounded by so many of them in my previous life. Her candor and bluntness were refreshing, especially as they didn't hide any malice or meanness.

"So far, he's proving to be really sweet," I concurred as we casually strolled on the sidewalk.

"He absolutely is!" she said with a firm nod. "Have you seen how he handles the animals he cares for?"

I nodded, my chest warming as his interactions with the adorable little Joree replayed in my mind. "He's so big and so strong, the gentle way he handles those pets is mind-boggling," I said pensively. "It's reassuring, although his size still intimidates me."

Belle chuckled while smiling sympathetically at me. "I hear you. I was quite worried about that, too, with Bayron. But we adapt. When the time comes, Krogal will be super patient and careful with you. It'll be fine. In fact, I have no doubt it will be great."

I gaped at her, and my cheeks felt on the verge of bursting into flames. "Oh my God! I didn't mean *that*!"

Belle's jaw dropped, and her pale skin turned a bright shade of crimson. "Oh! Oops, sorry," she said with an embarrassed giggle. "I misunderstood."

Despite my own embarrassment, she was so incredibly cute that I just wanted to hug her. To my shock, my mouth also ran away with me.

"But since you've brought it up…" I said, my cheeks heating a bit more.

She snorted and gave me a knowing smile filled with mischief. "All I can say is that you two are soulmates. Therefore, you are made for each other, and all the parts that matter will fit as they are meant to. I'm sure it will be intimidating at first, like it was for me. But Zamorian males take their roles as a protector very seriously, and Krogal is definitely no exception. He won't rush you, and he'll take great care of you."

I nodded, feeling a little baffled that such a thought would even enter my mind so early on in our relationship. Still, it was great having someone I could discuss this with.

"And don't worry about him being double endowed," she added with a nervous giggle, her smile broadening when I visibly flinched. "There's no need to use both at the same time. It took many months before we eventually got around to that, and even then, there's no obligation to ever do it with both simultaneously."

"Oh, God!" I said, pressing both palms against my burning cheeks.

"Sorry if that was too much information!" she added sheepishly, although the teasing glimmer in her eyes hinted that she was enjoying embarrassing me.

"You're not sorry at all," I countered, playfully glaring at her.

"I am!" Belle exclaimed, with an exaggerated air of innocence. "Well okay, not totally but at least a little bit."

I snorted and shook my head at her. Although it had indeed been way too much information, I welcomed it as that question had plagued me. Receiving confirmation that this could be a gradual process gave me a major sense of relief.

"So I guess it's safe to say that you're happy with your husband?" I asked, eager to shift the topic to a less spicy terrain.

"I'm over the moon!" she exclaimed with a huge grin. "When I went to Kayog so he could find my Beast, I never imagined he would match me with a Zamorian. But Bayron exceeded all my wildest hopes."

"Your *Beast*?" I exclaimed, taken aback as we were closing in on the shopping mall.

She laughed and gave me a sheepish grin. "Yes. I am what you could call a proud monster fudger. My whole life, I dreamt of marrying a strange alien. I wanted to be Belle, like in the fairy tale, but where the Beast would not turn into some pretty human, and remain exactly how he was when she first fell in love with him."

I burst out laughing. That woman was a riot. "I will grant you that I also thought the Beast was way hotter in his monster form than as a human."

"Totally! My perfect mate didn't turn out to be as beastly as I imagined, but he's more than alien enough for me. And above all, he's the most amazing husband I could have ever dreamt of."

My heart melted at the wistful and dreamy expression on her face as she thought of her husband. Belle was truly in love with him, and I could only pray that my own 'Beast' and I would achieve the same type of happiness.

"Bayron really helped me deal with my body image issues," she added, emotion seeping into her voice as she absent-mindedly ran her fingertips over her exposed belly.

I couldn't help a glance before quickly averting my eyes.

She chuckled. "It's okay to look. After all, there's a reason I'm wearing a crop top and a low-waist skirt like most Zamorian females here," Belle said teasingly. "I've always been chubby. Having two Zamorian babies—each of whom are quite massive —gave me extra skin and a lot more stretch marks. I was so ashamed about it. But Bayron put an end to that real quick."

My curiosity piqued, I glanced back a bit more openly at her stomach. She was undeniably plus size, but nowhere near anything that would be deemed unhealthy. A network of stretch marks crisscrossed her belly, which was wrinkled from excess skin. On Earth, women would indeed be shamed into hiding it, or would hurry to have surgery to remove it. With today's technology, it would easily be done and leave flawless skin behind.

From the moment I'd seen her walk into the clinic in her colorful outfit, I wondered why she didn't get that surgery. After all, between her own successful artistic career and her husband's countless formidable hunts, they had plenty of credits to afford such a simple procedure.

"My mate said that they were my battle trophies and demanded I flaunt them. He wanted me to show off to the whole world how my small body handled his massive twins without faltering when nobody thought I could pull it off," she said, pride shining brightly in both her voice and expression. "On Earth, I would have hidden it. Here, I am praised and admired for it."

"Because they truly are trophies," I said, with the oddest mix of admiration and shame.

My instinctive far-too-human reaction had indeed been to think she should hide what we stupidly qualified as imperfections.

She beamed at me. "You're going to love it here. Everything and everyone are awesome, and especially supportive. Women are highly respected and protected. The fact that this is a matriarchy certainly plays a role in it. But they seriously have a lot of things right here."

"I'm glad to hear it," I said with a grin.

As we reached the large doors of the shopping mall, Belle and I exchanged an uncertain look. Both of us waited for the other to step in first as the doors automatically parted before us.

"I'm the newbie here," I said preemptively.

She scrunched her face at me. "But you're the taller one," she argued.

I snorted and shook my head. "That means nothing. Krogal entrusted me in your care. I'm lost and clueless about this world. Therefore, I totally depend on you."

Belle once more made a face and muttered something under her breath. Chuckling, I followed her inside as we made our way towards one of the countless fashion boutiques.

Saying I loved the sexy outfits the women here normally wore would be quite the understatement. While I wasn't the exhibitionist type, I liked looking hot and showing a bit of skin, without being vulgar. I had great legs and a nice figure, so miniskirts and tight-fitting dresses were usually my go to. Here, the skirts ranged from very short to ankle-length for women, and kilt-length for males. Long skirts usually had thigh-high slits that gave a naughty glimpse of a woman's legs with each movement. Crop tops of every style and size, as well as cut-out dresses were also a thing.

Although they could, females rarely wore pants on Xoccoris. I didn't mind as I'd always been the girly-girl type.

I spent the next eternity modeling an obscene number of outfits for Belle. I couldn't remember the last time I had this much fun just hanging out with a female friend. My throat tightened once again at remembering just how much Liam kept me isolated, slowly but surely driving away anyone I knew, cutting off my entire support system so that I became entirely dependent on him.

"Have you ever thought about modeling?" Belle suddenly asked, chasing away my somber thoughts.

"I've done some," I said shyly while running my hands over the soft fabric of the blue dress I just tried on. "Before I launched into a singing and dancing career, I modeled for some magazines and fashion shows to get my name and face out there."

She pursed her lips with a speculative glimmer in her blue eyes. "You're so beautiful, I think you would make a wonderful model posing with some of the cute pets right here on Xoccoris. I would love to make a collection with you."

My eyes nearly popped out of my head while images of me cuddling with the adorable little Joree flashed before my mind's eye.

"Really?! That would be super cool! I love animals—well, the cute and cuddly ones," I added with excitement.

"Yes, absolutely! I would pay you for it, too, at the standard model rate," Belle said with enthusiasm.

I couldn't wipe the grin off my face. Aside from the thrill of modeling with cute pets—which I had done on a few contracts in the past—the perspective of earning some money of my own while I studied had me over the moon.

"You've got yourself a deal," I replied.

"Awesome!"

We finished shopping in an amiable atmosphere. As Krogal warned me, when we went through the cash, they automatically charged my purchases to his account. Considering the many outfits, accessories, and shoes I bought, a sliver of guilt wanted to worm its way inside me. Belle insisting I had actually been too reserved in my spending made me feel a little better.

We headed back home to drop off our purchases—Belle having acquired a few things for herself as well. Knowing that she lived only one floor above us in the Skortheatis fortress was an added bonus. That meant we could hang out often when she wasn't traveling the stars with her hunter husband.

The setup of the city was pretty cool with each main bloodlines of the clan owning their individual fortress within the city. Although our fortress was the most impressive—which made sense as it housed the clan's Matriarch and her husband the Clan Chieftain—the others also rivaled in style. Furthermore, the head of the family of each of those other bloodlines served as one of the Chieftain's generals.

We entered the building—which reminded me of the cyberpunk version of an industrial castle—through the massive entrance doors. On each side of the large hallway, life-size statues of Zamorian warriors lined the walls at regular intervals until we reached the intersection. It gave access to the corridors on the left and the right which led to the elevators to the individual dwellings. Straight ahead, about twenty meters in front of us, another set of adorned heavy doors hid the Gathering Hall where we would convene shortly for the assembly.

We entered the left corridor and hopped inside the lift to my house floor, one level below the penthouses where Bayron and Belle lived. When we reached our destination, the elevator doors opened with a soft swish on a tall Zamorian female, waiting to go down. For a split second, I thought she was Feidin. But she didn't have the Matriarch's midnight-blue hair and yellow eyes. Hers were both black.

"Hello, Talin," Belle said as the female took a few steps back to let us out.

My polite smile froze on my lips under the intensity of her gaze.

"Hello, Belle," Talin said without glancing at her, too focused on examining me like a foreign creature that defied logic. "So… you're Krogal's mate."

I didn't know how to interpret her tone. It wasn't contemptuous, but it also didn't qualify as warm or welcoming. Confused, I gave Belle a sideways glance.

"Talin, this is Farah Toussaint, Krogal's mate. Farah, this is Talin, Krogal's mother," Belle said, a sliver of tension in her voice.

My spine immediately stiffened. While Krogal had given me a general idea of the source of the tension between him and his mother, he never mentioned how she felt about our union. Did she disapprove of a human for her firstborn? She seemed cordial enough with Belle, who didn't display any dislike towards the female, only unease likely due to Talin's fallout with Krogal.

"Hello, Talin," I said politely.

She pursed her lips and gave me a slow once-over that made me want to squirm. As much as I could now see the resemblance between her and her sister Feidin, her expression held none of the warmth and charisma of the latter.

"You're pretty enough," she said in a semi-approving tone. "I can see how you would stir the protective instincts of one such as my Krogal. But you're too small and fragile. I don't see how you will ever be able to bear him any offspring."

That struck me hard. Even though she spoke the words more as one would when musing out loud, and once again without any apparent malice or disdain, it still hurt and offended me. Before I could respond, Belle rushed to my defense.

"You all said the same thing about me," she countered force-fully. "And yet, aren't my children thriving? Did I not carry twins to term without faltering? Do not underestimate us human women. We may be fragile in appearance, but we're tough inside and when it matters."

I could have hugged her right then. But the grateful and affectionate smile I cast her way immediately faded when Talin huffed this time with audible disdain.

"You're better padded. She's just skin and bones," she replied dismissively.

This time I bristled and placed my hand on Belle's shoulder to keep her from speaking when she opened her mouth to respond.

"I see you don't approve of me," I said sternly as I lifted my chin defiantly.

"Why would I?" she hissed. "You cost me my son!"

"Like hell I did!" I exclaimed. "You did that on your own by trying to force him to be someone other than who he is. Your actions drove him away. Whether me or another female, whoever he chose would have still landed you in the same position because you're trying to impose your will and desires on him."

"I'm trying to better him, you ignorant girl! He's wasting his time bandaging pets and wild animals instead of being a proper protector," she snapped. "As his wife, you should push him to do better. Is that truly the type of mate you want?"

"Yes!" I exclaimed. "Bashing skulls, using violence, and intimidation are easy paths for a male to follow. Believe me, I know it all too well. Only a truly strong man can rein in such primal urges. I've just met Krogal, but the past forty-eight hours are the safest I felt in the past seven years. All of that is thanks to him! So yes, Madam, he is exactly the mate I want, just the way he is."

She shook her head at me as if I was a hopeless case. The depth of disappointment in her eyes cut me to the core, reflecting the one I had seen far too many times in my own mother's eyes. And yet, instead of breaking me, it sparked an even stronger urge to fight, to stand up for my man.

"I don't have my mother anymore," I suddenly said, my throat tightening as an old pain resurfaced. "She pushed me away by trying to force me to follow a specific path that I didn't want for myself. She was doing it out of love, but she only made me resent her, and drove me into the arms of someone even worse. My ex crushed me, slowly eroded who I was to shape me into what and who he wanted me to be. I lost any sense of self and was slowly dying while he kept me sequestered inside a gilded cage until I finally found the strength to escape before he completely destroyed what was left of me."

"If you had listened to your mother—" Talin interjected.

"I would have also lost myself, but in a different way. Both were destroying me for their own agendas and desires. Now, she's dead. I will never be able to tell her that despite how much she hurt me, I still loved her. You cannot understand how deeply it crushes the soul when the person who's supposed to love you the most is constantly bringing you down, belittling you, and criticizing you because you don't fit what *they* think you should be."

"I am sorry you lost your mother, but the Zamorian culture is different," she said in a slightly gentler tone.

"Every culture is the same when it comes to the love that should exist between a mother and her child, and the support we need from our parents," I said in a tone that brooked no argument. "You want your son back? Stop trying to squash the parts of him that don't fit your ideals. Love him. *All* of him, just the way he is. The distance between you hurts him."

"He doesn't care," she said dismissively, although I could see the hurt and pain she was trying to hide.

I'd seen that look on my mother's face when she tried to get back into my life after I severed all ties with her.

"Yes, he does," I said more softly, my anger giving way to a sliver of sympathy—not to say pity. "Krogal only told me that you didn't support his career choices. But I could hear the pain in his voice and see it on his face. I understand that pain all too well for having gone through it myself. It's too late for my mom and me. Don't let it be too late with your son. Whatever you may think, he really does love you. Now if you'll excuse me, I have to get prepared for the assembly."

With one last nod, I squeezed past Talin and headed for our apartment. I didn't trust myself not to start bawling my eyes out. This was too vivid a flashback of a terrible past I worked so hard at burying. At the same time, there had been something cathartic about voicing this aloud.

I didn't turn back until I reached the door, the pitter patter of Belle's feet following in my wake. When I opened the door and stepped inside, holding it for Belle, I caught a glimpse of Talin, still standing in front of the elevator, head slightly bowed and hugging herself with her two sets of arms. My heart constricted further for the female. I didn't know her, but I believed she genuinely loved Krogal in her own clumsy and heavy-handed way.

In that instant, I swore to myself I would get those two to patch things up.

The minute we crossed the antechamber and closed the inner doors behind us, Belle squealed before giving me the biggest hug. Stunned, I instinctively returned it. Although brief, it did wonders for me.

"Oh my God, woman, you were every shade of badass!" Belle exclaimed. "Talin is a freaking dragon! People usually cower before her, but you were all like 'Nuh-uh! I ain't putting up with your shit' and held your ground. That was epic!"

I couldn't help but laugh in front of such enthusiasm. "No

kidding, she's quite intimidating. Honestly, I can't believe I spoke to her like that. But this gaslighting, this bullshit about blaming him for her faults, I just couldn't take it."

"That sounds personal," she said in a gentle tone.

I heaved a sigh and nodded as I headed towards my bedroom to drop the bags. "As you probably heard, I ran from an abusive relationship that lasted seven freaking years. In the past year spent in the shelter, I was lucky enough to have access to some therapy to help me recognize and call out gaslighting. He was so good at doing terrible things and then making me feel like I was the bad one, that *I* made him do it. Man, it felt so good calling that shit out."

"You go girl!" Belle exclaimed. "I absolutely loved it. I'm so glad Krogal found you. There's no question in my mind the two of you are going to be extremely happy."

"I hope so," I said sincerely while freeing her of two of the bags she carried for me. "He seems really nice. I just need to relax and let him in instead of constantly having my guard up."

"Farah, take your time," Belle said this time with a gentle seriousness that sharply contrasted with her usually exuberant ways. "Krogal will wait however long you need. He's in no rush. He's just happy to have finally found you. You should have seen what a nervous wreck he was while waiting for your arrival. My only advice is for you not to waste any cuddle opportunities."

I chuckled as heat creeped into my cheeks. "He does give some of the best hugs."

"I totally believe it. I can't get enough of my Bayron cocooning me in those massive arms of his. You know, you should sit in his lap at the assembly," she said with conviction.

"Oh, my God! I can't do that!" I exclaimed.

She looked at me as if I had said something so dumb she was starting to question my intelligence. "Of course you can *and* should! It's going to make him extremely proud. Above all, it's going to make the others so jealous. They tease Bayron and me constantly for it, but I can see them all drooling with envy. Do it!"

I grunted in a noncommittal fashion in a way surprisingly similar to how Krogal responded when I would say things he didn't fully agree with, like adopting little Joree.

That made me smile.

Maybe sitting in his lap wouldn't be so outrageous…

# CHAPTER 10
## KROGAL

Throughout the short flight back home in my personal shuttle, a sense of thrill and anxiety warred within me. I couldn't wait to participate in the assembly for the first time with my mate. The vain side of me I never even knew existed also burned with impatience to show off my gorgeous wife and my beautifully adorned braid.

But this also meant likely facing my brother Demar and my father.

We hadn't spoken since I requested to sever the bond with Mother. I wasn't hiding from them. They'd simply been on a hunt from which they returned this morning. Of all the unpleasant things I could do without, the inevitable conversation I'd have with them ranked at the very top of that list.

After landing on our terrace, I called out Farah's name, overly disappointed not to find her home—not that it surprised me. I couldn't tell whether she had not yet returned from shopping with Belle, if they'd already gone down to the gathering hall, or if they'd gone upstairs to my cousin's dwelling. I suspected the latter.

I took the lift down to the main floor. To my dismay, I

stepped out of the cabin to find my brother in an animated conversation with Kraslo right in front of the elevators. My stomach dropped as I made eye contact with Demar.

No words were needed. The single glance he cast towards our friend sufficed for Kraslo to get his meaning.

"I'll see you both in a bit at the assembly," Kraslo said in a friendly tone, although I didn't miss the glimmer of sympathy in his eyes.

With a final nod, he turned around and walked away. I braced, looking at my younger brother. He approached me with an unreadable expression.

"Walk with me, brother," Demar said.

"Now is not the time," I replied in a calm but firm tone. "My mate will be waiting for me at the assembly."

"She's not there yet," he countered dismissively. "She's with Belle in her dwelling. This won't be long."

I kicked myself for not following my gut and going to check Bayron's penthouse before coming down. Annoyed, I gave my brother a stiff nod and followed as he walked towards one of the courtyards surrounding our bloodline's fortress.

It was a nice open space with a simple garden, with lots of benches, a few picnic tables, and green areas for people to relax in. With everyone either already at the assembly or preparing for it, there was thankfully nobody present to witness the imminent unpleasantness.

"Okay," I said as we came to a stop under the shade of a large tree. "Give your speech and let us be done."

Demar snorted and gave me the strangest smile with a strong teasing edge. "There's no speech to be given. I merely wanted to say that I'm proud of you."

My brain froze, and my jaw dropped. I studied his features so similar to mine in search of any sign of mockery or sarcasm. When I failed to find any, I blinked, more baffled than ever.

He chuckled, his face softening into a sympathetic expression. "It was about time for you to finally stand up to Mother," Demar said in a factual manner.

I frowned, battling to reconcile his words with my expectations. "But you always agree with her stance on everything!" I argued.

He smiled and shook his head. "Although I can see why you would perceive it that way, you misunderstand me. I don't agree with her stance, especially where you are concerned. Mother and I just happened to share the same interests. I love hunting, competing, and the pursuit of fame and glory. I would kill to have your body and your skills. Can you imagine how famous I would be if I possessed all your attributes?"

I nodded, my innards twisting once again with that nauseous feeling that always washed over me whenever this topic came up. Everything about me had been built for battle. Had I been born with even a tenth of Demar's passion for hunting and combat, I would indeed be legendary. But my little brother possessed the standard height and body mass of a Zamorian male.

"Believe me, Brother, I've wished many times that you had inherited my body instead."

"Don't," he replied with a gentle smile. "I learned years ago to stop wishing for the impossible and accept my reality the way it is, with both its good and bad sides. Mother just keeps clinging to a dream that can never come true. You don't see me arguing with her because I want the same thing she wants for myself. But it's okay for *you* to want something else."

I felt faint as I stared at my brother as if I was seeing him for the first time. None of this made any sense.

His face took on a faraway expression as he seemed to search through his memories.

"You were always such a contradiction," he said pensively before refocusing on me. "Despite Mother's constant nagging and semi-veiled threats, you stood your ground in order to pursue your veterinarian studies. But otherwise, you put up with the borderline abusive way she tried to coerce you into submitting to her wishes."

"She's our mother," I said in a slightly defensive tone, as if that alone sufficed to explain my behavior.

"And you're her son," he countered forcefully. "She should nurture *you*, not *herself* or her own aspirations."

Completely befuddled, I ran a nervous hand over my braid, my mind still reeling from this most improbable conversation.

"So I don't disappoint you?" I asked, hating the hint of vulnerability audible in my voice.

"Not anymore," Demar said in an affectionate tone. He smiled in a reassuring fashion when I flinched at his words. "I was never disappointed in you for the male you are or for choosing a different path than what everyone else wanted to impose on you. I was disappointed in you for putting up with the abuse. It was high time you stood up for yourself and told everyone to either take you the way you are or to fuck off."

"Wow!" I breathed out. "I expected you to give me an earful about how I brought shame to our house yet again, what a huge let down I was, and how I had better get my shit together to do right by our parents."

He snorted and waved his hand. "How little you know me, big brother," Demar said mockingly. "That earful will come to you from Father. He's furious because Mother is upset. But just so you know, as much as he doesn't understand you, Father actually doesn't mind that you want to follow your own path. He just doesn't like when Mother is unhappy."

"Father will never forgive me," I said grimly.

Demar shrugged. "He will, once Mother gets over it."

I gave him a 'Are you serious?' look. "*She* will never forgive me!"

He chuckled. "Oh yes, she will, once the two of you make up."

"Which is exactly why I say she never will. I'm not going to cave in to her demands. There will be no grummoll slaughter, and I will never change careers," I said in a stubborn fashion.

"I know," Demar said with an indulgent expression as if I was acting like a petulant child. "Mother will come around. For now, she's going through the various stages of grief. And your mate helped her right along."

"My mate?!" I exclaimed, my spine stiffening at the thought Mother had gotten to Farah.

Demar raised his palms in an appeasing fashion. "Relax, Brother. All is well. Your female gave Mother a stern talking to."

"What?!" I shouted, my head jerking towards the side entrance of the fortress as I readied to run back inside to go check on my mate.

"Calm, I said!" my brother reiterated. "Your mate is fine. She seriously impressed Mother."

He burst out laughing at my gaping expression. I didn't need a mirror to know how flabbergasted I looked.

"Mother spent the past hour complaining about how a little wisp of a human chastised her," Demar said in an amused tone. "She berated you for lying about your mate being fragile and broken."

I snorted. "Meaning she's mad she wasn't able to bully her!"

"Correct," Demar said laughing. "It appears Mom got spanked by your human."

I laughed. "Kromor's teeth! What I wouldn't have given to witness such a thing!"

"Me, too!" he replied, still laughing. "And I see your mate is doing right by you in more ways than one," he added, glancing with admiration at my braid.

My chest swelled with pride, and I ran a hand over my braid. "She most certainly is."

Demar smiled then his face took on a serious expression. "You know, for all her griping, Mother approves of your woman.

She won't admit it, and it will be difficult for her to show it and to cast her pride aside. Mother loves you, and she wants you back. It will take time, but she now understands that she has to change. Promise you won't give up on her."

I blinked away the tears pricking my eyes and smiled at my brother. "I won't. However insufferable she may be, she is my mother, and I do love her."

"Good!"

"Thank you, Brother," I said, my throat constricting.

"No, Krogal. Thank *you* for finally breaking those chains and becoming the male I always knew you were inside."

"I'm supposed to be the big brother," I grumbled to hide my embarrassment.

"You have been. Even though you let her get away with a lot of shit over the years, you were never weak. You taught me to follow my dreams and stand my ground, despite peer pressure and naysayers."

I opened my mouth to respond, but words failed me. Instead, I pulled him into my embrace, which he returned. Khivolt smite me! For the first time in years, I felt like I got my baby brother back. From the moment I first expressed an interest in pursuing veterinary medicine instead of the warrior path our parents wanted for me, an increasingly great distance had settled between Demar and me. It shouldn't have taken me this long to understand it hadn't been disappointment in me that set us apart but merely diverging interests.

I intended to reclaim the lost years with my sibling.

"Come on, let's go back inside before my female sends a search party for me," I grumbled.

He smiled, his eyes sparkling with mischief. "I cannot wait to meet that little terror of yours."

I burst out laughing, my chest swelling with pride as we went back inside the fortress. We had just walked past the elevators and were about to step into the main hallway when the lift chime went off. I glanced over my shoulder to see my woman and Belle coming out.

"Wait!" I told my brother, pressing a hand to his shoulder as I turned on my heel to head back towards Farah. I beamed at her. "There you are! I hope you had a good time?"

She nodded with a big grin. "I had a blast. Belle is fantastic!"

"Of course, I am," Belle replied, flicking her hair over her shoulder like a diva, making us all chuckle.

I turned sideways and gestured at my brother who was standing a couple of steps back. "Farah, this is my younger brother, Demar. Demar, meet my mate, Farah."

"It's a pleasure to meet you," Farah said in a friendly tone laced with a sliver of shyness.

The moment Demar's face took on that familiar bratty expression, I gave him a warning glance that he completely ignored.

"Hello, Farah. So you are the little human who terrorized our mother..." he said in a speculative tone.

"What?! I... No! It's..." Farah said, with an air of total panic.

"Demar!" I scolded.

He burst out laughing while Belle snorted.

"Relax, Brother. You know I'm only teasing," he said mockingly before turning a much gentler gaze towards my mate. "Mother is a very hard female to impress. She has many faults but good hearts. I may not have witnessed your meeting with her, but it is clear that you stood up for my brother, for your mate, against someone as intimidating as our mother. For that, you have earned her respect and mine. Welcome to the family, little sister."

The powerful emotion that descended over my mate's beautiful face reflected the one swelling inside me. I prayed for a warm welcome for my woman from my family. I couldn't be more grateful for my brother's words right now.

"Thank you," Farah said with gratitude. "That means a lot to me. I didn't mean to upset or offend your mother."

Demar waved a dismissive hand. "Don't worry about it or about Mother. You may not realize it, but you are hers now. She may bark at you, but anyone else who dares mess with you will also have to deal with her. She will fight for you to the death if needed."

And she would.

My hearts filled with affection for that female, difficult to love and yet fiercely devoted to her family. The four of us headed into the Gathering Hall. The large doors stood wide open as people steadily trickled in. Most of those who planned on attending had already taken their seats on the tiered benches surrounding the central floor. Our numbers always varied between one and two-thirds of the residents of the fortress, with a vast majority being males. The middle of the floor had parted so that the brazier could extrude and act like the bonfire around which our ancestors used to gather for similar social meetings in days of old.

My mate immediately slipped her dainty hand into my much bigger one and stepped closer to me when every eye settled on us. As much as her seeking reassurance from me pleased me, that she felt intimidated whipped my protective instincts into a frenzy. I gave her hand a gentle squeeze and wrapped my secondary right arm around her waist. Farah instantly relaxed, although she moved even closer against my side.

Oblivious to it all, Belle made a beeline for her husband. After nearly seven years of marriage, my cousin no longer had any qualms drawing his woman into his embrace and publicly kissing her.

"Ah! Here is our new human clanmate!" Ugrul exclaimed with his booming voice.

I smiled at my uncle as we came to a stop in front of him.

This event being informal, he was sitting on one of the side benches with the rest of our clanmates.

"Farah, this is our Clan Leader, Ugrul, Feidin's mate. Uncle, clanmates, meet my Farah," I said proudly.

She whispered a greeting and shyly waved at everyone.

"That is one impressive braid you're sporting, Cousin. Is now when all our single males start complaining about not being allowed to present for her?" Varkuth said.

Bayron's older brother—and Ugrul's heir—had quite a mischievous streak of his own. I made a show of caressing my adorned braid to further show it off, then playfully glared at Varkuth while our clanmates laughed. The approving glimmer in their eyes as they ogled my braid had me puffing out my chest even more.

"Seriously, it's rather unfair!" Kraslo said with false outrage. Considering he was already wooing a female of his own, this was merely him teasing me.

"With all due respect, after the display I witnessed in the Plaza yesterday, I'm happy to pass on anyone presenting for me," Farah said, scrunching her face. "Anyway, I'm already spoken for," she added, smiling at me.

"Bah, humans are no fun," Kraslo playfully mumbled.

"We're the coolest thing under the sun!" Belle countered, making a face at him.

"You are very pretty and delicate," Ugrul said kindly to my mate. "You have my protective instincts going into overdrive, and I can see the same feeling reflected in the eyes of my clanmates. When you bless my nephew with your first offspring, our people will fight like crazy over who gets to babysit them like with my Bayron's little ones. I suspect they'll do so even more with yours."

"Ugh!" Belle exclaimed, rolling her eyes, which had everyone laughing. "It's great having so many willing babysitters. But it's exhausting dealing with all the complaining about who gets to do it more often than others."

"That sounds like a good problem to have," Farah said teasingly.

"It is," Belle conceded begrudgingly as she settled in Bayron's lap.

I led my mate to an empty spot near my cousin.

"So, are you going to snuggle on your man, too, little Farah?" Varkuth asked teasingly as I sat down on the bench.

"Where she sits is her business," I snarled at my cousin, who chuckled shamelessly.

I gestured at my mate to settle next to me. She stared at the spot, chewed on her bottom lip, and glanced hesitantly at me. My hearts leapt, and I held my breath upon realizing she was actually considering sitting on me. It took every bit of my willpower to force a neutral expression on my face, neither pleading nor foreboding.

After a split second of hesitation—that felt like an eternity and a day—Farah took on an air of determination and sat in my lap. The wave of happiness that swelled within nearly choked me. My mate glanced nervously at me over her shoulder. My silly grin wiped out any concern she may have had about how I felt. She relaxed, returned my smile, and comfortably leaned back against me.

I possessively wrapped my arms around my woman while the others playfully mumbled about it.

"You're just jealous," I said tauntingly, before giving Farah a gentle squeeze.

She snuggled a bit more deeply against me with a satisfied sigh that filled my hearts to bursting.

Everything was finally as it should be.

# CHAPTER 11
### FARAH

My first week with Krogal swept me away as if I'd landed into a fairy tale. Deep inside, a nagging little voice kept harping at me that this was too good to be true. Sooner than later, the other shoe would drop, and shit would hit the fan. Everyone acted so incredibly nice to me, and my man showered me with attention and cuddles, proving himself more than worthy of the gentle giant title.

Belle exceeded all my hopes of having a great friend here. Humble, full of life, and with a heart the size of the moon, she made me rediscover what it was like to just be oneself, not trying to pretend to be what others expected, or trying to fit within a mold imposed on us. She just embraced me the way I was and gave me back who she truly was, no pretense.

I didn't see Talin again. It was only a matter of time, and I would lie by saying it didn't unnerve me a little to wonder how that encounter would turn out. However, I did run into Krogal's father. Thankfully, he addressed me in a very polite fashion, if a little distant. He seemed mad at Krogal. It didn't take a genius to figure out why. That royally sucked. But I intended to fix it. In time, I felt confident I could help them mend the rift. The fact that Krogal still clearly loved his mother—and I perceived the reciprocal sentiment from her—further fueled my conviction everything would work out.

On a different note, Krogal gave me the bittersweet news that Joree recovered enough to return to her owner Cyric, and her mother welcomed her back. This meant the adorable little Nulia would be able to undergo a proper training and fulfill a meaningful life for one of her species. The selfish part of me continued to mourn the loss of the companion with whom I had felt instant chemistry. But maybe it was just the little girl in me who had been rejected by her mother who saw a kindred spirit in Joree.

In between all that, I lightly started looking into schools I could attend or what new career I could pursue. I hadn't devoted too much time to it as I had been too busy discovering my new home and new people's culture. As Krogal would resume his regular work hours next week, I intended to look more seriously into it then.

But our shuttle taking flight drove those thoughts from my mind. We were venturing outside the city for the first time since my arrival on Xoccoris. Krogal was taking us to the beach for a little picnic and a swim. Once more, I marveled at the beauty of this new world. Despite us living a jet setter's life, Liam never took me off-world, even though he owned multiple casinos and clubs on various planets and space stations. It was one thing to see alien landscapes on vidscreens and during holodeck sessions, but to be surrounded by it in the real world took it to a whole other level.

Krogal made a slight detour to show me the neighboring fortified cities as well as some notable landmarks. He weaved in humorous anecdotes that had me laughing to tears, especially those involving trouble Bayron, Demar, and he used to get into growing up.

We landed at the edge of the forest. He shunned the spots

closer to the beach where he could have parked the shuttle and purposefully chose this area so that he could give me a little tour of the forest. Naturally, my offering to carry some of the countless items he brought earned me a stern glare that had me giggling. While he was nowhere near as much of a braggart as his cousin and many of the other Zamorian males, my Krogal loved showing off how strong and skillful he was for me.

His efforts to impress me and to earn my admiration were beyond adorable. The silly man didn't seem to realize what a huge crush I was steadily developing for him. Even with a temperature-controlled crate containing our food under his arm, a bag with various accessories in one hand, fishing equipment hanging over his shoulder, and a deployable parasol in his third hand, Krogal still managed to have a spare hand to hold mine as we strolled through the woods.

"This is where Bayron and Belle found Ferach during their first trip to the forest," Krogal suddenly said, indicating an inconspicuous area nearby. "The poor pup had been in such a horrible state, it still blows my mind that he survived. Even as a veterinarian myself, I would have put him down had I found him like this. But Belle pleaded so fervently for us to give him a chance that neither Bayron nor I had the hearts to refuse her."

"And you saved him!" I exclaimed proudly.

He hesitated. "In a way, I did, but Belle really deserves the credit. She believed in him, and I think he felt it. The bond he formed with her was phenomenal. I could only do so much for him. It was the Ordosians, a snake-like species that managed to fully heal what I could not. What I wouldn't give for the opportunity to go train with them for a few days!"

"Oh! You should ask!"

His face fell. "Not a chance. Belle and Bayron are one of the extremely rare off-worlders to have ever been allowed inside their sacred lands. Even when they took in Ferach to heal him, Belle had to remain at the hunters' base on Trangor, the Ordosian homeworld, while they treated him. It took Bayron getting stung by the Atreall Queen he saved for him to earn that privilege."

My heart constricted at his dejected expression. Bayron's rescue mission had gone viral and significantly helped shift the generally negative opinion people used to have about Zamorians. Now that he mentioned it, I vaguely remembered hearing about how territorial the Ordosians were and how people trespassing would be executed.

*I'll need to ask Belle if there's any way she can put in a good word for Krogal.*

In my short time here, Krogal had already done so much for me, I'd love to be able to return the favor or to at least help make one of his own dreams come true.

"I wonder if I will ever meet Ferach in the flesh," I said wistfully. "I've only ever seen him in some of the paintings and drawings Belle made of him."

Krogal nodded. "He returned to the wild where he belongs. Ferach now leads his pack, has a mate, and offspring of his own."

"It must have been hard for Belle to part ways with him," I said with commiseration.

"It was," he concurred. "But he visits from time to time. He even came to introduce his young to Bayron and Belle."

"That's awesome!" I exclaimed. "With luck, I'll get to see them, too, one of these days."

The tree line parting before us put an end to this conversation. My jaw dropped at the sight of the magnificent beach that sprawled before us. The grass gradually faded, giving way to the strangest sand I had ever seen. It was extremely fine and felt more like walking on powdery snow than actual sand. Surprisingly, it didn't stick to my shoes. Its pale gold color shone like a sea of gems under the bright rays of the sun. Crystalline water, a light shade of turquoise, spread as far as the eye could see.

Unusual trees, resembling a cross between a giant cactus and a palm tree with vines covered in purple flowers, rose in random areas of the beach, their roots buried under the sand. I could only presume they went deep enough to find proper soil to get the necessary nutrients from. Krogal made a beeline for one such tree before setting down the bags and containers he was burdened with. He laid down a picnic mat under the shade of the giant leaves of the tree. Thankfully, the prickly needles that gave it the cactus-like appearance didn't start before at least two meters from the base of the trunk.

To my delight, there was no one else in sight. Then again, we were in the middle of the week in the morning hours when most people would either be in school or at work. According to Krogal, it was possible to find secluded areas for those seeking a bit more privacy. But the risk of someone stumbling on you remained during peak hours.

Without a word, Krogal began stripping out of the sleeveless vest he was wearing and then his pants. Saying I wasn't getting an eyeful would be a bold-faced lie. Yeah, I was shamelessly checking him out. As I stripped out of my own clothes, I didn't miss the subtle glances he was casting my way. My man was totally checking me out, too.

A part of me wanted to tease and put on a bit of a show, but I felt oddly self-conscious. It didn't really make sense, considering I'd been blessed with a rather nice body and an amazing metabolism. It was all the nicer now that Liam no longer forced me to stay on the skinny side. God, I used to hate how much he controlled my food intake. He claimed it was necessary as a performer to have a perfect figure. To me, in person, I looked more like a walking bag of bones back then. But it did come out looking really nice in photos and videos.

Since my escape, I'd gotten to what I considered a healthier weight, but I suspected Krogal wouldn't mind me putting on a few additional pounds. With the gourmet food he kept preparing for me, I could see that happening sooner than later. And I intended to enjoy every moment of it.

"You are breathtaking, my mate," Krogal said, his black eyes looking even darker as they greedily roamed over me.

The coral bikini I chose looked gorgeous against my brown skin. It left just enough to the imagination while also accentuating my narrow waist, the flaring of my hips, and my endless legs. I had decent breasts, firm and perky. I wouldn't have minded them being a bit bigger, but I couldn't complain. Anyway, considering the massive size of Krogal's hand, no boob could ever be big enough to fill his palm. He could cover my entire face with it.

"You look pretty hot yourself," I said sincerely but with a hint of teasing.

Deep down, however, I couldn't stop thinking how badly I wanted to lick him all over. His body was beyond perfection. For a male this massive, I would have expected him to be a little too bulky in places. But everything was properly proportioned, each muscle flawlessly defined without that unhealthy, oversized swelling that bodybuilders who abused steroids possessed. Even his double set of arms flowed aesthetically. Those chiseled abs had me drooling, and the small buds of his nipples had my mouth watering.

The only thing unnerving about him was the bulge between his thighs. The tight bathing black shorts he wore hugged his twin peens a bit too closely. That they would form such a noticeable mound while clearly not yet erect made me want to squirm just trying to imagine how massive they would be once ready for action.

My cheeks all but burst into flames when I glanced up at Krogal's face to find his four eyes studying my reaction as I stared at his crotch. To my relief, he seemed slightly amused.

"Do not fear anything about me, my Farah. We are soulmates," he said in a soothing voice. "This means we were meant for each other in every way. When the time comes, I will take good care of you, and you'll see that I truly deserve the title of cuddly dragon."

I snorted, my embarrassment fading at the same time a wave of affection swelled within me. Things were always so easy with him. Krogal had a way of making me feel safe and helping me realize that things that seemed overwhelming or insurmountable really weren't that big of a deal. Despite being still early in our relationship, I believe at a visceral level that he would take good care of me.

Truth be told, I was getting ready to spice things up a bit. I wouldn't go all the way just yet, but my hands were seriously itching to do a bit of wandering, beyond just braiding his hair.

"Come, my mate. Let's get you wet," Krogal said with a mischievous expression that made it clear this had been a deliberate innuendo.

I chuckled, shook my head at him, and took his hand. As we approached the water, I licked my lips nervously and gave him a sideways glance.

"You should probably know that I'm the worst swimmer in the entire universe," I said sheepishly. "I've been in pools and at the beach more times than I can count, but I never got the hang of swimming. Even just treading water is a major display of incompetence."

"That's terrible!" he said with an exaggerated air of stupor. "We must fix that. In the meantime, I fear I'll have no choice but to sacrifice myself and serve as your personal lifesaver. It will be a great hardship for me, but I will let you hang on to me."

I made a face at him and playfully elbowed him. "Just for that, I'll wrap myself around you like a squid!"

"Oh no! The horror! Whatever will I do?!" Krogal exclaimed, the huge grin on his face belying the fake despair in his voice.

Tugging on my hand, which he still held, Krogal pulled me

to him before sweeping me up in his primary arms. My yelp of surprise shifted into laughter as he broke into a run while carrying me like a bride. I hung on to him, my brain struggling to pick what overwhelming emotions to focus on.

My innocent side reveled at the childish, carefree fun of being carried by a behemoth, racing at dizzying speed towards the clearest water. I laughed and squealed, both eager to get in the water and apprehensive about how cold it would likely be. It had been far too long since I'd indulged in such activities without worrying about projecting the right image. Liam demanded I keep my laughter discreet, my voice calm and soothing, and my appearance flawless, with not one hair out of place. That meant no running down the beach or diving into the ocean.

My naughty side latched on to the amazing feel of Krogal's bare skin against mine. Sure, we hugged plenty before. With him mostly shirtless, it was a pleasant experience. As I'd always been dressed, my clothes had gotten in the way. But right now, my barely-there bikini was giving me greater contact than ever, and I instantly craved more. His skin was so warm, so silky against mine, I wanted to rub my face all over him.

A high-pitched shout escaped me when water splashed under his feet before quickly engulfing us. It was cold but not freezing. However, listening to me squealing, one might believe I'd been dunked into a pool of ice. The way Krogal moved through the gentle waves, you'd think he felt no resistance at all, which further testified to his incredible strength.

"How do you run so fast in the water?" I asked.

"Part of the warrior training every male undergoes as of the age of five involves racing in various heights of water, including fully submerged."

"Damn, that explains a few things."

Far from distracting me from the arousal such close proximity to my man awakened in me, the coolness of the water had me pressing myself even more tightly against him to seek his heat. It wasn't a conscious reaction, but I didn't fight it once I realized I was doing it.

It didn't hurt that Krogal seemed to appreciate having me clinging to him.

"Take a deep breath!" he warned while removing his arm from behind my knees to hold me chest to chest against him.

He didn't have to say it twice. Although we hadn't gone far from the shore, we were already deep enough in the water that my feet couldn't touch the bottom. Standing still, Krogal had water up to his shoulders. If I let go of him and let myself sink, I'd be completely submerged.

As soon as he saw me hold my breath, Krogal dove forward. His secondary arms wrapped around me kept my body aligned with his. He kicked his feet and used his primary arms to propel us forward under the waves. Eyes closed, my cheek pressed against his, and my arms hugging him, I surrendered to the caress of the water against my skin as we shot through it like a rocket.

Long before my lungs could start burning from lack of oxygen, Krogal swam back up to the surface—which had only been about a meter above us. As soon as we emerged, he spun us around so that he could swim on his back while I lay on top of him. My jaw dropped when I noticed how far he had gotten us from the shore in such a short time.

Still using his primary arms, he leisurely swam around, his black eyes studying my features with an air of awe while a happy smile stretched his lips. Eyes locked with his, a wistful smile on my face, I played with the small hairs around his nape as the water gently licked my arms and back. It struck me then that my legs were instinctively adjusting their movement to his.

"You're undoubtedly one of the best pool floats in the universe," I said teasingly.

He huffed, playfully offended. "I'm not 'one of the best floats' in the universe, but *the* best! How many floats do you know who can carry a conversation with you? Hold you securely on top of them while taking you on a scenic tour? And above all, also act as a theme park attraction?"

I never got a chance to respond. Krogal's secondary arms released their embrace around me. He held me by the waist before tossing me up in the air like I weighed nothing. I screamed, my arms milling in the air as I tilted into a vertical position. Seconds later, I fell into the water, Krogal catching me before I got submerged.

He lifted me back up, holding me over his head at arm's length. On instinct, I spread my arms and legs as if I were a plane. With the dexterity of a synchronized swimmer, Krogal rotated in place while still keeping me propped up. I laughed and squealed with delight.

I couldn't say if he was trying to show off his strength, but my man quite literally turned himself into a theme park ride. With his insane muscle power, he would put his primary palms under my feet and launch me at least three meters into the air. I quickly went from petrified the first couple of times to bold and daring, performing acrobatics before splashing back into the water. Other times, he would have me riding on his back while he used his four arms to zip through the ocean, butterfly style. It almost felt like riding a bull without fighting not to be brutally bucked off. Even when he would dive and execute a few wild moves with me still latched on to him, I never felt scared or destabilized.

By the time he swam back closer to the shore, my entire being buzzed with happiness and excitement. Krogal had no idea what a wonderful gift this was. For years, I'd been deprived of just enjoying the moment, no holds barred, no judgment, no fear. Every day, every moment alongside Krogal healed a bit more of the lingering scars of the mental cage Liam had kept me trapped in for years.

Above all, I felt safe, wanted, protected, and free. Free to be who I truly was, and free to become whatever I wished.

When he stopped a few meters from the shore and put me on my feet, a whirlwind of emotion surged within me, constricting my throat. I couldn't tell what expression he read on my face, but his mischievous smile faded, giving way to an air of tenderness laced with sympathy that turned me upside down.

A silent communication passed between us. I couldn't have put it into words, not that it mattered. Without thinking, I hoisted myself onto my tippy toes and pressed a kiss at the corner of his jaw. Krogal slightly stiffened in surprise. I buried my face in his neck and wrapped my arms around him. The infinite tenderness with which he returned my embrace had me melting from the inside out.

Seriously, four-armed hugs were freaking awesome, especially when given by the gentlest giant.

I loved how attuned Krogal seemed to be to my feelings. Most men would have started asking what was wrong upon noticing my sudden mood swing—assuming they even noticed. Although it was important to encourage people to open up about things that troubled them, sometimes, you really didn't want to talk—or even need to. You simply wanted your special someone to just be there with you and give you a world-class hug like this one.

*Who would have thought such a behemoth could be so empathetic?*

Then again, Krogal was a renowned veterinarian. No doubt his profession taught him to recognize when a wounded animal only craved the silent comfort and reassurance of a protector. This whole interaction could have been super awkward, but my man handled it perfectly.

With much reluctance, I eventually loosened my hold and took a step back to glance up at him.

"Ready for your first swimming lesson?" he asked.

"Oh boy! Why do I feel like this is going to be an epic disaster?" I said, partially horrified.

He chuckled and squeezed my shoulder reassuringly. "It won't be so bad. Worst case scenario, you'll be at the same point and still not be able to swim."

I made a face at him which only made him laugh further.

For the next eternity, he tried to get me to tread water. Despite religiously following his instructions, my performance qualified more as pathetic flailing. Considering my light weight, you'd think I'd float to the surface like a twig, but gravity made it a point to remind me who's boss. Although baffled by my inability to master such a basic task, especially for an accomplished dancer as I was, Krogal displayed the patience of a saint. Not once did he seem aggravated or discouraged in the face of my consistent failure.

He not only made a game out of it but teased me in a way that had me laughing instead of growing mortified over my shortcomings. We eventually switched things up. With his palms under my stomach, keeping me at the surface of the water, Krogal made me practice breast strokes. Remaining focused on his instructions grew increasingly harder. After all this time spent playing in the water with him, I should have been over getting aroused by physical contact with him. Yet, all I could think about was the calloused feel of his large palms on my stomach and how badly I wanted them roaming all over me.

After a while, Krogal put some distance between us and requested that I swim to him. I complied with as much grace as a cat tossed into a pool. But as that distance grew, the more erratic my swimming became, and the more water I swallowed. He finally took pity on me when I all but sank after crossing a measly five meters. He scooped me out of the water and held me in his reassuring embrace. I clung to him, coughing and sputtering.

Peering up, I gave him a dejected look. "You're either the

worst teacher in the universe, or I'm the most hopeless student to have ever set foot on Xoccoris."

He chuckled. "I think it's both."

I gaped at him in false outrage. "Hey! You're supposed to do the gentleman thing and take the blame, claim it's all you!"

He laughed some more. "Sorry, you're right. I'm a dreadful teacher. You are great. I'm just failing to bring out your potential."

I made a face at him and playfully elbowed him. Krogal smiled, his arms holding me tightening in a possessive fashion. I couldn't tell what triggered it, or when the change occurred, but the mood suddenly shifted. The dark depths of his eyes appeared to swallow me whole as our gazes locked. I melted against him as I returned his embrace. It was only once our mouths touched that I realized one of us—or maybe both—had leaned towards the other.

A bolt of fire exploded in the pit of my stomach as the plush cushion of his lips pressed against mine. It was soft and a little hesitant, as if he didn't want to frighten me. With a will of their own, my hands glided around his sides, up his chest, and then clasped behind his muscular nape. Emboldened by my positive response, Krogal increased the pressure of his lips against mine, and his palms cautiously caressed my back.

I had never kissed a male with tusks before. A part of me always assumed it would be awkward. Sure, it felt a little strange, but not in an unpleasant fashion. The fact that they were on the small side—nowhere near as massive as those certain orcish species possessed—certainly helped.

His tongue teased the seam of my mouth, and I parted mine willingly, welcoming it in. He tilted his head to the side to deepen the kiss as our tongues made each other's acquaintance. His was a little rougher than a human's, the odd but delightful sensation resonating directly between my thighs. A dull throbbing awakened in my nether region, gradually increasing in intensity as our kiss grew more passionate, and his hands on me became more feverish.

A yelp escaped me, swallowed by his voracious mouth, when his secondary hands grabbed the back of my thighs and lifted me up. I instinctively wrapped my legs around his narrow waist and sank my fingers into the silky strands of his dark hair. My stomach quivered when this new position had me feeling the hardening length of his shafts straining against his swimming trunks. My nipples began aching while my pulse seemed to be palpitating into my clitoris, which was quickly perking its head up in need of attention.

Krogal broke the kiss, his mouth continuing to roam over my face and the side of my neck as he gently bent me backward. As a result, my pelvic area rubbed against his twin cocks. It felt as if my clit had been struck by lightning followed by electric tendrils spreading outwards throughout my body. A moan tumbled out of my throat. That seemed to set something off inside him.

My man responded with a moan of his own, although it sounded more like the low, threatening growl a wild beast emitted as a warning not to come closer if you valued your life. It vibrated through his broad chest, making my skin tingle. It should have frightened me and been my cue to end things before they got out of control. Instead, it had moisture pooling between my thighs.

Krogal's mouth traced a blazing trail down my neck to my chest. A choked cry escaped me when it settled on my left breast, over the thin fabric of my bikini top. My inner walls contracted, and I involuntarily rubbed my pelvis against his. His stiff cocks grazing my clit had another spark of lust surging through me. Krogal's secondary hands tightened their hold behind my thighs, pressing me even more tightly against his twins.

He reclaimed my mouth in a voracious kiss, while his huge primary right hand slipped under the fabric of my bikini top to close around my left breast. I moaned against his mouth as our tongues mingled. He fondled my breast, his thumb teasing the nub as it painfully hardened.

It took me too long to notice Krogal had been on the move. Only once the sudden coolness of shade descended over us did I realize he had walked us out of the water and back to our picnic mat. Without breaking the kiss, he laid me down on the mat before lying on top of me. The small voice of reason at the back of my mind was timidly saying now would really be a good time to stop.

But the voice of lust had a completely different idea in mind.

With a will of their own, my legs parted open so that Krogal could settle more comfortably over me. He supported his weight with his secondary forearms so as not to squish me, while his primary hands explored my body with increasing boldness. Surprisingly, they didn't venture under the thin pieces of fabric hiding my naughty bits. Although he caressed my sides and even went further south to my thighs, Krogal steered clear of my sex.

Thinking he was waiting for an unequivocal signal to proceed from me, I began caressing his broad back with both hands, allowing them to journey down to the firm and round mounds of his behind. Krogal had the sexiest butt. It should be illegal to achieve such perfection. I gave his cheeks a firm squeeze while lifting my pelvis to press against his. Even as I did this, that little voice protested a bit more loudly without becoming assertive.

It had been too long since I'd been with a man, and even longer since I'd actually *wanted* to be intimate with someone.

*Am I rushing into it for the wrong reasons?*

Krogal's throaty growl resonated directly in my clit. When he broke the kiss and buried his face in my neck, I thought he would venture down like he had previously done when we were in the water. To my dismay, he merely pressed his lips on my pulse there, rubbed his face in the crook of my neck, then lifted his head to look at me.

His obsidian eyes shone with a lustful haze laced with infinite tenderness.

"You are far too tempting, my mate," he said, his voice even more rumbly from desire. "Let's feed you before I lose what little control I still possess."

I almost blurted out for him to go right ahead and lose control. At the same time, the stupid voice of reason heaved a sigh of relief. I didn't want him to stop, and yet I loved that he was going at a slow pace, making sure I was in the right head-space every step of the way.

I gave him a shaky smile as he got up and helped me to sit up. As he went to the other side of the mat to start retrieving the various dishes he had prepared from the temperature-controlled containers, I couldn't help but steal a few glances at him. Naturally, my gaze zeroed in on the massive bulge that his wet bathing trunks hugged in the most indecent fashion.

My inner walls once more contracted, but this time a hefty dose of apprehension seeped into the frustrated arousal that still lingered. Nevertheless, that he could show such discipline when he was clearly uncomfortably erect did wonders to reassure me I was truly in good hands.

The sexual tension quickly gave way to the laidback and amiable atmosphere that always reigned between us. I smiled while greedily buttering one of the homemade spiced buns Krogal had baked for us.

"It's been such a long time since I've been on a picnic like this," I said wistfully while taking in the generous spread before us and our fairy tale surroundings. "In fact, it's also been far too long since I've been able to enjoy so much good food without being told I've had enough."

"Oh?" Krogal said, a slight frown marring his forehead.

Despite his obvious curiosity, my man was forcing himself not to pry, showing enough interest to encourage me to continue without feeling pressured to do so. That was yet another thing I loved about him. He let me be and never demanded more than I was ready or willing to give. But it was time for me to open up.

"Liam, my ex, controlled everything. I was so young and impressionable when we first met that I was too mesmerized to see what was happening," I said, looking at the ocean without seeing it. "By the time I finally opened my eyes, I had already fallen far too deep down that rabbit hole. He controlled what food I ate and how much of it, the clothes I wore, my weight, my finances, and even who I could be friends with. My life was no longer my own, but entirely dictated by him."

"How did you meet?" Krogal asked in a gentle voice.

I sighed and ran a hand over one of my braids. "As far as I can remember, I always loved singing and dancing. Like most teenagers, I wanted to become a superstar. As you can guess, my mother didn't approve," I said with derision.

"So she forbade you from doing it?"

I shook my head. "No. She didn't mind it as a form of social activity. She believed a well-rounded person had some artistic knowledge or gift. Mother simply didn't want me to pursue it as a career. Like many Haitian parents, even in this day and age, Mom wanted me to become a nurse, a teacher, or a lawyer. Those were proper professional options for a woman."

The commiseration in his eyes touched me deeply. He, more than most people I knew, understood perfectly what it was like to have a parent try to impose a specific future on their child.

"The problem was that I totally sucked at school. I did well enough with general topics like literature, geography, and history. But math and sciences did not agree with me," I said with a shudder. "But I would do some small singing and dancing gigs on the side. I even had my own band for a while. One day, they held one of those reality shows singing competitions. I decided to participate, not holding high hopes that anything would come of it."

"But it did," he said. "You blew them away, didn't you?"

I snorted. "I wouldn't go that far, as I didn't win. But I did reach the semifinals. The beauty of those types of competitions is the amount of exposure they give you. Often, runners-up end up achieving even bigger careers than the actual winners. And that's exactly what happened in my case. So many contracts started flooding my way, it was overwhelming and very hard to choose."

I took a sip of wine as memories of those early days came back to the fore. Once again, Krogal didn't rush me as silence stretched between us for a few moments.

"Despite getting many record deal offers, I ended up accepting contracts in fancy clubs, hotels, and casinos. I loved the more intimate settings of those places. And truth be told, as much as I enjoy performing, the thought of being on the road doing music tours really did not appeal to me. It just so happened that Liam owned many of the venues where I was featured."

"So he saw you perform and approached you?"

I nodded. "He didn't start off flirting with me or anything like that. Liam was very professional in the first few months. He understood the type of career I wanted and offered to take me under his wing. Naturally, I couldn't accept fast enough. He was a legend in that arena. That he was also incredibly handsome, filthy rich, and twelve years older than me gave him a mythical aura of authority and power that was mesmerizing to the naive eighteen-year-old that I was back then."

Despite the slight frown creasing his forehead, Krogal nodded slowly, indicating he fully understood how all of this had come about.

"How did your mother feel about this?" he asked.

"Ugh! She was totally unhappy about it all. She wanted me to stay in school and get what she considered a 'real job' instead of this nonsense. But I was of legal age, and Liam was offering me the type of contract people would kill for. And he truly held his end of the deal. He had me performing in some of the most sought-after venues and A-listing events. Money was pouring in, and all I had to do was to follow his instructions."

"What type of instructions were those?" he asked in a suspicious tone.

I shrugged. "The type of things agents and managers often request, from being careful with my weight, taking good care of my image down to the clothes I wear and the way I do my hair, and picking the right type of crowd to hang out with, as all of those things could affect my career in both good and negative ways. But it gradually grew more and more extreme to the point I became isolated and no longer had a say as to who was allowed inside my inner circle. He even took over my finances. Initially, he offered to help me invest my earnings so that the day I decided to end my career, I would have a comfortable nest egg and never have to worry about the future."

"But he stole your money instead?"

I hesitated. "Honestly, I can't really say that he stole it because it's still there, and he hasn't touched or spent it. However, he had all the accounts set up in a way that I cannot make withdrawals without his consent. As he made sure I never needed to spend any of my own money, since he had tabs anywhere I was allowed to go, it never even dawned on me that I had no access to it until the day I decided to escape. Liam essentially has me under a form of conservatorship that has no ending date. We would need to go before a court to get it lifted. But the process would drag on for so long that God only knows what he could do to me in the meantime."

"So the wealth your singing career generated is still available but under his control?"

I nodded. "Like I said, everything happened so gradually and in such a subtle fashion that I got completely blindsided. Liam kept everything platonic between us for the entire first year. Meanwhile, he was increasingly isolating me. But as I had turned into his official arm candy for every event he participated in, we naturally evolved into a couple. Obviously, I was flattered that such a man would pick me of all people as his woman. My mother was livid. With her constantly nagging me, and Liam encouraging me to cut her out of my life if she couldn't be supportive, it not only made me double down pursuing my own path, but also drove me to sever all contacts with her."

"Was her issue the career you were pursuing or the man you were involved with?" Krogal asked.

"Both. Mom definitely wanted me to pursue a more traditional profession, less reliant on the whims of a fickle public. She hated the fact that he was much older than me, but I think she hated how powerful his influence was over me even more. Things were going so well for so long that I never even saw when the first rifts began. One day, I was living a fairy tale, and the next I abruptly woke up inside a nightmare."

"What happened?" Krogal asked, genuinely intrigued.

I shifted on the mat, and crossed my legs into a Lotus position as I gathered my thoughts.

"I started asking questions and challenging him," I said, bitterness seeping into my voice. "Three years into our relationship—which is four years after he took me under his wing—the number of performances I did significantly dwindled. I became more his companion than the star he was supposed to turn me into. The only shows I did were huge ticket events. But I asked to take part in various smaller events that supported causes dear to my heart, and he systematically refused. If I insisted, he got angry. He never hit me, but the verbal cruelty started, with him reminding me that I was an uneducated little girl with nothing more than a high school diploma. That I should let my betters make the decisions."

The feral anger that flashed over Krogal's features should have scared me. Instead, it acted like a balm on the many scars that still lingered from all the ways in which Liam put me down, belittled me, and undermined my fragile confidence as a young woman.

"As if to punish me for questioning him, my number of performances dwindled even more. I believe it was a dare on his part, to teach me a lesson. As I disliked the two-faced snakes who constituted our inner circle, I mostly kept to myself. Anyone outside of that circle that I dared befriend would get fired or suddenly disappear. Even Lorna, a lovely maid who had started working at our penthouse, was punished because I liked her."

Krogal frowned. "How so?"

"Liam came home to find us laughing about some joke I don't even remember. He was livid. He told her to get back to work, that he wasn't paying her to chat. I figured he had a tough day to display such an irrational reaction to something this innocent. But less than thirty minutes later, I heard Lorna crying and pleading while she was being escorted out."

"Escorted out?" he echoed, confused.

"Liam fired her. She was a single mom and desperately needed that income. When I confronted him about it, he got even angrier. I asked what the hell was wrong with him, how was me liking her a crime? He told me I was too stupid to see when people were trying to take advantage of me, like Lorna had been. He said that I was the one who changed. I used to be so pure and so sweet, but I was allowing people and fame to corrupt me. For my own sake, he would have to be more selective of who I could hang out with."

"That's insane!" Krogal exclaimed, anger audible in his voice.

"It certainly was. Liam was the master of gaslighting. Thing is, what he described as me being pure and sweet was me being naïve and mesmerized by him. I was his trophy, and the narcissist in him loved how I was constantly fawning over him. When that stopped, he thought he could make me go back to that girl by becoming more and more controlling. My life became hell from that moment forward. If I expressed admiration or envy for any other artist, he would ruin them. If I smiled or showed any kindness to anyone outside of his inner circle, he would fire them or hurt their business, whatever field they were in."

"He wanted to be the center of your universe," Krogal said with sudden understanding.

I nodded grimly. "From the start, Liam made it clear he didn't want children. At first, I simply thought he feared I would try to trap him with a baby. After all, he never wanted us to get married, which seemed to contradict his need to otherwise fully own me. But children would have taken my attention away from him, and marriage would have given me rights and powers he didn't want me to possess over him."

"So what prompted you to finally leave him?"

"The straw that broke the camel's back was when we attended one of the biggest UFC championships," I said, hugging myself as my stomach roiled at the horrible memory. "Gabriel had been an up-and-coming UFC fighter who everyone believed would break every possible record, he was that talented. Before the match, we got personal introductions, as was often the case with Liam. Gabriel made the mistake of complimenting me and saying how beautiful he thought I was. I merely smiled as a thank you, but Liam felt disrespected."

"You can't be serious? A simple smile in response sufficed for him to be angered?" Krogal asked, shock and disbelief filling his voice.

I nodded, a shudder coursing through me. "He'd been growing increasingly paranoid. For him, the fact that I smiled was a form of encouragement, of me welcoming another man's attentions. I told him I was merely being polite, but Liam insisted I disrespected him and that he couldn't allow that to go unpunished."

"Do I dare ask what he did?" Krogal asked in a gentle voice.

"They stopped the match halfway through the first round so

that Gabriel could be rushed to the hospital," I said, my voice constricted. "Liam had his opponent bust his kneecap. The bones of his jaw and cheeks had been shattered in multiple places thanks to the metal plates hidden under his opponent's hand wraps."

"Surely that was easily proven! They didn't prosecute him?!" Krogal exclaimed in outrage.

I shook my head. "Liam owned the venue. The security guards worked for him. And Gabriel's agent and family were *very strongly* encouraged not to make waves or ask too many questions. That's when I realized that Liam was involved in even darker things than I thought. From that day forward, I planned my escape in earnest. As I had no money, and no way of withdrawing any without him being immediately alerted, I had to get creative."

"Couldn't you just go to law enforcement?"

"No. He had too many friends and too many connections everywhere. The risk of them ratting me out was much too high. As I could never leave the penthouse without an escort, even to go shopping or for a medical appointment, I had to find a way to sneak out unnoticed."

"Kromor's teeth! How did you manage?"

"I escaped in the one place no one would ever think to look. When the cleaning service came to pick up the curtains, duvet, and all other items that required an industrial washing machine, I hid inside one of the laundry bins. The whole way out, I thought my heart would burst at the prospect of being discovered. As Liam often worked from home, I pretended to be taking a long bubble bath while he was having a meeting, so that no one would come looking for me for at least an hour or two."

"Were the employees in on it?" he asked, looking impressed.

I shrugged and once again ran a hand over one of my braids. "Honestly, I don't know. A part of me believes they suspected it. I'm not all that heavy, and some of the curtains weighed a ton.

But I'm sure they felt a difference while carting the bin around. Either way, I snuck out the minute they dropped the bins at their facilities. As far as I know, no one noticed me coming out of the bin, but I was spotted walking out of the building. I doubt the staff recognized me, but I'll never know."

"What did you do then? How did you get to Khendis?"

"I didn't want to go to the cops, so I went straight to a pawn shop and asked to be put in touch with the Enforcers. The owner was obviously reluctant both to take the jewelry I wanted to pawn and to contact the galactic peacekeeping forces."

Krogal snorted. "I can imagine. Considering he was likely running a shady business of his own, he wouldn't want the Enforcers sniffing around his affairs."

"Exactly. He only consented because I agreed to a ridiculously low price on the pieces I had. I reeked of desperation, so he knew I would accept pretty much anything. Although he pretended not to recognize me, I'm certain he knew who I was."

"Didn't you fear he would rat you out?" Krogal asked with a frown.

I shook my head. "I specifically went to him because Liam majorly screwed him over in the past. He wanted to get even or to at least hurt him in some way. Helping him lose his woman would undoubtedly be satisfying for him. In the end, he gave me a throwaway phone so that I could contact the Enforcers myself."

"So that's how you ended up leaving Earth," Krogal said with understanding.

"Barely," I said with bitterness. "The Enforcers didn't believe I was a victim of domestic violence. In fact, they denied me the status, which made my life a lot more difficult on Khendis. They believed I had been in on whatever criminal activities Liam was involved in and that, now that things had gone south between us, I was trying to play the victim to get a free ride out of there."

"But didn't they ask a Temern to confirm your honesty or deceptiveness?" Krogal argued. "I believe it is a standard procedure for most major cases handled by the Enforcers."

I nodded. "That's the only reason they finally allowed me to go to Khendis. But it was with much reluctance. They wanted to use me as bait to catch Liam."

"Are you serious?!"

I gave him a dejected smile. "Sadly, yes. They delayed as long as possible before allowing me to transfer to Khendis. Obviously, the first thing I did was to change my name and appearance. It was a good thing, too, because some of Liam's goons showed up at the shelter. That's what allowed me to obtain a restraining order against him. I just fear what will happen the day he eventually finds me again."

"So Farah Toussaint isn't your real name?" Krogal asked, surprised.

I smiled. "Yes, it is. But on Khendis, I went under a pseudonym and wore prosthetics on my face to change my appearance."

"Ah, I see. Do you seriously think he's still looking for you?" Krogal asked with genuine curiosity laced with concern.

"Absolutely!" I said with conviction. "I humiliated him by leaving. He will never forgive me for that. He will want to punish me. But he also considers me his property. And nobody is allowed to take or touch what's his."

"You are safe here, my Farah. You not only have me as your protector, but the entire clan will also stand by you."

"You don't know Liam, Krogal. You have no idea the types of lengths he will go to get what he wants," I said with a shudder. "For this reason, I also need to tell Belle that I can no longer model for her collection, unless she makes some major modifications to the pieces."

Krogal stiffened. It didn't take a genius to see my comment

highly displeased him. "You fear he will recognize you in one of her paintings?"

"There is no question he will. And then he'll come after me, which means he'll also come after you for touching what's his."

"Let him come," Krogal hissed, a dare in his voice. "I will take great pleasure in teaching him the error of his ways."

"No, Krogal. You do not want him coming here. The best thing is for him to never find me. Belle must agree to change my face and use a fake name if she wants to use me in her paintings."

"I do not wish for you to live in hiding, my mate. You realize that going this route is setting up yet another prison for yourself?" he asked in a gentle voice.

"This is the type of prison I'm comfortable living in," I said stubbornly.

"Is it?" he challenged. "Is this why you aren't looking into any of the music programs here on Xoccoris?"

I shifted uneasily but lifted my chin defiantly as I held his gaze. "Yes. My music career ended a long time ago. Liam is far too well connected in this field. The minute I perform again, he will find me."

"Do you not realize how much power you are giving him over you with this approach?"

My throat tightened, and I blinked back the tears pricking my eyes. "All I know is that pretending that Liam is not a threat is foolish. I will spend the rest of my days living in fear that he might show up again. With luck, he never will. But I certainly won't make it easier for him to find me. I just hope you can respect that."

My heart sank when Krogal clenched his jaw. Judging by the hard glint in his eyes, he wanted to argue. I braced for what would follow as he continued to stare at me intently.

He heaved a frustrated sigh, then pursed his lips into a disgruntled expression. "I do not agree with your stance on this matter. But I will never force you to go against your better judgment, even though I am not thrilled by your decision. If this is what you desire, I will stand by you."

A wave of emotions dominated by gratitude swelled within me. I rose to my feet and circled around the dishes sprawled before us on the mat to embrace him. Krogal wrapped his four arms around me. Despite the anguish and torment thinking of Liam always stirred within me, in this instant, I felt sheltered and protected.

"Thank you. Thank you for being my soulmate," I whispered, my face buried in his broad chest.

"Always, my mate. As long as I draw breath, I will always be by your side."

# CHAPTER 12
## FARAH

In the two weeks that followed our trip to the beach, things steadily heated up between us, with plenty of kissing, groping, and cuddling. At this point, I was more than ready to move to the next stage, but Krogal would always pause the minute we got close to truly getting down and dirty. Saying it annoyed the hell out of me would be the understatement of the millennium. I was no longer so thrilled about him not pressuring me. He was waiting for me to make it clear that I was ready, and subtle hints wouldn't suffice.

Who would have thought I'd resent my man being so considerate?

I'd never been the type to make the first move, but this time I had made my peace with the fact that there would be no way around it. And tonight, I definitely intended to cross that line.

I walked out of my bedroom, strutting my stuff in my brand-new outfit. As I loved the sexy fashion worn by the Zamorian females, I had not only adopted it, but also made it my own. Seeing Krogal's four eyes widen with awe as I sauntered into the living area where he was waiting for me had me tingling in all the right places.

"My mate, you look gorgeous as always. But you are particularly stunning in this dress," he said, opening his arms in a beckoning fashion.

I twirled and struck a pose first before going into his embrace.

"Thank you! It's a dress I bought at the store and modified on Belle's sewing machine," I explained.

"Belle's machine?! You need your own!" Krogal said, sounding offended that I didn't have everything I required.

"Relax," I said teasingly. "I already ordered one. It should be delivered on Monday."

"Good," he replied in a slightly grumpy tone, mollified. "I will not have my mate lacking for anything."

It made me chuckle. "Don't worry. I will abuse your tabs in every store, since you insist so much."

"You better," he said in a falsely menacing fashion. "But I didn't know you were so talented at sewing."

"I love it! In fact, before my musical career took off, I seriously considered going into fashion since I didn't have the brains for the medical field Mom wanted me to pursue. And law put me to sleep. It came in handy, too, because it allowed me to create my own stage costumes when I started singing. We weren't poor, but we also didn't swim in money."

"We have some great fashion programs here on Xoccoris," Krogal said carefully.

"I know," I said enthusiastically. "I actually started looking into them. There are many interesting ones. Belle offered to draw patterns for me to make custom printed fabrics. I'm super excited! She even suggested a collaboration with hair accessories. I would love it, but so long as I get to remain in the shadows on that front."

Krogal's smile immediately dimmed. Although he made a respectable effort to hide his displeasure at that last comment, I knew he hated my determination to remain in hiding. He hadn't flat out come out and said it, but I strongly believed he perceived my cautiousness as a sign that I didn't trust in his ability to keep me safe from whatever Liam might try to pull off—if ever. Obviously, that wasn't the case. He simply had no idea what a ruthless monster my ex could be. I could never live with myself if Liam hurt him or his family because of me.

Thankfully, he let it slide.

I wasn't so naïve as to think that would always be the case. Sooner than later, Krogal would force the issue. He would never allow me to spend the rest of my days living in fear of Liam potentially finding me. I didn't want that for myself either, but what other options were there? So long as Liam remained a free man, I would never be safe. He needed to get a life sentence without the possibility of parole—or better yet to be permanently put down—before I could stop looking over my shoulder.

*No, not death. I don't want him killed.*

That would be way too easy. I wanted him to live a very long time in the worst conditions possible. He deserved to enjoy purgatory in the real world followed by a one-way ticket to Hell for eternity once he keeled over.

Liam deserved to spend the rest of his days on the prison planet Molvi in the brutal care of one of the Hell Lords who ran it.

"I'm really impatient to get started with some of the classes," I said, wanting to shift back to a safer topic. "I'm self-taught. So I need proper training, especially with pattern making, stitching, embroidery, and draping, among other things. And then, on top of you having some of the coolest braids in the city, I'll make sure you're also the most fashionable Zamorian."

Krogal chuckled, his tension fading just as I hoped. "I'm more than happy to play mannequin for you, my mate."

"Did I tell you that you're the best?" I asked, my heart melting for him.

"I'm not sure," he said, pretending to be searching his memory. "Maybe you should remind me."

I chuckled and drew his face towards mine. He came willingly then immediately took control of the kiss. That suited me just fine. While I didn't exactly fit the submissive profile, I liked for my man to take control in the bedroom.

Then again, I didn't have much experience with men as Liam had been my first and only. But all thoughts of that rich wretch vanished as I savored the slightly sweet taste of my mate as our tongues mingled. His massive hands caressed the skin of my back and sides, exposed by my short crop top, attached between my breasts by a small knot. They glided down to my behind, each palm settling on my butt cheeks and giving them a firm squeeze. Despite the restraint he consistently displayed, Krogal was nonetheless growing bolder in his fondling, and I loved it.

Emulating him, I grabbed his perfect behind and pressed my pelvis against his—although it was technically against his thighs considering my petite stature in comparison to his gigantic height, even with me standing on my tippy toes. He picked me up, and I wrapped my legs around his waist. The thigh-high slits on both sides of my ankle-length skirt allowed me to do so without the fabric getting in the way.

As was his wont, Krogal quickly got me hot and bothered with the expert way in which he was kissing me. His primary hands teased all my erogenous spots, from my nape to the right side of the crook of my neck, the small of my back, and the sides of my breasts, right where they began to curve. Feeling his shafts hardening against my stomach also did a number on me.

Just as I was considering telling him to carry me back to his room, Krogal ended the kiss and locked eyes with me.

"Don't kiss me like that when we're on our way out," he grumbled with pretend frustration.

"First off, *you* kissed *me*!" I exclaimed. "And second, it's not my fault you started something you can't finish."

"Who says I can't finish?" he growled.

"The clock does," I replied mockingly. "But it's okay. Consider that your incentive to not get yourself demolished during the game so that we can pick up where we left off later tonight."

Krogal froze. Having his four eyes flicking between mine to make sure he wasn't misinterpreting my underlying meaning made me dizzy. I still occasionally struggled to figure out which eye to stare at when looking at him. Nevertheless, I pressed my chest against his and gave his bottom lip a little nip to make things clearer. His chest vibrating with a hungry growl had me instantly wet.

"Consider me properly incentivized, my mate. I *will not* get hurt," Krogal said in a rumbling tone.

My nipples pebbled in reaction to his heated expression, and my toes curled as he reclaimed my lips in one last passionate kiss before setting me back down on my feet. Taking me by the hand, he led me to our personal shuttle on the terrace. By the time we took off, my inner walls were still contracting and throbbing with frustrated need.

It was a short flight to the massive arena where the clan would be challenging our neighbors, Azamphir Clan, in the Zamorian's national sport called Fultar. I'd read up a little about it and seen some videos. It vaguely reminded me of a cross between rugby and no-holds-barred elements of wrestling.

The gist of the game was to grab a ball and carry it across the goal line of the rival team. Obviously, the opponent would use every means necessary to keep you from it, and better yet to steal the ball from you and score in your own end zone. What worried me was the semi combat allowed. You couldn't just start punching and kicking people. However, you wanted to toss your opponent to the ground and keep him immobilized there for a five-second count to put him in a forced timeout for a short while.

Each participant had a special node stuck to their backs, between their shoulder blades. Knocking down your opponent didn't suffice. You needed to get the actual node in direct and continued contact with the ground for those five seconds. Breaking that contact for even half a second was enough to reset the timer. But if you succeeded, the node would immediately send a signal to the player's nervous system, paralyzing him for thirty seconds.

While that sounded fairly brief, in a heated match, it would be an eternity, especially if multiple members of a single team ended up paralyzed at the same time.

As our shuttle landed, the worry I'd been trying to keep it bay reared its ugly head again. By all accounts, my man rocked this game, and so did our clan. They had won seven of the last ten championships, finishing second in the other three cases. However, the fact that the men wore none of the type of protective gear football players did unnerved me. Then again, rugby players didn't wear protective equipment either.

But they also didn't average 7 1/2 feet tall, 250 lbs. of pure muscle, and two sets of arms strong enough to toss an adult bull with one hand as if it was just a tennis ball.

The arena was already packed when we arrived. Krogal led me to the bleachers. As our Matriarch, Feidin, her husband, their children and their spouses normally occupied the VIP box, while the rest of the clan settled in the seats on each side of it. Today, exceptionally, Talin and I were invited to join Feidin, Belle, and Kari—Varkuth's wife. Since all our husbands would be duking it out in the field, it made sense we should be together to encourage them.

Today marked my fourth time meeting Talin since our first rough encounter outside the lift. Each time, we'd only see the other in passing. To my relief, she'd been content to give me a polite nod without engaging me in conversation. To my shame, the part of me keen on avoiding conflict at all cost welcomed it.

But like with Krogal's disapproval of my desire to hide from Liam, dodging Talin would only last so long before I needed to deal with it.

Thankfully, she once again acted courteous towards me, if a little distant. As much as I loved the motherly hug Feidin gave me, I couldn't help the sliver of guilt it sparked. Considering Feidin had taken her son as hers, I didn't want to rub it in Talin's face that she was also taking her daughter-in-law. In spite of her prickly disposition, I believed a sensitive and loving female lurked behind that hard exterior.

We settled in our respective seats with a perfect view of the massive arena sprawling before us. Seeing Belle shift restlessly in her seat brought a smile to my face. That woman truly was a ray of sunshine. She explained enthusiastically what was about to happen and gave me the lowdown on the friendly rivalry that opposed our clan to Azamphir since the beginning of time. Even Talin would cast the occasional amused glance at Belle, pitching in some juicy anecdotes about how our men stomped all over them during various encounters over the years.

The almost malicious glimmer that sparked in her dark eyes so similar to Krogal's revealed how much Talin was anticipating the havoc and mayhem that would soon ensue. My mate had initially worried about me attending the match. The silly man feared seeing him going feral against his opponents would make me fear him.

Obviously, I didn't want him ever becoming violent with me. But I had no problem watching him give a proper spanking to a rival team while observing the rules of engagement of a brutal contact sport. My only concern was that he might get injured. At least, with the Zamorians ranking among the top ten most advanced species of the galaxy, their medical technology could quickly fix the majority of injuries earned during such a match, even serious ones.

The sound of loud drums rising in a rhythmic pattern had the crowd go wild for a few seconds before a hush descended over the arena. A haunting melody resonated through the com system and a number of young women clad in traditional outfits in the colors of both competing clans entered the arena. They launched into a beautiful choreography with elements that vaguely reminded me of a mix of hula and a slower paced step dance. Their movements blended strength, sensuality, and a lethal confidence that had me mesmerized.

My mind overflowed with ideas for my own spin of choreographies inspired by their traditional dance. Some of the movements from our folkloric Yanvalou and Ibo dances associated with Vodou would mix perfectly with theirs. A part of me wished I was dancing right alongside them. I would have to look into joining them in the future.

The tribal melody gradually faded as the drums came back to the fore, their rhythm taking on a faster and more ominous pace. Savage cries resonated from each end of the arena as the females twirled and swirled their way out through the side doors. The two teams rushed in like two armies about to clash once they met in the middle. However, each team stopped on their half of the terrain, the twenty men of their respective units standing in four perfect rows of five columns each.

Heart pounding with excitement, I pressed my palms to the top of the stone railing in front of me and leaned forward to take in the show about to take place before us. My man looked so impressive, towering over everyone else on his team. Naked but for a tight pair of black shorts with a red stripe and cleats on his feet, he looked good enough to eat. The only other thing noticeable was the black node between his shoulder blades. From a distance, it merely looked like a five-inch square patch glued to his skin.

His team wore similar outfits. Ugrul—Feidin's husband—occupied the central position in the front row, flanked by his sons Bayron and Varkuth. My Krogal stood to Varkuth's right, while his father, Orym, stood at the other end, next to Bayron. They made for an impressive front line, not only by their sheer sizes, but also by the fierceness of their expressions.

Facing them, a few meters away on their half of the terrain, the Azamphir Clan were clad the same way, but in the forest-green and orange colors of their people. Ugrul emitted a savage war cry, echoed moments later by the rest of our men. Seconds later, they broke into a mesmerizing dance. Once again, elements of it undeniably reminded me of step dance, but it mainly resembled their version of Haka.

It lasted a little over a minute before they stopped in a menacing pose. The rival team responded with feral shouts of their own, then performed their own little dance. After a minute of this, the Azamphir team stopped, and the drums resounded over the arena. As much as I wanted to see the match begin, I felt disappointed that their dance had ended so soon. I could have watched a while longer—or rather drooled at—their wild display.

The crowd loudly expressed its enthusiasm as the teams took position, their respective twenty men loosely spread over two rows near the central line. Being the visiting team, Azamphir started with the ball. An older male from our clan I didn't know brought it to their leader, before moving to the sidelines.

The entire attendance appeared to hold its breath as the opponents glared tauntingly at each other while waiting for the signal. I yelped when the shrill sound finally went off. The deafening shouts of the crowd easily buried it as both teams charged forward.

A mix of pride and amusement surged through me when I realized that Tomu—the Azamphir Clan Leader, who also happened to be carrying the ball—was running as quickly away from Krogal as his strong legs permitted. His team scattered, charging forward deep in our territory, hoping for a pass. Seconds before Ugrul rammed into him, Tomu tossed the ball to one of his men on the left. The poor sod jumped to catch it but barely held it for half a beat.

Before he could land back on his feet, Bayron grabbed his legs, and slammed his back onto the ground. His opponent appeared winded by the force of the blow. With one powerful swipe, Bayron knocked the oval ball out of his hand, and pressed his foot on the male's chest, likely to activate the node that would paralyze him for a short while. His opponent obviously tried to fight back. As much as I wanted to see if Bayron would succeed in keeping the node against the ground long enough for paralysis to kick in, the ball flying in my mate's direction reclaimed my attention.

I caught myself shouting in frustrated anger when an Azamphir clansman caught the flying ball right in front of my man.

Big mistake.

Running at full speed, Krogal scooped him up and carried him under his left secondary arm like a giant log. Without slowing, Krogal yanked the ball away from him with his right hands then tossed the man like trash. Every Azamphir male converged on Krogal, who was running as if a swarm of rabid demons was hot on his tail. His teammates knocked many of their opponents out of the way, some of them engaging in full-on wrestling brawls to paralyze the others. A few blue lights went off, like a shimmering shield over the bodies of those who got their backs —and more specifically their nodes—pinned to the ground for five seconds.

But I only had eyes for Krogal.

I realized I'd jumped to my feet and was shouting my lungs out when Belle stood up next to me and alternated between yelling encouragement at her husband and cussing out the two Azamphir clansmen trying to trip him and pin him down.

I nearly lost my mind when Krogal crossed the last few meters into the goal zone, dragging one man who was clinging to his right leg, another pulling on his right primary arm, and a third monkey riding his back. The ease with which he kept running was beyond embarrassing for his rivals.

And it was hot as fuck!

Dejected, the men released Krogal, who raised his four arms in a victorious gesture. The crowd—and I—went wild. As both teams ran back to the center of the arena—which seemed a third longer than a standard rugby field—he glanced in my direction. The huge smile that stretched his lips when he found me frantically clapping struck me like an arrow to the heart. I blew a kiss at him, and he pretended to catch it and press it to his lips.

Yeah, I was falling hard for my behemoth.

This time, our clan was starting with the ball. Seeing a third of the Azamphir clansmen take position close to Krogal had people snickering. I couldn't decide if I was prouder that they acknowledged my man as the biggest threat, or more worried about how brutal they might get with him.

It was Ugrul's turn to take off with the ball. Although a few of their opponents made a beeline for him, at least a third of them either went after Krogal or hovered around him. It struck me as both flattering and silly. Taking the lead, Bayron and Varkuth barreled through anyone who even remotely looked like they wanted to mess with their father. A handful of our men also cleared the path for him. Realizing their mistake at focusing on my mate, the Azamphir clansmen started shifting towards our clan leader who was getting dangerously close to their goal zone.

Krogal, who had been luring his tails in a wild goose chase, seized the moment to burst into action. Seeing him effortlessly grab two men—one with his two right hands and the other with the left ones—and effortlessly slamming them on to the ground had me roaring with encouragement. They tried to fight him off, but miserably failed at lifting their backs in time. A third man jumped onto him again. Krogal rolled so that his attacker would lie on his back beneath him and kept him pinned down until his node also went off.

Perceiving this as their opportunity to temporarily take him out of the game, at least seven Azamphir men piled up on top of him. A flood of less-than-ladylike expletives poured out of me as Krogal fought them off as best he could. Whatever doubt I might have had about his phenomenal strength faded as I watched in disbelief my man push up to a sitting position on top of the paralyzed male beneath him, despite the onslaught. He surged forward, flattening one of the males in front of him trying to push him down. Crushed under his weight, his opponent never managed to free himself before the paralysis light went off.

With a savage roar, Krogal fought to get back on his feet, his muscles bulging as four rivals—two on each side—each held onto one of his arms and used their weights to try and keep him down. Seeing him drag them like heavy sacks had the crowd chanting his name. When he suddenly stopped moving forward, I briefly thought he'd grown too exhausted to continue. But only then did I realize he'd provided enough distraction for his teammates to score again.

The next few rounds turned out to be variations of the same, although Azamphir managed to score on a couple of occasions. Demar seriously impressed me. He didn't have the mass or strength of his brother and was clearly less imposing than Bayron and Ugrul. But my brother-in-law was fast as hell. More than once, him taking off in a random, less crowded space at dizzying speed, created the perfect opening for a pass that led them closer to the goal zone.

My Krogal managed to take the ball into the goal zone one more time, but it quickly became clear that the opposing team would continue to focus on trying to keep him out of the action. At first, it seriously bothered me. It felt as if they were picking on him. Thankfully, the joyous expression on his face put those worries to rest. My beast was having a blast. More importantly, despite the relentlessness with which they kept trying—and failing—to pin him down, the Azamphir clansmen all displayed a friendly type of sportsmanship.

Whenever a goal was scored, regardless of which team earned it, they would immediately release Krogal, some of them even appearing to apologize for their roughness or checking that he was unharmed. A few slapped him in the back with admiration, and others accepted the hand he extended to them to help them up after their paralysis faded. The obvious respect and admiration they displayed for my man moved me to the core.

It wasn't until ten minutes before the end of the match that the opposing team finally managed to pin him down long enough for his node to go off. While my protective side wanted to boo and hiss at them getting the upper end on my mate, I couldn't help but laugh at the Azamphir clansmen's reaction. The way they cheered and high-fived each other for succeeding was beyond hilarious. Even the crowd joined in, actually applauding their success at this nearly impossible feat.

And nearly impossible was quite accurate.

It took ten men to finally get the better of him. After five of them managed to trip him, he curled into a turtle position, his arms hooked into those of his opponents to make it harder for them to push him onto his back. More and more joined the fray, looking like they were trying to roll a boulder as they battled to get him onto his back. Even with that achieved, he kept shifting his shoulders just enough to break the node's contact with the ground long enough to reset the timer. It wasn't until the tenth man piled on top of him that it became too much for him to overcome.

Despite our team's clear superiority, Azamphir lost with a very respectable score, and after giving us a most enjoyable match. As I watched the men file out of the arena under the cheers of the crowd, my heart filled with possessive pride and affection for my mate. As I turned to head out of the VIP box and make my way down to the locker room to wait for Krogal to come out, my gaze landed on Talin.

The same pride I felt shone brightly on her beautiful features. She had every reason to be proud. Her husband and both her sons performed exceptionally well.

No doubt sensing me staring, she turned her head to glance at me sideways. Our gazes locked, and an unreadable expression fleeted over her face.

"Your mate played admirably," she said in a neutral but polite tone.

A dozen different responses burned my tongue. However, the one I ended up giving took even me by surprise.

"Of course he did," I said, matter-of-factly. "He is visibly the greatest warrior in this arena."

"He absolutely is," she replied, lifting her chin defiantly. "Which is why it is such a waste."

"How is it a waste?" I asked, my voice devoid of any antagonism. "Tonight, everyone got to see it yet again. Krogal doesn't have to flaunt it every day to establish his dominance. Actually, the less he shows it, the better."

Talin recoiled, stunned by my comment. Feidin, Belle, and Kari eyed me with curiosity, also wondering what I meant by that.

"How would showing it less help establish his dominance?" Talin asked.

"Humans have a saying about how familiarity breeds contempt. In some cases, it can even fuel resentment," I explained calmly. "As Krogal clearly demonstrated tonight, no one can beat him. If he always participated in every combat or physical competition, what would be the point or incentive for anyone else to partake, knowing they would only ever finish second, at best? It would make the event predictable and boring."

"Then they only have to train harder," Talin replied dismissively.

"Do you really think anyone could ever train hard enough to rival your son?" I challenged.

The way she pursed her lips and further lifted her chin screamed of motherly pride. Obviously, she knew no one stood a chance.

"Tonight, the way the opposing team interacted with him really opened my eyes," I said wistfully. "The fact that he rarely partakes in those events makes it a special treat for the crowd when he does and an honor for his rivals. Did you not listen to them? Did you not see how much they rejoiced and celebrated when they finally managed to get him paralyzed?"

"It took ten of them to achieve it!" Talin said with a sliver of outrage.

"Exactly!" I exclaimed as if it was self-evident. "Under normal circumstances, people would be ashamed that it would take so much of them to take down one guy. However, he is such a legend that those males not only derived great pride to have achieved the impossible, but they also felt in complete awe that his incredible strength required ten of them to succeed. This is true fame and honor for your house. People will be speaking forever about the Skortheatis behemoth who required the strength of ten elite warriors to be taken down. And those warriors will brag of having had the honor to be one of those ten."

Talin took on the troubled expression, having apparently never looked at it from that perspective.

"Krogal doesn't need to make a show of his prowess. All Xoccoris knows your son is the greatest warrior of this era. He doesn't need to devote his entire life to it to achieve what you wish. He's already done it," I said in a gentle voice. "He's happy. Isn't it all that matters?"

She pressed her lips into a thin line, as she controlled the somewhat mulish expression wanting to rear its head.

"You care about him," Talin finally replied, her tone a little grumpy as if trying to make a begrudging concession.

"Of course, I do," I replied in a factual manner. "We're soulmates. You raised the most wonderful male I have ever met. It was a blessing that Kayog somehow managed to bring us together and to make me a part of your family and of your wonderful people."

She gave me a stiff nod, once more fighting hard to hide her emotions—in this instance how much my words touched her. It took every ounce of my willpower to repress an amused smile in light of her misplaced pride.

"You should drop by our place one of these days," I said softly. "Krogal loves you and misses you."

She ran the fingers of her primary hand through her long obsidian hair, while her secondary hands hugged her midsection. This time, she failed to fully hide the sadness she felt at the rift between them.

"I love him, too," she replied as if it was self-evident. "He's my firstborn."

"Then tell him," I said in a gentle voice. "Our men should be coming out of the locker room any minute now. We should go find them."

Talin gave me another stiff nod then took the lead, walking out of the VIP box. I slightly frowned and cast a worried glance towards Feidin. Technically, as the clan's Matriarch, should she be deemed the protector of our little group?

But Feidin was staring at me, motherly love and approval shining in her golden eyes. She approached and gently caressed my cheek while winking at me. The fact that Zamorians did that with both their left eyes always messed with my head. I doubted a lifetime would suffice for me to ever truly get used to it. But the sentiment behind that reaction was all that mattered. Our Matriarch made no mystery she hoped to see the relationship patched up between her sister and her nephew. She was walking a fine line trying to help the situation along without coming out too forcefully or further alienating her sister.

As I watched her exit the box behind Talin, Belle came to stand next to me. With a big grin on her face, she gave me two thumbs up that had me snorting. That female was a riot.

We hastened after the two Zamorian females, weaving our way through the crowd talking excitedly about the match in the hallways. Their elation was contagious. You couldn't walk past it all without a huge grin plastered on your face. Getting patted on the shoulder for my husband's stellar performance—even though I had no merit for any of it—had me even more thrilled. But seeing Talin strutting like a peacock was hilarious.

A few men were already pouring out of the locker room when we finally reached it. Both our clanmates and the Azamphyr teammates were hanging outside the door, chatting happily. To my surprise, Tomu—the rival team's Clan Leader—stared at Talin with a taunting expression while she glared at him.

"Peace, Talinsaya Skortheatis," Tomu said in an amused voice. "I have not taken your son."

"But you tried!" she hissed.

"Of course, I did! Who wouldn't, given the opportunity?" he asked as if she'd said something silly. "I want no quarrel with you, female. Let the sound trouncing your males—and especially your son—gave us today be compensation enough for the offense."

Talin huffed haughtily without answering. Tomu chuckled, his dark-brown eyes, a slightly lighter shade than his hair, sparkling with mischief. Despite the scar running down the side of his left eyes, and his intimidating presence typical of Zamorian males, the Azamphyr clan leader seemed rather charming. That Feidin and Kari watched the scene with amusement confirmed this was all in good fun, despite Talin likely truly being offended by the situation.

As I understood it, when Krogal asked to sever his tie with his mother, had the request been denied, he would have chopped off his braid and joined the Azamphyr Clan instead with Tomu's blessing.

"And you must be his little human?" he asked, turning to me.

I smiled and opened my mouth to respond, but Krogal's voice behind him stopped me.

"Yes, she is. Stay away from my mate," he said with false severity.

Pretending to be intimidated—a stance belied by his grin—Tomu raised his palms in surrender and took a step back. "Apologies!"

To my shock, I instinctively ran and threw myself into Krogal's arms. He chuckled, caught me on the fly, and lifted me in his powerful embrace. My toes curled at the passionate and possessive kiss he gave me. Sadly, it was all too brief. Then again, I wouldn't exactly call myself an exhibitionist.

"You were amazing!" I said as he reluctantly put me back down on my feet. "Don't you agree, Talin?" I asked, glancing at her over my shoulder.

Although he kept a neutral expression on his face, Krogal stiffened in a very subtle fashion. Had my arms not been wrapped around him, I probably wouldn't have felt it.

"Yes, he was," she said in a soft, but cautious tone. "You were quite formidable, Krogal and did a wonderful job of putting a certain would-be usurper in his place," she added a bit more sternly while casting a sideways dark glance at Tomu.

The Azamphyr Clan Leader snorted, totally unfazed by the dig.

"It was just a bit of Fultar fun," Krogal said with an almost timid humility, which he tried to hide behind a smile.

Talin waved a dismissive hand. "It was more than that. You brought great honor to our house in our clan. But then, you always do."

My heart leapt upon hearing her making this genuine effort

to acknowledge her son's awesomeness. Krogal blinked, visibly taken aback by this unexpected compliment.

"Fultar is a team sport. Great teamwork makes all the difference. Father and Demar were formidable, not to mention the others," he said, looking a bit embarrassed before glancing at Orym and Demar who had come outside of the locker with him. "We make each other shine."

"Stop being so modest," Demar said, slapping the back of his shoulder.

Orym grunted his agreement, which seemed to move Krogal even more.

"I wasn't just speaking about tonight's Fultar match," Talin said a little stiffly, like she was feeling mightily awkward. "Even though we don't always see eye to eye on certain things, we… *I* am always proud of you."

It was like a nuclear bomb had just gone off. The loud and excited voices around us faded in the background while Krogal stared at his mother with a powerful emotion. Words were not needed. Eyes locked, they exchanged a silent but deep communication. After a few seconds that might as well have been a century, Talin blinked and averted her eyes before giving her husband a critical once-over. The way he looked back at his wife was the softest I'd seen from Orym, while Demar beamed proudly at her.

"Well, you certainly got properly bruised during the match," Talin said in a grumpy tone. "Let's get you patched up. There's a feast later, and I can't have my mate and second son looking all banged up like this. Farah, you go and fix your mate," she added in a commanding tone.

Belle snorted in amusement, while the rest of us bit the insides of our cheeks to repress our smiles. A part of me wanted to go give my mother-in-law a big hug. This wasn't easy for her, but I loved that she was making genuine efforts.

"Yes, Talin," I said in a slightly submissive tone that seemed to please her, making me want to smile even more.

"Come, my dear husband. Let's take care of those booboos," I said teasingly.

Waving everyone goodbye, I let Krogal lead me back to our shuttle.

# CHAPTER 13
## KROGAL

Every cell in my body vibrated with excitement and happiness as we flew the short distance back home. Aside from the adrenaline rush that always came with a brutal match of Fultar, having my Farah fawning over me like this had me over the moon. I'd been so worried that seeing me in that rather violent setting would set back the progress we had made so far. But my mate had been as rabid a fan and supporter as any pureblood Zamorian. Just remembering how she cheered for me and cussed out the opponents trying to pin me down still had my hearts filling with joy.

And my mother's words before our departure had been the culminating point of a perfect day. My mate's role in getting her to make such an admission only made me love her even more. She truly was my soulmate.

As soon as we landed on our terrace, Farah started fussing over me.

"Are you hurt badly?" she asked, concern oozing out of her voice as we entered the living area through the giant patio doors of the terrace.

Even as she spoke, she carefully touched some of the spots on my arms that had started darkening.

"Terribly," I said in an overly dramatic fashion.

I almost felt guilty when Farah stiffened and examined my features with genuine worry.

"Really? Should you see a doctor?" she asked.

I shook my head reassuringly. "No, that won't be necessary. A physician already examined us in the locker room before we were allowed to leave. I'm just very sore and bruised."

Farah's shoulders drooped with relief. As much as I wanted to feel ashamed about sparking concern for my welfare, seeing my mate so worried about me stroked the needy part of me and filled my chest with warmth.

"All right. Go take a shower, and I'll apply some healing cream on you," she said in a commanding tone that had me want to smile.

I loved how my mate was steadily becoming more assertive as she increasingly felt safe and confident in her right to express herself. Despite her delicate appearance, my Farah held a great deal of strength within. Soon, she would be bossing me around like our females tended to do. Oddly enough, I looked forward to it, if only to play martyrs like my fellow Zamorian males always claimed to be whenever they balked at their wives' requests.

In truth, the masochist in me couldn't wait for the day Farah would yank my braid—in that instance my leash—to impose her will on me. Considering the tense relationship with my mother, you'd think I would dread such behavior from my wife. But at a visceral level, I knew whatever demands my mate would make would not be unreasonable.

I made quick work of showering. I ended it with a good minute under ice cold water to cool the fire raging in my blood at the thought of my woman rubbing her hands all over me as she applied the healing cream. As much as I wanted Farah to know what burning desire I felt for her, walking out with both of my cocks fully erect wasn't how I wanted to communicate that I was ready and eager as soon as she was.

Under normal circumstances, I wouldn't bother using any cream. I had gotten banged up far worse than this in the past. Despite the bruising quickly darkening, it didn't actually hurt enough to even be worth mentioning. But I had no qualms playing the wounded puppy to have my woman fussing over me.

As I suspected she was onto me, it made the game all the more fun.

I wrapped a towel around my waist as I walked out of my en suite hygiene room. To my surprise, Farah was standing by my bed with a pot of healing cream in her hands. My brain froze as I registered the slight dampness of her hair at the nape and the bathrobe she had donned instead of the dress she previously wore.

My mate had showered as well and used a cap to keep from wetting her hair.

My stomach did a couple of backflips, and I groaned inwardly as my blood rushed to my groin at the thought of what this could mean. Farah's words earlier to the effect she wanted to give me an incentive not to get too hurt on the field replayed in my mind. Could it truly mean what I hoped it did?

"Oh, give me a moment to go put some pants on," I said, feeling irrationally nervous.

Farah shook her head. "No, keep the towel. Even from here, I can see some bruising on your legs. It will be easier for me to access with the towel."

She gestured for me to approach, and I complied. My stomach fluttered, and another wave of lust surged through me at the greedy way her gaze roamed over my body. It still boggled my mind that such a stunning female should find me attractive. By Zamorian standards, I would be deemed a very handsome male. But off-worlders found my species a little freakish, especially with our four eyes and arms.

"Wow, those are some really nasty bruises," Farah mused out loud as I stopped next to the bed a couple of steps in front of her. "They must really hurt."

"Horribly," I said in a piteous tone that sounded excessively fake even to my own ears.

She snorted and gave me a look that made it clear she wasn't fooled in the least. To my delight, she continued to play along.

"Well then, we're going to have to treat them. I can't have your mother chastising me for allowing her firstborn to endure such agony," my mate said mockingly. "Lie down on your stomach," she commanded.

Once again, I complied, wincing and groaning in a dramatic fashion as I did so. The musical sound of Farah giggling filled the room, putting a smile on my face. And yet, I turned my head sideways to glare at her before resting my cheek on the mattress.

"I'm not sensing a great deal of empathy from you, dear wife," I grumbled in a pouty tone.

She snorted and knelt on the mattress next to me. "You poor baby. Of course I empathize with you. Am I not here treating your terrible wounds?" she asked as she brushed my hair aside to expose my back.

I grunted in a non-committal fashion, which had her chuckling some more. The cool feel of the cream on my back wrested an involuntary moan from me. This time, I wasn't pretending. Until now, I hadn't realized how sore I actually felt. Considering ten mature males piled up on me multiple times during the match and desperately tried to wrestle me into submission, it wasn't surprising that I should feel so tender.

"That feels good, doesn't it?" Farah asked, her voice taking a genuinely sympathetic edge as she gently applied the cream on my skin.

I couldn't tell if the sense of well-being seeping into me came more from the soothing and numbing effects of the cream, or my mate's wondrous touch rubbing it into my skin. Whatever the cause, I savored every second, shamelessly purring as she applied the cream on my back, shoulders, arms, and legs. The wretched female naturally seized the opportunity to torment me, slipping her hands beneath the edge of the towel still wrapped around my waist. She carefully massaged the cream right below the bump of my ass, and at the back of my legs, her hands slipping provocatively between my thighs, just shy of reaching their apex.

"Wow, they really bruised you everywhere," she said mockingly while her fingers continued to tease me.

My frustrated grunt only had her laughing in an unrepentant fashion. And yet, my body couldn't decide whether to be aroused by her gentle and sensuous contact or become wonderfully languid as she continued to massage the healing cream into my skin, loosening the knots in my muscles along the way.

"Okay, you can turn onto your back now," Farah said after she was done giving me a foot rub.

I felt almost groggy as I rolled to the side and then onto my back. A single glance at my face had my woman burst out laughing. I didn't need a mirror to guess I looked completely drugged up.

"Ouch, that's one really nasty bruise you've got there," Farah said with a frown as she stared at my chest.

I glanced down at my right pectoral. During one of the pile ups, someone had rested their knee on my chest, right below my clavicle. It had hurt like hell.

"They brutalized me! I doubt even the healing cream can appease this," I said.

Farah snorted, and quickly repressed a chuckle. "My poor husband. Maybe I should kiss it better."

"It might help," I said a bit too eagerly.

My mate cast a mocking look my way before leaning forward. I held my breath while she carefully pressed her lips to my bruise. As she straightened, her braids brushed over my chest, sending a thrill down my spine.

"That's amazing," I whispered, my voice dropping an octave. "It works even better than that cream you used on my back."

"Does it?" Farah asked with an exaggerated air of surprise. "Should I do it for your other bruises?"

"It's worth a try," I shamelessly concurred.

Her beautiful brown eyes sparked with mischief as she once more leaned forward to kiss another bruise on my chest.

"Yes! Much better," I said with a purr. "It's almost miraculous."

She chuckled before moving to the other side of my torso. "And here?" Farah asked before kissing a spot right above my armpit.

I merely growled in approval.

My mate continued peppering my chest and stomach with little kisses, asking in between if that area also needed some attention. After she covered most of it, Farah lifted her head to look at me, her eyes darkened by what I could only assume to be arousal.

"And what about here?" she asked in a sultry voice, her index finger circling the areola of my left nipple. "I don't see any bruising, but I want to be thorough."

"It may not show, but it got badly mistreated. It's undoubtedly the most tender part and is in dire need of urgent care," I replied, pretending to feel major discomfort.

"You have no shame," she whispered with a chuckle.

"When it comes to you, my Farah, I have none whatsoever," I deadpanned, although a sliver of seriousness entered my voice.

I was falling hard for my woman. There truly wasn't anything I wouldn't do for her.

Farah kissing my left nipple had a bolt of lust exploding in my pelvic area. My abdominal muscles contracted when she didn't move away and poked her tongue out to lick the little nub before drawing a wet circle around the areola. I took a hissy breath as her lips latched on to my nipple, and she leisurely sucked on it.

I slipped my primary right hand through her soft braids to gently hold her head in place, but not in a way that would prevent her from moving away if she so chose. My secondary hands caressed her back through the thick fabric of her bathrobe. I reined in the urge to rid her of the garment. Although my woman was clearly signaling her desire to take our relationship to the next level, I wanted her to take the lead and set the pace. She needed to know I wouldn't push her farther than what she was ready for.

That didn't stop me from hoping.

My stomach quivered, and my cocks started to perk up when she let go of my nipple to pursue her journey south. Her mouth on my abdominal muscles had them involuntarily constricting. The timid spark of desire in my loins flared into a burning flame when Farah's hands started fiddling with the knot that held my towel bound around my waist. She was trying to be inconspicuous about it, distracting me by teasing my navel with her tongue. But there was no way I wouldn't notice such a thing.

I couldn't help the tension building in my back when she slowly parted the towel, exposing me bare. My mate had never seen that part of my anatomy, but the many times we had embraced, I'd felt her unease and worry about how thick my cocks felt against her through the fabric.

Farah moved further down until she was staring straight at my crotch. I swallowed hard and realized I was holding my breath as she unabashedly examined me. To my utter relief, she didn't appear traumatized by them. That didn't stop her eyes from slightly widening. She licked her lips nervously—although her face also displayed something that felt akin to wonder.

My breath hitched when she caressed my pelvis before brushing her fingertips along the length of my lower, smaller cock. Blood rushed to my groin, and I felt irrationally mortified as both my cocks thickened and lengthened as my erections steadily grew. Seeing her delicate hand wrapping around my lower cock made me realize just how massive I was in comparison to her.

That she wasn't running for dear life blew my mind.

With an air of fascination, she traced one of the 'necklaces' of my lower cock with her index finger. It referred to the pearl-like ridges that lined the left and right sides of my cocks. A shiver coursed through me, and I swallowed back the moan that wanted to rise in my throat as she boldly explored my lower cock and then the main one. While her fingers fell just short of touching around the former's girth, they came nowhere near with the latter.

And still, my woman didn't seem to panic.

Then again, she'd had a few weeks to mentally prepare for this moment. Clearly, she had put them to good use.

"Did they hurt you there as well?" she whispered, each hand wrapped around one of my cocks.

"Yes," I breathed out, my voice barely audible to my own ears.

Farah smiled, a mischievous glimmer sparkling in her stunning dark-brown eyes. "We can't have that."

A strangled gasp escaped me when she leaned forward and rubbed the side of her face against my length in a downward motion. On her way up, she turned her face to the side so that her lips would brush against the necklace on the left side of my lower cock. A violent shudder swept through me. I inhaled deeply then exhaled slowly to control my breathing.

My wife peppered a series of kisses all over it while gently stroking my main cock. The small fire burning low in my belly turned into a roaring brazier when she poked her tongue out and licked my lower cock from its base to the tip. An almost pained moan vibrated in my throat when she took my lower head in her mouth. She didn't bob at first, content to suck the head and tease it by swirling her tongue around it. The whole time, her right hand continued to stroke my main cock.

I emitted a needy growl when she took me deeper into her mouth, and as far back as her throat would allow. With a will of its own, my hand in her hair fisted her braids. Grinding my teeth, I forced my arm to remain relaxed so as not to restrict her movements. Careful at first, Farah gradually picked up the pace as she grew more comfortable with my girth. Leaning on my secondary forearms, I stared at her as she sucked me.

An inferno was raging in my loins, and it took every ounce of my willpower not to thrust upward into her mouth. Kromor's teeth, I fantasized for so long about intimacy with my mate, but I never would have imagined she would take the lead, and especially not with such boldness.

However, as much as I wanted to give myself over to the divine feel of her mouth on me, I only meant for her to familiarize herself with my body. Our first time together should be about her pleasure, not mine. I would be damned if I would find release before her.

Judging by the way she was accelerating her movements, even her hand stroking me, squeezing the base tightly on the way up, Farah was clearly trying to make me climax.

I would, but not now.

Silencing my selfish need to let her pursue her ministrations, I tugged on her braids to force her head away from me. She gasped and gave me a questioning and slightly offended look. It was quickly replaced by shock and the startled yelp when I effortlessly lifted her before laying her on her back in the center of the bed.

I claimed her lips in a passionate kiss. She didn't argue or challenge my taking over. Instead, she wrapped her arms around me, caressing my back with a possessiveness that messed with me. I loved the softness of her tongue swirling around mine, her sweet taste, and the way she followed my lead. I didn't want a submissive woman, but I couldn't deny having dominant tendencies in the bedroom.

Even though she already took things to another level with that fellatio, I moved slowly and first caressed her body over the thick bathrobe she still wore. My right hand glided down her side, past her narrow waist and the length of her upper leg before slipping under the hem. She shivered as my palm caressed her thigh in an upward movement. To my pleasant surprise, I didn't encounter any underwear.

I continued my journey upward, parting the left panel of her robe. But the belt tied at her waist kept me from fully opening it. I did quick work of untying it with my primary left hand. As the left one resumed its now unencumbered trajectory, I broke the kiss and lifted my head to lock eyes with Farah. She held my gaze unwaveringly as my palm caressed a path up her flat stomach and between her breasts.

Moving ever so slowly to give her a chance to balk or pull away, I covered her left breast with my hand, fondling it, then teasing the nipple with my thumb until it pebbled. Farah smiled and lifted her chest for greater contact. I returned her smile and used both my primary hands to push the fabric of her bathrobe wide open and over her shoulders. She slightly lifted her back to help me rid her of the garment. As she was pulling her arms out of the sleeves, I leaned forward to suck one of her taut nipples into my mouth.

Her sigh of delight resonated straight in my cocks. It was her turn to sink her fingers through my hair as I took my sweet time worshiping each of her breasts in turn with my mouth, while my hands freely roamed over the silkiness of her golden skin. I loved its soft texture, Fresh scent, and light saltiness.

With each touch, I studied her responses, making note of each of her sensitive spots and paying them extra attention. But the delicious scent of her growing arousal soon had my mouth watering. Unable to resist, I ventured further south towards my prize. Once again, I gave her every opportunity to stop me, but at this point, it was clear that she was all in. On the way, I paused at her outie navel. I couldn't help but nip at it, which had her giggling.

In our time together, I'd discovered that my woman was extremely ticklish. Most people seemed to be particularly sensitive to tickling on their sides and under their feet. For Farah, it was the crook of her neck and her navel. Sometimes, I only had to point my index finger at her neck, and she would already start giggling.

But laughter was the last thing my touch in her other sensitive area elicited. Her stomach quivered when I brushed her cleanly shaven sex with two fingers. The dark pink, almost purple color of her petals beckoned me like the sweetest treat. I blew over her slit, and a violent shiver coursed through her seconds before her skin erupted in goosebumps.

A smug chuckle escaped me to find her so responsive. I leaned forward and covered her mons with kisses, deliberately avoiding her clit, which was begging for attention. I didn't know why I wanted to tease her like this, but I pursued the game a short while longer. My index finger caressed her folds, circled around her slit and her little nub, always coming ever so close without ever touching them.

When I finally gave her clit a lick, Farah emitted the sexiest throaty sound. I gave it another slow lick, then proceeded to flick my tongue over it at increasing speeds. Soon, her voluptuous moans filled my ears, and the intoxicating scent of her musk tickled my nose. In no time, my mate's sex glistened with her arousal, further rewarding my efforts.

I slipped a finger then two inside her slit, their entry eased by how wet she already was for me. Her inner walls contracted around them, as if to draw them in deeper. I happily obliged.

I pushed them deeper and faster inside her, my mouth still

feasting on her clit. As her pleasure built, Farah began gyrating, her breath coming out in short, loud bursts that hinted at her impending climax. I inserted a third finger. It was a tight fit, but she quickly relaxed around them. I scissored them in and out to stretch her. Obviously, that wouldn't be enough to fully prepare her to receive me, but it would help ease penetration later.

When her legs started trembling around my face, I crooked my fingers to brush against her G-spot. To my surprise, Farah instantly fell apart. I had not expected for her orgasm to swoop in so soon—not that I complained about it. I lifted my head to peer at my woman's beautiful face. Lips parted, her face dissolved in an air of pure bliss, she looked like a goddess, swept away by the pleasure I had given her.

My hands continued to make love to her, the fingers of my left hand picking up where my mouth had left off so I could continue admiring her beauty in the throes of passion. It was only once she started coming back to reality that I pulled my fingers out of her. She looked at me with hooded eyes, and bit her bottom lip with a lascivious expression when I slowly licked her essence off each of my fingers.

Farah extended her arms towards me in a beckoning gesture. I crawled back on top of her, kissing and caressing her stomach and breasts on my way up. She spread her legs wide so that I could settle between them. I reclaimed her lips, my pelvis rubbing against hers in a slow movement, which also allowed me to coat my lower cock with some of her essence.

"Do you accept me, my mate?" I whispered against her lips.

"Yes, Krogal. I'm yours," she whispered back, her arms tightening around me.

I smiled and gave her another passionate kiss then started pushing my lower, smaller cock inside her. It barely went in a couple of centimeters before her body started resisting my invasion. As I'd expected as much, it didn't faze me. However, it made me monitor my woman's reactions all the more closely.

As much as I hungered for her and burned with the urge to lose myself inside her, keeping my mate safe overrode any other consideration. With careful and shallow thrusts, I gradually breached her resistance, lavishing kisses and caresses on her, interspersed with words of encouragement and affection. Despite that, Farah remained an enthusiastic and willing participant.

After what felt like an eternity, her body abruptly yielded when I was only halfway in. It burned, and I found myself fully sheathed. My woman gasped, and I froze, fearing I had harmed her. Eyes closed, her lips parted, she was breathing in short bursts. She was trying to adjust to my girth, but I couldn't tell what level of discomfort—or worse pain—she was experiencing. I wanted to believe that the mildness of the frown marring her forehead indicated that it was more than bearable.

Only once she opened her eyes and smiled at me did I finally relax.

She resumed caressing my back and lifted her behind to press her pelvis against mine, making her meaning clear. With infinite care, I began rocking in and out of her. The first stroke nearly undid me.

By Khivolt, she felt so insanely good!

Her inner walls squeezed me from all sides, their wet heat fanning the inferno raging in my loins as they caressed my length both on the way in and out. Waves of pleasure crashed over me, attempting to sweep me in a tidal wave. But I forced myself to focus on my mate and on her responses to me.

She was so fucking beautiful, with her lips swollen by my kisses, her cheeks flushed with pleasure, and her eyes darkened by passion. To think I feared we would struggle to come together, and that I would fail to make this an enjoyable experience for her. I never should have doubted us. We were soulmates, made for each other.

When my woman began to writhe beneath me, her hands feverishly caressing every inch of my body, I picked up the pace, taking her deeper and gradually harder. As she showed no signs of distress, I let myself go even more, without going all out. I didn't know how much she could take and was in no rush to test the extent of her limits. The night was young, and I intended for us to savor every minute of it.

With my main cock remaining outside of her, its underside massaged my woman's clitoris with each stroke, enhancing her pleasure. Accelerating the speed with which I took her only intensified that additional sensual stimulation. In no time, Farah was cresting again. I nearly spilled when she cried out, her nails digging into the small of my back, and her inner walls clamping down on my lower cock.

A savage growl escaped me through my clenched teeth as I fought the urge to give in to ecstasy. That didn't stop a few drops of precum from seeping out.

Khivolt take me, I would never tire of the magnificence of my woman as she fell apart for me. Head thrown back, eyes closed, and lips parted, Farah was moaning in between every other heavy breath. Even as she flew high, her hips continued to gyrate as she greedily welcomed me inside her.

As she slowly came back to reality, I slowed down the pace, and eventually stopped before pulling out of her. She gave me a surprise look that I hadn't found my own release. But I wasn't done with her yet. For the next eternity, I kissed and caressed every inch of her body, erasing any lingering doubt she might have about just how much I worshiped her.

Turning her to the side, I spooned her, holding her back to my chest as I lovingly brushed my lips along the sensitive spot at the edge of her nape. She shivered and emitted the most sensuous sigh that washed over me like a warm blanket.

With great care I pushed my main cock into her slit from behind. Sideways or on all four was the best position to make love to her with my main cock without the lower one getting in the way. That was unless we proceeded with double penetration.

Obviously, that was not an option for our first time together—assuming this would even be something she'd be open to. And while what humans called doggy style held an undeniable appeal, it screamed more of unbridled passion to me and less of the tender and intimate union that I wanted for our first coupling.

Even with my lower cock paving the way, it once more required for me to carefully work my way in as her body resisted the invasion of my main cock's greater girth. This time again, I distracted her from the discomfort by fondling her breasts, kissing and caressing her body, and massaging her clit.

Having four arms held undeniable advantages.

Thankfully, it took little time for her to welcome me in. I remained still, my arms possessively wrapped around her as I whispered words of love and encouragement in her ear. Only once her inner walls started contracting around me did I tentatively begin moving inside my woman.

Each careful and slow thrust inflicted the most exquisite torture on me. Lava swirled in the pit of my stomach, and liquid flames spread through my veins, setting my skin and each of my nerve endings ablaze. My rumbling growls of pleasure mixed with my mate's throaty moans. She reached a hand over her shoulder to sink her fingers into my hair as I gradually accelerated my movements. Even as I leaned into her touch, I continued to kiss the side of her face and neck while my hands relentlessly expressed their devotion to the perfection that she was.

Despite my determination to keep things gentle and tender, I quickly found myself taking my woman deeper and harder. Soon, passion took over any rational thought as I began to pound into her. Her voluptuous moans spurred me on. Nothing mattered anymore but the searing feel of her skin against mine and the overwhelming pleasure putting us on the verge of combusting.

Farah chanting my name as she neared the edge was whipping me into a frenzy. Although I saw her climax coming, it still took me by surprise when her body suddenly seized, and she cried out.

This time, I didn't resist the call of bliss clawing at me.

My orgasm struck me like lightning. The room spun, and my vision blurred. For half a beat, I felt as if my soul had been knocked out of my body. My skin tingled, anchoring me to my mortal vessel as liquid ecstasy shot out of me in powerful spurts. I continued thrusting into my woman, my movements slightly erratic as I filled her with my seed.

Once fully spent, I didn't pull out of my wife. Instead, I tightened my arms around her in a possessive hold. Farah snuggled deeply against me. She turned her head to look at me over her shoulder. The depths of emotion and affection in her eyes wrecked me. I leaned forward and reclaimed her lips in a passionate kiss that hid nothing of the powerful feelings filling my hearts for her.

"I am yours, my Farah," I whispered against her lips as our racing heartbeats slowly returned to normal. "Now and forever."

# CHAPTER 14
## FARAH

Emerging from the best sleep I could ever recall, I stretched loudly. After the wildest sex marathon with my man, I felt wonderfully sore and a little guilty we missed the after-match feast.

Only a little...

It still blew my mind that I managed to take him. No words could describe how massive he was or how impossibly full I felt with him inside me. By rights, this should have been a strenuous if not dreadful experience. But the gentleness and care my giant displayed, constantly focusing on my responses and reaction to him, rocked my world.

I couldn't have hoped for a more perfect male.

Krogal made me feel cherished, even worshiped. There was no doubt in my mind that he was falling in love with me, as I was with him. The prospect of our future together filled me with a joy impossible to describe.

This was what a healthy relationship felt like, with a partner who showed you respect, made you feel valued, and made your needs and welfare their priority. When someone treated you that way, you couldn't help but want to reciprocate, not out of duty or guilt, but out of genuine desire. I wanted to spoil him rotten. The challenge was what did you give a man who already had everything?

*Tons of cuddles and help mend the rift with his mother.*

That first part was a breeze. Krogal couldn't get enough hugs, and he was the best living pillow to snuggle with. Even now, I hungered for his powerful embrace.

I sighed as I glanced at his empty side of the bed. It saddened me not to have awakened in his arms. Granted, he got up early every morning for his training routine—alongside most Zamorian males. However, I would have expected him to skip it today, not only to give his body a chance to recover from getting seriously roughed up during the Fultar match, but especially to savor our first time sharing a bed.

Heaving another sigh, I forced myself to get up, a wicked smile settling on my lips as the lingering soreness made its presence known as a sauntered to the hygiene room. It didn't hurt. In fact, it was almost turning me on again just thinking how he had felt riding me. When passion finally got the best of him, and Krogal started pounding into me, it both thrilled and scared me. It should have hurt, but I'd shouted his name, begging for more. Even then, my man had kept control over his insane strength, taking me with unbridled passion while also keeping me safe.

*And let's not talk about double penetration.*

I had done anal before. Although it wasn't my favorite thing, I didn't mind it and even enjoyed it at times. But I didn't know if I would ever be able to handle it with someone endowed the way he was.

*I had fun last night riding his humongous club. Maybe I'll enjoy that with him, too.*

There was no point borrowing trouble. As the saying went, we would cross that bridge once we got there. For now, I wanted to enjoy further strengthening the bond between Krogal and me.

As I stepped inside the shower, I took in my surroundings.

Judging by the towel hanging on the wall, Krogal already bathed this morning. As I began to wash myself, a million thoughts flooded my mind. It was my first time entering his hygiene room. Or should I call it *our* room? After last night, did Krogal expect me to move into his bedroom? Did I want to? Was it too soon? Going back to my own room struck me as weird. But I also didn't want to come on too strong. And I suspected my behemoth would feel the same about not pressuring me into doing anything.

There was such a thing as being to considerate sometimes.

I quickly showered, got dressed, and headed into the kitchen. My heart melted when I saw a sumptuous breakfast already waiting for me on the plate heater. A card on top of the placemat on the table, next to a large, temperature-controlled covered plate displayed a holographic message which read 'Thinking of you.'

Damn the man for being so freaking awesome.

Liam never had that type of little attentions for me. Granted, he made sure I had all the material things I needed, and that service staff always waited on me hand and foot. But using your wealth and influence to buy comfort for your partner didn't compare to you personally doing things for your significant other to prove how much you cared.

I heartily devoured the feast, wondering where my dear husband could possibly be. He wore me out so much that I slept in. It was already 10:00 AM. Krogal should have returned from training more than two hours ago. Then again, considering his spectacular performance last night, it would make sense for him to have gone out a little later than usual.

I finished putting away the leftovers and was starting to rinse the dirty dishes to put them in the dishwasher when I saw our personal shuttle landing on the terrace. That took me aback. Krogal never flew out to train as our fortress—like every other with bloodline dwellings—possessed its own training gymnasium in the basement and mini-arena in one of the courtyards outside.

I all but shoved the dishes in the appliance and hastened to the large patio doors. They parted before Krogal, who reached them before me. I only meant to give him a warm greeting and let him set the tone to what our interactions would be. But I broke into a run and threw myself into his arms. His chest vibrated with a happy chuckle as he caught me and gave me one of those squishing hugs I loved so much.

We kissed with a mix of passion and tenderness that utterly wrecked me. Yeah, I was definitely falling in love with this man. Our tongues mingled, and our hands caressed each other with a depth of affection devoid of animal lust that confirmed the nature of the feelings spreading their roots between us.

He broke the kiss, buried his face in my neck, and inhaled my scent. My arms tightened around him as another wave of affection swelled through me. We remained in each other's embrace for a few moments longer before Krogal reluctantly released me and set me back down on my feet.

"Did you sleep well, my mate?" he asked in a gentle voice, although I didn't miss the sliver of worry.

"I slept wonderfully," I replied in a reassuring tone, my arms around his waist giving him a little squeeze.

He didn't need to spell it out for me to know the true nature of his inquiry. That, too, moved me to the core. He had been so gentle with me and still he worried about how I fared this morning.

"But I was sorry not to find you by my side when I awakened," I continued with a playful pout.

He grinned, an unrepentant—almost smug—expression settling on his features. "Believe me, my Farah, it took all my willpower to force myself away from you this morning. But I have a couple of surprises for you that I needed to finalize."

My eyes widened with curiosity. "Surprises?"

I looked over his shoulder at the shuttle outside, wondering if he had left them inside the vessel since he clearly didn't have them on him.

"They're not here," he said, guessing my thoughts. He glanced at the breakfast table, visibly pleased to find it empty. "I see you've had your meal. Then we can go now if you're ready."

"I did, and it was excellent, as always," I said truthfully. "You know, if I hadn't already married you, I would have had to claim you."

My chest warmed again upon seeing the air of pure joy that descended over his features in response to my words. It was insane how little he required to be happy. Knowing that my mere presence and acceptance of him were the cause filled me with a sense of purpose and worth that had been taken away from me in a slow and insidious fashion.

Liam convinced me that no one could ever love me just the way I was. He made me believe that I needed to fit a mold and follow guidelines dictated by my betters to be of any value.

"I am glad to hear it, my Farah. In case you have not noticed, I am falling madly in love with you. So had you not married me, I would devote every waking hour trying to convince you to do it. Instead, I will devote the rest of my days reminding you why marrying me was the best decision you ever made," Krogal said with fervor.

My throat constricted, and tears pricked my eyes. I'd never been the crying type, but this man was bringing out my deepest emotions. They had lain dormant or grown so stunted over the years that they now threatened to overwhelm me.

Realizing how his words affected me, Krogal smiled, cupped my face with his primary hands, and gave me a kiss full of love that left me weak in the knees.

"Come, my mate. Let me show you those surprises," he said in a gentle voice.

I smiled and let him lead me by the hand to the shuttle.

To my shock, he made me settle in the pilot's seat.

"Wait, what?" I asked, half confused, half panicked.

"Peace, my mate. All is well," he replied with a mischievous grin before closing the door and circling around to the passenger's side.

Was that his surprise? Teaching me how to pilot a shuttle?

"The controls are extremely simple," he said in a reassuring tone. "The artificial intelligence handles most of it. It's no different than driving a hovercar. You only have to steer in the direction you want and set the speed. The A.I. will automatically kick in if your flight becomes erratic or dangerous. But you can also fully set it on autopilot, just sit back, and enjoy the ride."

"Oookay…" I said carefully, still confused as to why he felt the need to make me do this.

"To answer the question in your eyes, I'm getting a second personal shuttle for you," he said with a smile. "You're going to need it to move around freely when I go to work."

"Move around to go where?"

He gave me a shit-eating grin. "That's part of the surprise."

"What the heck kind of surprise is that? Where are you taking me?"

"*I* am not taking you anywhere. *You* are taking us," he deadpanned, making me want to throw something at him. "And you'll find out soon enough. Come on, get this thing airborne."

I muttered under my breath but complied. Sure enough, piloting the shuttle was a breeze. Playing video games offered far more challenges than this. I literally only had to move the stick left and right to turn, or forward and backward to go up or descend. Speed could either be controlled with a pair of buttons on the stick, or pedals under the navigation board.

I went with the pedals, which were more natural for me.

It ended up being a good ten-minute flight, taking us to the edge of the fortified city to a new sector under development. They'd just completed Phase Three of a massive complex, with the fourth beginning construction in a couple of weeks, and the final one in about six months. As I understood, the entire complex would be devoted to creative arts in all their forms, including a Fine Arts school, academies dedicated to dance, music, and performing arts, a fashion section, and digital arts specializing in holograms and virtual reality.

"Were going to Penlam?" I asked when he indicated for me to begin our descent towards the huge underground parking lot of the Phase Three building.

"We are," he said smugly. "The Third Phase contains new lofts dedicated to students, artists, and young entrepreneurs in art-related fields. The upper floors are reserved as housing whereas the lower ones can be used as studios or shops."

My eyes widened with growing suspicion laced with excitement.

"And you want me to become comfortable piloting so that I can make the trip here often?" I asked, trying to make him spill the beans at last.

"Exactly. You can switch to autopilot here, if you want," he added pointing at the navigation board's interface. "The parking spot is already programmed in the shuttle. And it will park it for you if you so wish."

He didn't have to suggest it twice. Although I felt relatively confident I could safely land it myself, I had nothing to prove, and would rather not blow us up or this place by risking it. He chuckled at the swiftness with which I activated the feature.

Seconds later, the vessel settled down in our reserved spot. The place was quite empty, which would have unnerved me under different circumstances. But it was well lit and open, eliminating the gloomy and claustrophobic vibe underground parking spaces often had.

"Are you finally going to tell me what we're doing here?" I insisted as he helped me out of the shuttle.

"Patience, my love. Just a few more minutes, and I will show you," he said with a thrill in his voice.

As contagious as his excitement was, my mind remained locked on the fact that he had called me his love. It was the first time he'd ever done so. It didn't mean that he was in love with me just yet. After all, I'd only been here a month. But I knew that he had not used that term of endearment lightly.

I smiled and let him lead me by the hand to the elevator, which took us to the 4th floor of the fifteen-story building.

"This is the highest floor authorized for any space that could have commercial activities," Krogal explained as the doors of the lift parted.

My jaw dropped at the sight of the spectacle that awaited us as we stepped out of the cabin. It almost looked like I had entered a mix between a huge shopping mall and a fancy office building, with doors and windows lining each side of a humongous central area that could serve as a gathering place or indoor Plaza.

From where I stood, I could see a few glass walls revealing the interior of some kind of store being set up. Others had solid walls which hid what was happening inside. The signs above the doors hinted at the type of business they intended to run there, while others revealed nothing at all.

Krogal turned right, leading me to a wide set of fancy wooden doors at the back. At a glance, I suspected that the room behind it occupied at least half of the back wall. As we approached, my mate's smugness gave way to a growing air of nervousness. It always messed with my head to see this vulnerable side of him. Remembering how intimidating, savage, and powerful he had been last night during the match, it seemed impossible that he should be so worried about how I would react to his surprise. You'd think someone like him would be ruthless and cocksure.

He opened the door and stepped in, beckoning me inside. I

smiled at his air of inquisitive anticipation, typical of people who awaited the verdict of a particularly picky customer once they presented the work they did for them.

But the room took my breath away. It was huge, with pristine white walls framed by exposed black wooden beams, and ceiling-high French windows on the back wall that flooded the room with light. A pair of doors to the right gave access to two more rooms, while another on the left led the way to a fourth room.

"This place is beautiful, Krogal!" I breathed out.

A huge smile lit up his face, and his broad shoulders relaxed. "I'm happy you like it, because it's yours! Come, let me show you the other rooms!"

"Mine?" I echoed even as I fell into step with him as he led me by the hand to one of the rooms on the right.

"Yes, yours to do with it what you please," Krogal said proudly. "There are four rooms, all of which are fully soundproof. So you can have a dance studio, a singing or recording room with perfect acoustics, a sewing and design room, and a storage area."

He opened the second door to the room that would be a perfect place for a recording studio, with acoustic walls. Here too, a large window allowed plenty of light in. But the total absence of sound coming from the outside confirmed it had been specifically designed for it.

"You expect me to do all of that?" I asked, unsure if I felt excited about this perfect space to do whatever my heart desired, or worried that he was trying to force my hand to do things he felt I should, regardless of my preferences.

"No, my Farah," he said, taking on a serious expression as he turned to face me. "I want you to be able to pursue whatever passions you have. Our dwelling isn't suited for you to be able to dance and sing freely the way you might want without risking injury. You're also extremely cramped at home trying to work on the fashion articles you want to make. There's no reason for you to be restricted in how creative you can be due to lack of space. This allows you to do exactly that. You can fit the rooms however you please, whether it's to pursue one or all of those activities. But if you do not wish to do any of them, it's also entirely fine."

"You wouldn't mind if I said I didn't really need this space?" I asked cautiously.

He shook his head and held my gaze unwaveringly to confirm he was speaking truthfully. "This is a gift to make your life easier, not a burden to coerce you into anything. If you have no use for it, then I'll just cancel the lease."

"So this would be my playground, if I decide to keep it?" I asked, trying to hide the excitement in my voice.

He nodded. "Absolutely. You can keep it for personal use, turn the main room into a shop to sell your clothes, or a studio to give dance lessons, should you so desire."

This time, I dropped my mask of wariness and threw myself into his arms.

"I freaking love it!" I exclaimed before crushing his lips with a kiss.

He chuckled and gave me another of his amazing bear hugs while spinning us around.

"Are you sure you like it?" he asked.

"Absolutely! I really needed more room for the designs I want to work on. And after last night's match, I'm seriously itching to get back to dancing and experimenting on some choreographies inspired by the Zamorian traditional dances."

His happiness at my response filled my heart to bursting. My behemoth was truly going out of his way to give me everything my heart desired. The silly man didn't realize that the wonderful husband he was proving to be already accomplished that.

"Why are you so perfect?" I whispered.

"Because I like seeing you smile… and hearing you call me perfect," he deadpanned.

I snorted and lifted my face to give him another kiss, to which he responded passionately.

"Come, let's check out the other two rooms and your second surprise," Krogal said enthusiastically.

He put me back on my feet and led me to the third room. It had clearly been set up as a potential dance studio, if only for the giant mirror that covered the entire south wall. My mind was already bubbling with ideas on how I would decorate each of those spaces, although the main room—which I intended to turn into the sewing room—claimed most of my thoughts.

We crossed it on the way to the other side where the storage room was located. When Krogal opened the door, my first thought was that it was huge enough to serve more as someone's primary bedroom than a storage area. But all such musings flew right out of my mind when a familiar yipping sound filled my ears.

"Joree!" I shouted, shock and wonder washing over me as I gazed upon the little Nulia.

She was lying on a large cushion on a built-in shelf by the large windows at the back of the room. A full bowl of water and food rested next to her. She took flight towards me at the same time I ran towards her. I caught her, and she snuggled in my arms, rubbing her furry face against mine while I laughed and cooed at the little beauty.

I couldn't believe she remembered me after that single visit nearly a month ago. Then again, maybe her warm response was in reaction to what her empathic abilities revealed about my feelings towards her. She yipped and purred, her small paws patting my cheeks.

"She's officially your new companion," Krogal said in a soft voice behind me.

I jerked my head over my shoulder to look at him in disbelief as he closed the distance between us.

"My companion?" I repeated, not daring to hope. "Her mother rejected her again?"

He shook his head and smiled as he reached a hand to scratch the back of Joree's left ear.

"No. Her mother fully embraced her. Even though she's a little behind compared to her siblings, Joree's training is progressing nicely. She can never achieve the levels the others will since she started later than would have been ideal, but that wouldn't have stopped her from being someone's companion. Since you love her so much, and you imprinted on her at my clinic, it wasn't too hard convincing Cyric to let you have her."

"You're serious? I get to keep her?" I asked with a shaky voice.

He nodded, his eyes filled with affection.

"Oh, my God! You're the best!" I exclaimed, pressing myself against him.

Although I was careful not to squish Joree between us, she wiggled free of my embrace and climbed on top of Krogal's shoulder. She booped his cheek and then stretched her neck to rub her cheek against mine. Tears pricked my eyes as I held my man even more tightly.

"Your happiness is all that matters to me, my Farah. And I was overdue for having a pet at home," he said in a rumbling voice meant to hide his shyness. "But be warned that she still needs training. She's coming to you to start strengthening the bond between you. For now, she won't live with us as she still needs her mother."

"Oh!" I said with a sliver of disappointment as I caressed Joree's head, who was still perched on Krogal's shoulder.

She licked my hand before leaning into my touch.

"She will come and go until she can live permanently with us. Over time, she will stay for longer periods," Krogal explained before pointing at a small window in the top right corner of the room. "She will be able to come in and out on her own through this window. As we speak, a similar one is being installed at home."

"Oh, my God! I love you!"

I hadn't meant those words that way, but I also didn't feel guilty about using them. Anyway, I was well on my way there.

"Of course, you do! I'm beyond lovable and huggable," he said smugly, making me chuckle. "But be warned, woman. Don't expect me to give you every pet you find cute in the future."

"I won't!" I said in the least sincere fashion.

He snorted and shook his head at me.

# CHAPTER 15
### FARAH

A month later, we had settled into a delightful routine. Not only was I steadily falling in love with Krogal, but I was growing closer to his mother Talin. She would forever be prickly, but once you looked behind that defense mechanism, you discovered a deeply loyal and loving female. Although things weren't fully mended between her and Krogal, they were now interacting in a friendly fashion. Talin and Orym even came to our place for dinner on a few occasions.

While there was no rush for Krogal and me to finalize our union, I'd already decided that the day we went through a formal Zamorian wedding, I wanted Talin to be the one giving me her son. It was a relief that Feidin had hinted as much as well. The clan's Matriarch was both a wonderful leader for our people and a loving sister.

I just needed to get my mother-in-law onboard with the idea that not only our wedding would not be a traditional one, but that I also wanted Joree to play a part in it. I didn't know what it would be, but we'd figure it out sooner than later.

The not so-little-anymore Nulia was thriving. In the past week, she slept half her nights in our home. Surprisingly, although she was technically mine, Joree spent a great deal of time at Krogal's clinic. At first, I thought she was forming a stronger bond with my husband than with me. It shamed me to admit that I felt a bit jealous about it. However, I quickly found out what a far different reason motivated that behavior.

Joree's empathic abilities drove her to comfort those who needed it. During her short stay at the clinic for her own illness, the Nulia realized she could help the other pets being treated there. She would not only help soothe them but would also help communicate what pain they felt through mental imagery telepathically conveyed to Krogal or one of his assistants.

The strength of the bond she was forming with both of us manifested itself through the increasing clarity of those telepathic communications, but also the distance from which she could reach us. As much as I selfishly wanted to benefit more from her presence, I loved that she found a fulfilling way to put her abilities to good use while doing so much good for the helpless creatures who needed it.

She still cuddled with me plenty of times. But the cute little baby she had been had now grown into the size of an adult cat. According to Krogal, once fully mature, she could grow as big as a Maine Coon. She certainly shed just as much fur. I didn't mind, that mild inconvenience was well worth it in exchange for the unconditional love and fluffy snuggles she generously gave.

To my shame, as she began spending more and more time with us, I admitted that I worried how awkward it might get when my husband and I wanted to get a little frisky. Unlike a cat, Joree's intelligence made her a lot more like a person than a pet. But her empathic abilities always kicked in when needed. The minute Krogal or I got aroused, Joree would make a discreet exit and remain scarce until we were done. I couldn't tell if I felt more relieved than mortified that she knew we were going at it like rabbits.

Once again this morning, I woke up to find Krogal already

gone. A glance at the clock told me he'd be back any minute now. I jumped out of bed and made my way to the hygiene room, hoping he would join me there. It had become a part of our routine.

A grin stretched my lips when the hygiene room door opened as I was starting to rinse the soap off me. I looked over my shoulder to find Krogal standing in the doorway, his expression darkening in a way that had my knees instantly wobbly.

"You look good enough to eat, my mate. And I'm rather starved after my training. May I join you?" he asked.

My skin erupted in goosebumps at the sound of his deep voice, my stomach flip-flopped, and my breasts instantly felt heavy. I extended a beckoning hand towards him. He kicked his shoes off and removed his pants before coming to me.

Good God, it felt so good in his arms! He instantly claimed my lips in a passionate kiss, his primary hands roaming over me with an impatience that had my inner walls contracting with anticipation. You'd think we'd been separated for months, even years, instead of a few hours.

He lifted me, and I wrapped my legs around his waist. His quickly engorging cocks pressed against my core, making my toes curl. Our tongues warred, and I savored his sweet taste and the dominant way he kissed me. I gasped against his lips when his primary right hand caressed my behind, circling around my cheeks to reach my sex. His thick and long index finger teased my slit and then my clit. It massaged it for a moment, until my breath became labored with pleasure. He then dipped that finger inside me, a second one joining the fray as he began scissoring them in and out of me, stretching me.

I felt wetness pool between my thighs that had nothing to do with the water raining over us. My inner walls spasmed, wanting more. Krogal broke the kiss and tilted me back so that he could take one of my nipples into his greedy mouth. With both his secondary hands holding me, and his primary right hand still fingering me, he fondled my other breast with his remaining hand. Simultaneously, he rubbed the length of his second cock against me, the friction over my clit sending electric sparks down my legs.

I slipped a hand between us and closed my fingers around his primary cock—or at least tried to. The damn thing was so damn thick, I couldn't reach around its circumference. That had another jolt of anticipation resonating straight between my thighs. Even after all this time, Krogal needed to be careful with his initial penetration before I adjusted to the massive girth of his primary cock.

His mouth still wrapped around my nipple, Krogal grunted in approval as I stroked him. He pursued his ministrations a few moments longer before bending me back further. His mouth ventured over my stomach and lingered at my navel, licking and nipping at it. Although it tickled, I was too focused on the waves of pleasure quickly building in response to his wicked fingers between my legs.

Krogal suddenly straightened me and effortlessly hoisted me upward. I let go of his cock, both my hands flying to his shoulders for support. But my surprised gasp shifted into a rapturous moan when he settled my legs on his shoulders and buried his face between my thighs. Had he not been holding me up, I probably would have toppled over. Instead, my nails dug into his shoulders as he licked and sucked my clit with the voracity of a starving man.

A pool of lava swirled in the pit of my stomach, bliss radiating outward to each of my nerve endings as I neared the edge. His fingers slipping inside my slit as he devoured me was the final push I needed. The moment he crooked them and grazed my sensitive bundle of nerves, I threw my head back and cried out as my orgasm swept me away.

Krogal continued to pleasure me with his mouth until I started coming back down. The whole time, his fingers scissored in and out of me, preparing me to receive his considerable girth.

He eventually took me down from his shoulders. Still holding me in his arms, my body pressed against his and my legs wrapped around his waist, my man gave me a long and passionate kiss in which he poured all his passion and devotion. He rubbed his pelvis against mine, the friction on my clit sending electric sparks throughout my nether region.

My inner walls spasmed with impatience, aching to be filled. Krogal lifted me up a bit and aligned his secondary cock with my opening. With great care, he pushed himself in, using shallow thrusts until he was fully sheathed. While it had taken an eternity the first time for my body to give in to him, it now took less than a minute before he could start rocking in and out of me.

Good Lord! I was addicted to how incredibly full he made me feel and the amazing sensation of the pearl-like ridges along the sides of his cocks. His primary cock, pressed against my clit, acted like a clitoral stimulator with each thrust, doubling my pleasure. With his legendary control, Krogal kept a steady pace, his secondary hands holding me propped up while his primary ones caressed every inch of my body.

He was everywhere at once, in and around me, making me feel both helpless but to yield to his passion, sheltered by his strong arms and body, and utterly worshiped. My blood heated as the inferno raging in my loins sent liquid flames coursing through my veins. The sound of his growls of pleasure, vibrating through his chest in an almost continuous flow, turned me on even more.

My legs shook around him as I began to crest for the second time. Sensing my impending climax, Krogal accelerated the movement. His cock struck my G-spot with deadly accuracy, tearing one strangled moan from me after the other until my spine seized. With a sharp cry, I tumbled down an ocean of bliss as another orgasm swept me away, and my inner walls clamped down around Krogal's cock.

I distantly heard him cry out, and his hands painfully tightened their grip around me. My man was fighting the urge to yield to his own orgasm. But my inner walls squeezing him from all sides were challenging his ability to resist.

He didn't give in, but something finally broke inside him. Even as I continued to fly high, I felt him taking me deeper, harder, and at a more frantic pace. In no time, he was pounding into me. His primary cock, still rubbing over my clit had me on the verge of combusting. Before I could even finish recovering from my second climax, a third one engulfed me. I threw my head back and would have crashed onto the tiled floor if not for Krogal holding me with a bruising grip.

The room spun, and pleasure almost too much to bear swelled through me, setting each of my nerve endings ablaze. In my lustful daze, it took me too long to realize Krogal had pulled out of me, turned me around in his embrace before ramming his primary cock in with one powerful thrust. It felt like a distant burn, and even my strangled cry sounded far away to my own ears.

Keeping me twisted like a pretzel, my back to his chest, and his secondary hands holding my legs to my own chest, I had no choice but to take everything he was giving me. While his mouth kissed my neck and shoulder, his primary right hand frantically rubbed my clit, and his left one fondled my breast.

The sound of the water raining over us, the rhythmic slapping of flesh meeting flesh, my voluptuous moans, and his nearly feral growls filled the room as I gave myself over to my mate. He was wrecking me, physically and mentally, the excess of bliss threatening to fracture my mind. I never saw that ultimate orgasm creep up on me. It slammed into me with the violence of an erupting volcano. A blinding light exploded before my eyes, and I felt as if my soul had been torn right out of my mortal vessel.

Moments later, the deafening sound of Krogal's roar resonated in my right ear, and his seed shot out into me in powerful spurts, bathing my battered insides. I felt boneless and utterly destroyed as he continued to rock in and out of me at a slower pace, until he was fully spent. Through it all he gently caressed me and whispered words of love and devotion in my ear.

He eventually pulled out and thoroughly washed me with infinite care. I felt like a queen when he dried my body, then my hair, and even plaited it for me. I reciprocated the favor, then enjoyed the copious breakfast he made for us. Somehow, the wretch multiplied the ways to be the one cooking for me, even on my days. And I couldn't even complain.

Joree joined us and feasted on a mix of various nuts, grapes, apples, and wild berries. Later, I would treat her to some oatmeal raisin cookies, her favorite treat.

"So you're spending the day with Mother?" he asked, a mix of amusement and sympathy audible in his voice.

"I am," I replied, lifting my chin defiantly as if to dare him to make any type of disparaging comment. "Talin can be a handful, but I've learned how to handle her. And I have some workers coming over to discuss the plans for the shelves I want installed for my custom fabrics, and drawer units to store the threads, buttons, sequins, and all that other good stuff. Your mother will cow them into submission if they try to pull a fast one on the clueless off-worlder."

Krogal snorted. "Fair point. On that front, Mother will eat them alive if they even think to con you. Well, I better get going. I've got a busy day ahead."

We exchanged one last passionate kiss, and I waved him goodbye as he took flight. To my delight, Joree stayed with me. It was always a coin toss who she decided to spend the day with.

I went to Talin's apartment across the hall, and we flew in her shuttle to my studio. Joree comfortably balled herself up in my lap and half-napped while Talin and I chatted amiably.

She couldn't help trying to dictate how I should run my life. At this point, I made my peace with the fact that Talin would never change on that front. But she was also acknowledging this somewhat toxic trait in her and was making genuine efforts to rein it in when called out about it.

"So, have you reconsidered joining one of the dance troops who expressed interest in you?" Talin asked with false innocence.

I gave her a sideways glance that made it clear she wasn't fooling me. "I haven't, because I no longer want to perform on stage."

I didn't add that Liam killed my passion for public performance. Granted, I still liked dancing and joined the other Zamorian females during informal group dances, often held in the city's Plaza. But it wasn't the type of career I wanted to pursue.

"But you are bringing a unique spin to our traditional dances that has people very excited," Talin argued. "It is a waste of a great potential that could leave a lasting mark in our cultural evolution."

"I didn't say that I wouldn't continue experimenting with a crossover of Zamorian traditional dances and music, with Caribbean rhythms and moves," I replied in an indulgent tone. "I did set up a proper dance studio in Penlam. I'm more interested in remaining in the shadows and license the use of my songs and choreographies to those interested. But for me, this will be a side gig so that I can continue dabbling in one of my former passions."

*Without the baggage and trauma...*

As she parked the shuttle in my reserved spot, Talin pinched her lips, displeased by my answer. She was the biggest braggart in the entire city, more even than her nephew, Bayron. If you wanted to make her cringe, you only had to hint at your desire to remain backstage and let someone else stand in the spotlight. She was definitely one of those people who lived their dreams vicariously through their children and relatives. Being able to brag about my music and choreographies being used by big-name artists didn't hold the same pizzaz as being able to shout from the rooftops that your daughter-in-law was the actual big-name artist herself.

"I might even give some dance classes at the studio," I continued. "There's been enough requests to justify putting a group together. But that's not a priority. For now, I really want to focus on fashion. I'm super excited about starting my own line and have a billion ideas just demanding to come to life. And Milna is absolutely brilliant. Thank you for finding her for me."

Those words immediately mollified my mother-in-law. She smiled and nodded in acknowledgement, although I didn't miss the pride she tried to hide. Milna was one of the city's most famous seamstresses and fashion designers. Although she retired a couple of years prior, Talin convinced her to take me under her wing as my private tutor until the next semester began.

We entered my studio, which I had renamed Medjine's after my late mother. I didn't welcome customers here just yet, and probably wouldn't for quite a few months to come. We were still furnishing and setting up the space. And it would take a while for me to build a large enough collection to open to the public. I just loved that Krogal gave me the means to work on this project with no time or financial pressure. And modeling for Belle provided me with extra income for the more extravagant things I might want to throw into it.

Speaking of which, while visiting a few weeks ago, Belle drew a sketch of me playing with Joree in my living room. I found it so adorable I sweet talked her into making a giant version of it on the wall in the main room of my future store. It was Talin's first time seeing it. For some silly reason, the glimmer of approval in her eyes moved me deeply.

"You are a beautiful woman, Farah," Talin mused out loud. "Belle did a wonderful job of capturing the moment between you and your companion. This is how you should be portrayed in all the pieces she's painting of you. Do you not see how tragic it is that you insist she hides your face? Even the name of your fashion line bears no direct tie to you or our family!"

"You know I wish to maintain my anonymity," I said with a sliver of irritation. "And my fashion line is named after my mother. Even there I hesitated because it is a link to me. I know how important fame and honor is for you. But in this instance, I would really appreciate you respecting my wishes. You have no idea what it's like living in fear of what a psychopath could do if he found you. You take pride in being a protector, then act as such. Grant me the peace of mind I seek by not trying to force me to expose myself to danger."

It was a bit of a low blow, but it was also honest. I hated how she flinched upon hearing my words, putting in question her protective nature for selfish reasons.

"Whatever you may think, Farah, your safety and welfare do matter to me," Talin said in a slightly clipped tone.

It wasn't anger at me pushing back that motivated that reaction but hurt that I should imply she might deliberately put me at risk merely to satisfy her personal ambitions.

"Do not doubt that I understand your motivations. But I believe they are wrong," she continued. "You can only hide for so long before the demon chasing you eventually catches up. No one can run forever. If that abusive human is going to come after you, let it be on your own terms, and not on his when you least expect it. Tell him where you are and dare him to come after you again. He will find out the hard way that you do not stand alone. It is every member of the Skortheatis Clan and every Zamorian on this planet who will teach him that no one messes with one of ours. And you, Farah Toussaint, are *ours*."

My throat tightened, and tears pricked my eyes. The day of my first confrontation with Talin, Demar told me that his mother claimed me as hers. Today, for the first time, she made it official. It had been far too long since I truly belonged to a family who wanted what was best for me, even when awkwardly expressed.

I didn't know what expression my face displayed, but it moved my mother-in-law. As she hated showing weakness or tender emotions, she scrunched her face and shifted the subject to a safer topic. It made her even more endearing to me, and I had to summon all my willpower not to go give her a bone crushing hug.

"Anyway, I don't think the shelves you have ordered will suffice," she said in a slightly grumpy tone.

I smiled as I followed her around the room and listened to her many suggestions as to how *she* would set up the place if it was her decision to make. The female was hopeless, but she was growing on me. In truth, she'd become a fun challenge to handle, and I wouldn't change her for anything.

Feeling mischievous, Joree decided to make a pest of herself, flying to whatever location Talin was discussing and striking a pose. Working with Belle for her paintings, the little Nulia had become quite the diva and attention whore. In this instance, she was deliberately trying to irritate Talin because she could feel it amused me. She had become quite attuned to me and fed on my emotional loop. The happier I was and the more she thrived.

A knock on the door put an end to her antics. She flew to one of the two large worktables I had set in the main room, settling on top like a sphinx. Her large blue eyes locked on me, she casually wagged her fluffy tail from side to side as I went to open the door.

To my surprise, a Zamorian male I had never seen before stood outside. He measured about seven feet, which was on the shorter side for his species. In his early forties, with silver eyes, and dirty blonde hair, he had the more slender physique of an artist.

"Hello?" I said with a slight frown, indicating my confusion at finding him here.

"Hello. You are Ms. Toussaint, correct?" he asked in a polite tone.

"Who wants to know?" I asked, instantly defensive, even though I had no reasons to be. But since Liam, anytime a strange man approached me, I automatically became suspicious… if not paranoid.

"My name is Teral," he replied in the same calm and professional voice. "I am Niven's colleague. A last-minute situation kept him from coming personally. He asked me to replace him."

"Oh, okay," I said, tension bleeding out of my stiffened back. "He was only coming here to take some measurements. But I also wanted to talk with him about a few other things."

"Whatever you wanted to discuss with him, I can handle. I've got you, Farah," Teral replied with a smile. "I will take good care of you."

A cold shiver ran down my spine. Something in the way he said that made me uneasy. No doubt in reaction to my discomfort, Joree yipped and became a little agitated. Before I could respond, Talin stepped forward with an outraged expression.

"What do you mean, Niven can't make it? What could be more important than for him to see to my daughter's needs?"

Teral stiffened. "Your daughter?!" he repeated in surprise.

"She means her daughter-in-law," I answered in her stead, my tone making it clear his reaction to her comment was out of place.

To my shock, his face hardened as did his voice. "I thought that union wasn't official, yet."

I recoiled, both baffled and offended by his words. Everyone in the city pretty much knew of the situation since Krogal was part of our clan's ruling family. They didn't know my personal story, only that Krogal and I were not an officially married couple yet.

"Not that it's any of your business, but we are legally married in all the ways that matter. We only have the Zamorian wedding to finalize in the next few weeks," I said in a clipped tone.

"Is that so?" he retorted, a hint of disgust seeping into his voice.

A sense of dread washed over me. Although he had a different voice and a completely different appearance, this man had spoken Liam's favorite line in the same way he did right before he would exact some terrible retribution or punishment for a perceived slight.

"Is there a problem?" Talin demanded, taking a menacing step towards the Zamorian male.

Teral never got a chance to answer. Joree hissed and suddenly charged forward, attacking him.

"Joree, stop!" I called out as Teral ducked to avoid having his face clawed off by the Nulia.

She barely missed and circled back to attack him again. To my horror, Teral pulled out a blaster and fired at her.

"You fucking flying rat!" he shouted.

Two of his shots made contact, one of them clipping Joree's wing and the other her left leg. She screeched in pain and nearly plummeted to the floor.

"No!" I yelled and rushed towards Teral who was still aiming at my pet. "Joree, get out!"

Bleeding, and visibly in serious pain, she flew erratically out of the building through her access window. Just as I was about to strike his arm to stop him from further shooting at her, he swiped his arm at me in what I believed to be a defensive reflex.

Since I could barely fight my way out of a wet paper bag, the blow sent me flying back, and I fell hard on the floor.

"See what you made me do, Fae?!" he shouted as he stared at me in horror.

My blood drained from my face and turned to ice in my veins.

Fae… That was Liam's pet name for me. Farah, his little Fae, his delicate fairy.

Talin's war cry drowned the inner voice yelling for me to run for my life. Even as she rushed him, my mother-in-law hurled things at him from all four hands. On instinct, the disguised Liam raised one arm before him to block the incoming projectiles while blindly shooting at her. As soon as she reached him, she tried to rip the weapon out of his hand. He fought back but eventually lost his grip. The weapon fell, and he quickly kicked it behind him.

"Run, Farah!" Talin shouted as she began hand-to-hand combat with Liam.

I gaped in awe at the strength, speed, and dexterity with which she fought him. Under each blow, Liam's holographic disguise waivered, giving glimpses of the shorter human male behind it. While she was attempting to subdue him, he was trying to free himself long enough to reach for his blaster. For a split second, I thought about going after it. But the damn thing was next to the door. I would have to come within range of the two pugilists to recover it.

My ex had always been fit. On top of regular fitness training, he had a black belt in martial arts and was a skilled boxer. I couldn't help but cringe every time he landed a blow on Talin. But she didn't fall apart, taking it like a champ, and giving back as good as she got.

"Run!" she shouted again, anger seeping into her voice that I remained there paralyzed.

I ached to go help her, but I would only get in the way, and likely get myself seriously injured. Silently berating myself for not taking some self-defense classes, I turned around to run into the dance studio, intent on calling Krogal for help.

Just as I started running, I glanced over my shoulder to see Liam swipe his right leg at Talin. His shin struck right behind her knees knocking her off her feet. She fell hard. The way the back of her head hit the hardwood floor, I feared she had cracked her skull open. Despite being clearly dazed by the impact, she pushed herself up, but not fast enough to keep Liam from grabbing the blaster.

He shot directly in front of me. I screamed and veered to the left, away from the impact. He fired wide enough not to hit me, but close enough to make his warning clear.

"Farah, stop and get back here!" Liam shouted.

Shaking with terror, I froze, my eyes flicking between the door of the dance studio only three meters ahead, and my tormentor ten meters away. He never raised a hand to me. No matter how furious he was—and he certainly was right now—I knew with bone-deep certainty that he would never shoot me.

No doubt guessing the thoughts crossing my mind, he shifted the blaster, aiming it straight at Talin's face, who was still crouching in front of him.

"Run, and I'll kill the Zamorian bitch," he hissed.

Talin tried to lunge for him, but he fired.

"TALIN! NO!" I shouted, rushing forward.

I almost wept with relief when she didn't collapse or lose consciousness. Instead, with phenomenal resilience, she got up on her feet and placed herself between Liam and me. Her secondary right hand pressed on the bleeding wound of her left shoulder.

"Step aside, female," Liam hissed at Talin, his voice dripping with contempt as he deactivated the now defective disguise that kept glitching around him. "Fae, get your ass over here. Come home with me, where you belong, and the bitch lives."

"She's my daughter! You can't have her!" Talin replied defiantly, her voice devoid of the pain one would expect in light of her wound.

Liam scoffed and gave her a disdainful glare. "I offed the last female who made that claim. I have no qualms doing the same with you."

My blood turned to ice, and a sharp pain lacerated my heart. "It was you," I whispered in disbelief. "It was you who killed my mom?!"

Even though I stated it as a question, I didn't need him to answer. A part of me always suspected, knew even. But I had been in such denial that it had been easier to convince myself that the man whose bed I shared for a total of seven years couldn't have ordered or committed such a horrible crime.

"I freed you from a leech," he spat with anger. "I've given you everything, laid the world at your feet, and this is how you thank me? How dare you leave me? How dare you whore yourself to one of those freaks? All these years, I've worshiped you and been faithful to you. And you let one of these animals touch what's mine? You let him defile you?"

Each of his words felt like a punch in the gut. For all his faults, Liam had indeed been faithful to me during our entire time together. In his own sick and obsessive way, he loved me, or rather the image he had of me. Truth be told, Liam loved the person he tried to mold me into, not the real me.

"I've moved on, Liam. You have to let me go," I said in a pleading tone.

"You don't move on without me," he snapped. "You *need* me! And I *own* you!"

My stomach dropped, and the look of madness in his eyes sparked genuine fear within me. His knuckles turned white while his fingertips went red from how hard he was holding his blaster. This man would lose it any minute. I needed to find a way to bring down the temperature. I could only pray that Joree was okay, and that she found help for herself and hopefully for us as well.

I opened my mouth without truly knowing what I wanted to say. But Liam interrupted me. As always, he didn't care about what I had to say or what I desired. In the end, he simply wanted to dictate everything, from what I did all the way down to what I thought.

"Where's the necklace I gave you?" he demanded, his voice cold as ice.

He stared at me with a hardness that would fool anyone into thinking he was merely stoic. But I knew that look. He was seething with fury and had reached his breaking point. This was yet another question he didn't really want or need me to answer. In this instance, I didn't doubt he already knew the truth of it. I wanted to lie, if only to try and appease him. But it would make matters worse… if that was even possible.

"You already know I pawned it," I said in a shaky voice.

He clenched his teeth and silently glared at me with murder in his eyes.

"I had no choice, Liam," I said pleadingly. "You control all my money. How else was I going to pay for transport off-world? What was I supposed to live off of?"

"Is that why you whored yourself to a Zamorian?" he snarled. "You ran out of money, so you spread your legs for a—"

"Enough!" Talin shouted. "Leave her alone! What kind of a pathetic male tries to force himself through menace on a female who clearly doesn't want him? Leave with your life while you still can, human. The wrath of all of Xoccoris will soon descend upon you."

"Shut the fuck up, you cunt!" Liam said in a calm, almost conversational tone.

My heart stopped. Whenever he used it, it was him handing down a death sentence. Time slowed as I watched him fire at Talin's stomach. I didn't recall bursting into action. It was only once my hands pressed onto her left shoulder and shoved her out of the way that I realized I had attempted to save her.

From the corner of my eye, I saw the flash around the weapon's muzzle then an intense pain struck the base of my spine. My legs went numb and collapsed beneath me. I pitched forward, my scream of pain dying in a choked gasp when a second atrocious pain exploded next to my left shoulder blade. The floor rushed towards me, and I slammed against it face down. Winded, I tried to scream again from the excruciating pain radiating through my upper body as I couldn't feel anything from the waist down, or rather nothing more than a strange tingling.

"Farah! My love! No!" Liam screamed, pain and horror filling his voice.

Talin roared with rage, and the sound of more fighting filled the room as I struggled to remain conscious. But the tingling kept spreading, and I felt myself becoming lighter as if I was floating out of my body.

Four hands pawed at me. Through the fog enshrouding my mind, I realized Talin had picked me up. She ran inside a room with me, I couldn't say which one as my vision had gone blurry. The impact of each of her steps as she ran sent a stabbing pain up the length of my spine.

As I lost the battle to remain conscious, I heard the muffled sound of Liam shouting my name and the terrified voice of my mother-in-law.

"Fight, my daughter. Don't you dare die on us. Fight for my Krogal. He cannot lose you."

My Krogal… His beloved face flashed before my eyes as darkness engulfed me.

# CHAPTER 16
### KROGAL

I growled in annoyance as I glared at my monitor. For the past thirty minutes, I tried in vain to make sense of the data of the blood tests I performed this morning. I needed to quickly confirm the nature of the flu-like outbreak spreading amongst our Yeskas herds. The bovine species constituted one of our main sources of meat. If we didn't promptly eradicate the disease, things would get ugly.

Except I couldn't focus to save my life. My thoughts kept wandering back to my mate. Every time I tried reading the information on my screen, the lines blurred, and Farah's beautiful face floated before me.

By Khivolt, I was obsessed with my wife and falling madly in love with her. And judging by her reactions to me, my woman was also falling in love with me. Although I had known it to be inevitable since Kayog had deemed us soulmates, I still struggled to admit that this was real. Such happiness, such complete harmony felt impossible. I kept fearing this perfect life unfolding before us would suddenly get shattered.

Things were even getting great with my mother. It blew my mind how masterful my Farah had become at handling her.

Despite Mother's haughty and prickly demeanor at times, she adored my mate. She always lamented not having a daughter of her own. But now, she fully claimed one. It was all the crazier that Farah did not meet my mother's expectations for a daughter. She always envisioned a battle maiden, well-versed in combat, an adept hunter, and a fierce protector. My female couldn't have been farther from that description. She didn't need to. Her force of character shone bright. And that had been another lesson for my mother. Strength didn't have to come down to one's skills with a weapon or at bashing skulls.

Although she was too old to ever fully change her ways, Mother had come a long way and was still making efforts to be less controlling and demanding. It pleased me tremendously, as I was counting the days before bringing up the topic of a formal Zamorian wedding with Farah. My gut said my woman was ready and willing to proceed. But the wretched insecurities plaguing me kept whispering that maybe I should give her a bit more time before asking her to set a date. While I still had no intention of having a traditional ceremony, I wanted that date to be perfect for Farah and me. And that meant for Mother to be a willing participant, different though it would be.

I groaned again as images of potential ways our ceremony could unfold filled my mind. I really needed to get my head back on the task at hand. The sooner I got it done, the sooner I could indulge in my daydreaming without it being disrupted by guilt.

Taking a deep breath, I refocused on the data before me. Within seconds, a sudden pressure manifested itself behind my eyes. I blinked and shook my head. For half a beat, I thought it faded away, but it returned and quickly grew in intensity. I frowned and rubbed my eyes over my closed eyelids. The pressure not only continued, but blinding white flashes started appearing before me, both with my eyes opened or closed.

I got up from my chair, not sure with what intention, but a wave of dizziness forced me back down onto my seat. White blanketed my vision. The panic blossoming inside me gave way to stupor when Farah's face appeared, floating in the pristine void.

It confused me at first as it faded within seconds, only to reappear. This time, she looked terrified. Hearts pounding, I examined what I could only call a vision as my woman's face continued to fade in and out of existence before my mind's eye. To my shock, a Zamorian male I had never seen before replaced her. There was something off about him. As if his skin was too big for his skeleton. It appeared to melt, like a wax statue under intense heat.

Horror descended over me when it revealed a human face beneath the melting exterior—the face that had been haunting my wife's nightmares.

The vision, illusion, or whatever the fuck this had been vanished, as did the pressure that had heralded it. I sat there in shock and confusion before I felt my blood drain from my face.

*Joree?! Did she message me this?*

A sense of dread washed over me even as I berated myself for taking so long to realize what could be happening. I whipped out my com to call Farah. It immediately told me there was no signal. My blood turned to ice as I tried again with the same result. Remembering that Farah was spending the day with my mother, I called her instead. No signal either.

I jumped to my feet, relieved to find myself steady, and rushed out of the lab to the reception.

"Dhalgal, try to call Farah and my mother!" I ordered my receptionist. "I think something bad is happening. I'm going to Penlam. If you do not hear back from me in thirty minutes, send the peacekeepers."

"Yes, Krogal," she replied, her eyes round with shock and worry.

Thankfully, she didn't press me with questions—guessing accurately that I didn't have time to waste on that—and immediately reached for the com. I darted into the elevator while calling my brother. As the cabin flew up to the roof, I gave Demar a quick rundown of what was happening. He didn't ask any questions, only confirming he was on his way.

Our father had gone to a neighboring clan for the day and would take far too long to return. Everything in me prayed that I was overreacting and that our females were fine, but my gut told me otherwise. Losing either one of them would break me. Losing both would destroy us.

The ten-minute flight to Penlam from the clinic almost drove me insane. When I finally reached the venue, I almost crashed in my haste to land inside the underground parking. If not for the AI kicking in, I very well might have.

I couldn't decide if I felt more relieved than panicked when I found my mother's shuttle still parked in Farah's reserved spot. Very few other shuttles, a pair of hoverbikes and a handful of hovercars could be seen in the vast space. Although fully leased, the complex was still mostly unoccupied. New tenants were slowly trickling in, and a majority of them only planned to go into full business in the next three months.

Just as I was disembarking, the now familiar pressure behind my eyes returned, and my vision blurred.

*"Joree?! Is that you? Where are you?"*

Those questions no sooner popped up in my mind than the image of a stone pavement surrounded by grass and a yellow tree flashed before me. Whatever doubts I still had faded. In the two months since she'd been with us, Joree occasionally communicated with me. But as we were always in close proximity, there was none of this unpleasant pressure, and the images were crystal clear to the point I almost felt like I could reach out and touch them. This was weak and blurry. I didn't know if the distance caused it. But a new image showing a trail of blood and her mangled wing answered my unspoken question.

Joree was injured. She crashed somewhere outside and was communicating what she was seeing: her own damaged wing.

I hated that I could not directly communicate with her. The Nulia could only sense my emotions and interpret their meaning. That didn't stop me from thinking about what I wanted to convey to her and hoped she would get it.

*"I'm coming. Is Farah with you? Is she okay?"*

I kicked myself for throwing out so many questions at once. But I couldn't help the panicked thoughts flooding in.

Her response was swift and unequivocal. She did not want me to come for her, but for Farah first. Joree did so by showing me her broken wing before it faded to darkness and then flashing urgently an image of my mate lying in a pool of blood.

"NO!" I breathed out in horror.

Having likely realized I understood the priorities—or being too weak to continue communicating with me—Joree disconnected from my mind. With my normal vision returned, I broke into a run towards the lift. My senses immediately went into high alert when I spotted two males I'd never met before—one human and the other Zamorian—standing near the elevators.

A small number of humans and various other species regularly visited Xoccoris. Therefore, his presence in our city wasn't shocking in itself. While I obviously couldn't claim to know every Zamorian on this planet, as a member of the ruling family, I knew or had seen most people in our city and many others from the neighboring clans. I had never laid eyes on this one.

The trouble was that neither of these two should be here in Penlam. This complex was exclusively reserved for our local population. Off-worlders and visiting clans could have business in the Phase One complex, but not here in Phase Three.

More importantly, what were they doing just standing there? Were they loitering or standing watch?

As I approached, both males made a beeline towards me,

which had me even more suspicious. I berated myself for not taking a weapon in my haste to get here.

"Hello, friend," the human said in a friendly tone. "My companion and I are a little lost. We're looking to rent, but—"

"I'm sorry," I said in a sharp tone, interrupting him. "I'm in an extreme hurry."

To my dismay, he shifted to block my path when I tried to circle around him. His rather handsome face framed by unruly blond hair took on an offended and disappointed expression. He was respectably tall and fit by human standards. Not bulky and markedly muscular like a bodybuilder, but strong and solid like a bodyguard. His Zamorian companion was on the smaller side. Although his features had the full maturity of an adult, his height and the broadness of his shoulders would have rather belonged to a male in his late teens.

"Hey! It's rude to dismiss someone in need of help," the human said in a patronizing tone. "I just have a couple of questions."

"I said I don't have time," I snapped. "Go to the admin office."

As I tried to push past him, the human took a couple of quick steps back and reached for a blaster tucked in the back of his pants. I lunged at the Zamorian, who tried to corner me from the right, and yanked him in front of me as a meat shield. To my shock, my hands sank into the holographic disguise that made him look taller and bigger than he truly was. By the unexpectedly light weight of the disguised male, I could only assume he was also human.

Without sparing it a second thought, I immediately adjusted to that new situation and charged the blonde man while restraining his companion with my secondary arms. Even if he chose to shoot, his buddy would take the brunt of the damage.

Panicked, he retreated quickly while trying to aim at my face. But I zigzagged in a way that made it impossible.

"Dennis!" The blonde man suddenly shouted, looking at someone behind me.

I glanced over my shoulder to see a third human partially hidden by a parked shuttle, his blaster trained on me. I dove into a roll just as he fired. The disguised man still trapped in my arms shouted in fear when I flowed with the motion to get right back on my feet. I grabbed him by the wrist and, using my momentum, I spun on myself and flung him towards the shooter by the shuttle. Although my blind aim seemed accurate enough, I didn't wait to see if he hit the target. The third male ran out of the path of his companion while I rushed the blonde male.

He tried to shoot me, but I violently slapped his wrist. His pained cry as the weapon fell out of his hand was cut short when I rammed into him. I continued running over a couple more meters while carrying him, then lifted him up before slamming his body onto the hard parking floor. Blood shot out of his mouth, his wet scream of pain accompanied by the delightful sound of bones shattering.

I would have stomped him into a pulp, but a blaster shot grazing my right shoulder forced me to dodge into another roll and run for cover. Luckily, the blonde man's blaster slid in the same direction as the corner wall enclosing the elevator. I grabbed it on my way before slapping my back against the wall. I cursed up a storm as the last man standing prevented me from coming out of cover, shooting every time I tried to make a move. Sadly, I was in a dead end, unable to circle around and sneak up on him from behind.

Only a few seconds lapsed, but time was of the essence. My mate could be dying right now. Thankfully, the solution came rolling in on a hoverbike. Blaster raised, Demar zipped past the shuttle, shooting the human with deadly accuracy.

I ran out of cover just as my brother was jumping off his bike.

"Thank you, Brother," I shouted while calling the lift.

I quickly apprised him of what new images Joree had shared with me. My hearts ached for the little Nulia. I could only pray that she last long enough for us to rescue Farah and then come for her. Under different circumstances, I would have sent Demar to search for her. But if we faced guards here, chances were more of them awaited us upstairs.

I didn't wait for Dhalgal to call the peacekeepers after the thirty-minute timer I had given her. Our little encounter below sufficed to justify them having to send someone over. Demar placed the call just as we reached the fourth floor. I almost went on the offensive when the elevator doors opened on a male standing in front of it. He recoiled at my menacing stance and only relaxed when I did, after recognizing his face. I didn't know his name but had run into him quite a few times before.

"What's going on?" he asked warily at the sight of blood on me.

"Off-worlders are attacking my mate," I growled while exiting the cabin.

"What?! I'll help!" he offered.

"Warn the complex' security guards, and please go check the courtyard by the paved path. I believe you will find my mate's Nulia there, injured," I replied while hastening towards Farah's shop.

"On it!" the male replied before jumping inside the lift.

My hearts pounding, I ran up to the door with Demar hot on my trail. If the soundproofing of these studios had been one of their major selling points, I now resented how they effectively prevented the neighboring studios from hearing whatever drama might be unfolding inside.

Kromor only knew what kind of welcome awaited us within. I doubted the three guards below had a chance to warn Liam—or whoever else might be inside—of our approach. That we still couldn't reach Farah's and my mother's coms implied that they had some kind of disruptor active. I could only hope it also affected their own.

I waved my hand in front of the biometric lock. It recognized me and unlocked the secure door. With much care, I pushed it slightly open. But the loud sounds that immediately reached us had me throwing all caution to the wind.

"Cut that fucking wall open!" Liam shouted at two humans.

They were working diligently with lasers to carve an opening in the wall separating the main room from the dance studio. The studio's door had been all but destroyed as they had visibly attempted to kick it in. However, various heavy objects on the other side had been pushed against it to keep anyone from breaking in. Cutting a new door in an unencumbered area would be much faster. Judging by their progress, they'd been at it for a while and were seconds away from succeeding.

My hearts seized in my chest upon seeing the large amounts of blood staining the wooden floor. The two humans cutting up the wall seemed totally unscathed. Despite Liam having clearly gotten into a savage fist fight, there was too much blood for it to have come from him. This meant my mate, my mother, or both were seriously injured. A smaller trail of splattered blood led to the window which served as access for Joree to come and go as she pleased. The large smear around the frame confirmed that the Nulia as well was hurt.

It only took a few seconds for my brain to register all this information. Blind fury surged through me, and a savage roar tore out of my throat. The humans jerked around in surprise and fear. As one, my brother and I fired at the two men cutting the wall. The one on the right dove to the side. My brother's shot grazed his flank. He cried out and blindly fired back. But Demar quickly put him out of his misery. The one on the left, closer to Liam, instinctively surged forward.

Bad choice.

My shot landed right above his clavicle barely an inch next

to his jugular notch. His attempt at firing back went wide as he slapped his left hand on his throat to stem the blood gushing out of the wound. He fired a few more random shots as he gurgled, choking on his own blood. They were not deliberate attacks but triggered by the spasms of death.

Thinking quickly, Liam activated the energy shield from his bracer, raising it in front of him while unloading his weapon on me. I rolled out of the way and took cover behind a chest of drawers near one of Farah's two worktables. While he continued firing at me, he started kicking backward at the cut-up wall with the power and dexterity of a skilled martial artist. I pushed the chest of drawers towards him, still using it as cover. Unfortunately, it only took three brutal kicks from Liam for the wall to cave in.

A few more seconds, and I could have reached him.

Without hesitation, Liam jumped inside the room, still firing at us. I heard my mother cursing menacingly at the intruder. My hearts soared with relief that she still lived. But the absence of any sound from my mate whipped my blood into a frenzy.

Liam dodged as a heavy object I couldn't identify flew past his head. Still rushing forward, I lifted the chest of drawers and threw it with all my strength through the opening at Liam. Still destabilized from trying to duck whatever my mother had thrown at him, he failed to avoid it. It struck him hard, sending him flying back. He crashed a few meters away onto the floor with a loud thud.

To my surprise, he didn't lay there completely stunned, like most people would have. Instead, using the power of both his legs and arms, he shoved the chest of drawers crushing him back towards me. Under different circumstances, I would have been impressed by his strength and resilience. Farah mentioned he was a seasoned fighter. But a human, no matter how talented, didn't stand a chance against a Zamorian—and even less so against me after you've threatened my loved ones.

He straightened into a half-sitting position and shifted his aim towards my mother.

"Stand down, or I'll shoot her!" he shouted, anger rather than fear filling his voice.

Once more, that commanded a begrudging respect. Under similar circumstances, most people would be wetting themselves, begging for mercy, or pleading for compromise. But that would not spare him from my wrath. He didn't fear because the fool genuinely believed in the righteousness of his endeavor. He believed he had rights over my soulmate.

I would make him rue the day he ever laid eyes on her.

Another projectile from my mother thwarted his threat within seconds. He ducked only to see the chest of drawers flying right back at him as I simultaneously kicked it in his direction. He tried to roll out of its path, but it struck his leg right on the kneecap. His roar of pain sounded like the sweetest music to my ears. By the way his leg bent in the wrong angle, the force of the impact had snapped it.

He never got a chance to raise his blaster at me again as I was already upon him. I kicked the weapon out of his hand before stomping my foot on his left shoulder. The sound of the bones snapping was literally orgasmic. I dropped to my knees in front of him and slammed my primary fist onto the left side of his face. The cheek collapsed, and blood and teeth flew out of his mouth.

"KROGAL, NO!" my mother shouted. "Do not kill him!"

But I wanted blood.

I lifted both my primary hands to beat him into a pulp, but Demar rammed into me, knocking me off Liam. A savage roar escaped me as I threw my brother off me to get back to my prey. He wrestled to restrain me, even knowing he would never be strong enough to succeed.

"Farah is dying!" my mother shouted when I wouldn't relent.

Those words pierced through the feral rage that had taken

over me. I'd been so focused on taking out the threat that I barely registered the state of my female. My mother partially sheltering her with her own body had hidden the worst from my line of sight. My bloodlust faded as I crawled towards Farah.

"No! No! No! No!" I whispered when I saw the ashen-gray color that her usually golden-brown skin had taken.

She was covered in blood, and her body was shaken by the occasional spasm. Her skin was clammy, her breathing shallow and rapid. I lifted her eyelid only to find her eyes had rolled to the back of her head. She was likely going into shock from blood loss.

Without a word, I picked her up and ran out. Just as I was exiting the shop, the elevator doors opened, and a peacekeeper unit came rushing out. A single glance at me had their unit leader call for a medic to come at once.

My arms tightened around my mate's unconscious form, excruciating pain lacerating my hearts at the thought help might arrive too late.

"Hang on, my love. Hang on. Help is coming. Please, don't leave me."

# CHAPTER 17
## FARAH

Hushed voices in the distance pierced through the fog shrouding my mind. I couldn't make out their words. I felt heavy, as if gravity was hellbent on sucking me into the Earth's core.

*Earth? No... not Earth.*

I left Earth a long time ago. I fled it to escape Liam.

My eyes jerked open as memories flooded back in. The brightness of the room blinded me. In my panic, I refused to close them and blinked frantically instead in the hope of quickly adjusting. I wanted to sit up and investigate my surroundings but feared revealing to whoever was talking that I had awakened.

My heart leapt at the sound of a familiar yip. With a will of its own, my head jerked to the left. Although it didn't hurt, the movement caused an odd discomfort at the base of my spine. I wanted to focus on it, but all such thoughts evaporated at the sight of my beautiful Joree lying on a cushion on a table a meter away from me.

"Joree!" I whispered, my voice rough from disuse.

Tears of joy pricked my eyes when the Nulia spread her

wings and flapped them twice to cross the short distance between us. She landed next to my shoulder and booped my cheek.

"Joree! What did I say about flying?" Krogal's stern voice said on my left.

She tucked her head between her shoulders with the cutest guilty expression and pressed her wings against her body. Normally, I would have melted at this adorable tableau, but I only had eyes for my man.

"Krogal!" I said, my vision blurring with tears of happiness.

"Welcome back, my mate," he said with a world of affection in his obsidian eyes as he settled at the edge of my bed.

He leaned down and gave me a long and tender kiss that had my throat tightening with emotion. He broke it and straightened, then took my hands in his secondary ones.

"How I missed seeing your beautiful eyes," he said, his primary right hand caressing my cheek. "Don't ever scare me like that again, woman. I thought I was going to lose you."

The guilty smile that wanted to settle on my lips stiffened as a horrible thought crossed my mind.

"Talin?!"

"Mother is fine," he said in a reassuring tone. "She's waiting outside to come see you. Everyone is okay, and Liam will never threaten you again."

I exhaled a shuddering breath, too many conflicting emotions rushing through me, from relief to shock and disbelief. But above all, an impossible sense of being free at last washed over me.

"What happened? Where is he? I just recall being shot and your mother carrying me to safety," I said, my voice still shaky.

He gave me a quick breakdown of Joree's valiant effort at contacting him and putting my welfare before hers. My heart filled with love for my little companion. She felt it and rubbed her face against mine. I whispered words of gratitude while scratching the side of her ear.

Krogal petted her as well as he continued recounting the events until he got me out of that room. Although it shouldn't have surprised me, it boggled my mind that Liam came with five of his goons to abduct me. While relieved to learn Krogal didn't murder him in the end, it baffled me that he allowed him to live.

"Believe me, I wanted nothing more than to shatter every single bone in that wretch's body," Krogal said, a sliver of anger seeping into his voice. "But getting you medical aid was my priority. By Zamorian law, I could have demanded a duel to the death to make him pay for harming my mate. Mother made a very good point that for once I actually sided with."

"Oh?" I said with curiosity.

"Death would be too lenient a sentence for him," Krogal said. "Even if I took my sweet time making the torture last, he would still be free of his misery in minutes or hours. He made your life a nightmare for years and took your mother from you. He deserves a lifetime of the same. We made sure he would get a one-way ticket to the prison planet Molvi. No one ever escapes it. And the Hell Lords who run it will be sure to make it particularly painful. As I understand it, he's being sent to Warden Dakon's playground—the worst possible sector for any inmate to serve their sentence."

The glimmer of cruelty that I'd never seen before in his eyes should have frightened me. But the same malicious glee at the thought of the fate that awaited my former abuser swelled through me. I heard of Molvi. People preferred to take their lives than to serve there. Liam kept me in a cage. It was poetic justice that he should end up in one of his own.

I shifted only to be reminded of the discomfort in my lower back. The memory of my legs going numb after getting shot resurfaced. Frightened at the possible meaning of this, I tried to wiggle my toes. A choked sigh of relief escaped me when they responded. It was still awkward, but at least I wasn't paralyzed.

"How bad was it for me?" I asked warily. "And what is my current status? If Liam has already been sentenced and is on his way to Molvi, I must have been out a long time."

Krogal nodded and smiled reassuringly while gently caressing my arm. "It was pretty bad. You suffered a serious spinal injury. Both the shot and your fall shattered a couple vertebrae. The damage to your spinal cord was greatly increased when Mother picked you up to take you to safety in the dance room, and when I carried you out of there to look for help. Bone fragments wreaked havoc in there. You also lost a lot of blood from both blaster wounds."

"But I will make a full recovery, right?" I asked, the tension in my voice audible.

"Yes, my love. You will." The confidence in the tender smile he gave me wiped out my lingering worries. "They had to put you in an induced coma for twelve days to treat you. Spinal repairs are extremely finicky. They needed to remove all the bone fragments, mend your vertebrae, and repair your spinal cord. You had more nanobots in your system than some of the most advanced cyborgs out there."

I chuckled. "Does that mean I now have super strength and can lift you with one hand?"

He snorted and shook his head. "No such luck, my mate. Over the past couple of days, they flushed the nanites out of your system. You're just going to have some physiotherapy for the next few weeks to be completely back to your old self. And so will she," he added, giving a pointed look to Joree.

The Nulia responded with a yip that struck me as a pout, making me smile.

"How is she faring?" I asked.

"That shot seriously damaged her wing. It's a miracle she managed to fly out as far as she did," Krogal replied with admiration. "We had quite a bit of reconstructive surgery to do, including some artificial bone replacement. But her feathers are growing back nicely, and she should make a full recovery, or close enough that it will be hard to tell the difference. She just needs to let her wing heal instead of constantly flying around. Someone will get harnessed if she keeps misbehaving."

I laughed as Joree yipped again and bumped her snout on Krogal's hand in what I interpreted as a playful tap.

"So when can I go home?" I asked.

"Either later today or tomorrow, after the doctor has evaluated you," he said.

A knock on the door interrupted him. When we bid the visitor come in, Talin poked her head in. The expression on her face wrecked me. She was always so fierce, strong, and borderline intimidating, that this subdued almost shameful demeanor fucked with my head.

"Talin! Come in," I said warmly. "I'm so happy to see you are well."

She gave me a hesitant smile then clumsily approached, her gait devoid of its usual confident fluidity and elegance.

"I will give you a moment to talk. In the meantime, I'll let the doctor know you're awake," Krogal said in a gentle tone.

He leaned forward and gave me a tender kiss that had my still tingling toes curling. Although I smiled as he walked away, it struck me as odd that he should think his mother and I needed some privacy. Her own demeanor baffled me.

She brought a chair next to my bed, and sat down, a hint of wariness on her noble features as she studied my face.

"How are you feeling, Farah?" she asked in a hesitant voice.

I slightly frowned, more baffled than ever. You'd think she was here to give me some bad news. As Krogal stated that I would make a full recovery, and that Liam would never be a threat to me again, what could possibly trigger such a behavior?

"I'm feeling surprisingly well, considering the ordeal we just went through. But in the end, it sounds like it all worked out for the best," I replied in a friendly tone.

Talin clasped her hands in her lap, swallowed hard, and nodded in response to my words. The air of shame that fleeted over her face threw me for a loop.

"It was indeed quite an ordeal. I'm sorry you got injured. I'm sorry for so utterly failing you," she said, her eyes cast down.

I gasped in shock. "For failing me?" I repeated, flabbergasted.

"I was your protector. No harm should have come to you. Or at least you shouldn't have sustained the most grievous injuries. My failures almost cost you your life. I should have—"

"Oh, hell no!" I interrupted, disbelief and outrage filling my voice. "I will not let you blame yourself for whatever harm I faced because of Liam's actions. What injuries I sustained, *he* inflicted upon me. Not you. You saved my life, Talin. If anyone should apologize, it should be me for having brought this threat to your home."

"Saved you? You were bleeding out in my arms!" she argued.

The trembling in her voice struck me hard. This strong and stalwart woman was showing her real vulnerability for the first time. But more importantly, she was revealing the depth of the affection she now bore me.

I reached for one of her hands and gave it a gentle squeeze. "Yes, I was. But that was because I pushed you out of the path of the blaster and got hit instead. You tried to shield me with your own body. You put your life on the line for my sake."

"As is my duty as a protector!" she exclaimed as if it was self-evident.

"Which you performed admirably," I countered, making it clear it should be obvious to her as well. "Do you not realize that I'm still here today thanks to you? Had Liam dropped by yesterday when I was alone over there, he would have abducted me with no one being the wiser. You delayed him long enough for help to arrive. When I was injured, you took me to a safe room and tried to stem the flow of my blood so that I could hang on until rescue got there. The skilled and fearless way you fought him, even though you were weaponless, was a thing of legend. You're my fucking hero!"

She gaped at me, then pressed her lips together, no doubt to hide their quivering. Talin blinked rapidly, but it didn't hide the glistening in her eyes.

"Don't you dare question how you handled this situation. For as long as I live, I will forever be grateful that you were there, and that you stood up for me. Thank you for saving my life."

To my surprise, Talin dropped all pretense of control and stoicism. A powerful emotion settled on her face as she carefully drew me into her embrace. Although it once again stirred a slight discomfort in my lower back, I felt no pain and gladly recipro-cated. My throat tightened, and I buried my face in her neck. It had been too long since I received this type of truly maternal hug.

I didn't know how long we held each other. When she released me, Talin studied my features as if she was seeing me for the first time. She then gently caressed my cheeks and my hair in that same motherly fashion that turned me upside down. To my left, Joree was purring approvingly.

"You are my daughter, Farah. There is nothing I wouldn't do to ensure your happiness. I have many faults, but this was yet another lesson that I must keep my arrogance in check," Talin said with a humility that left me reeling.

She smiled at my confused expression, kissed my forehead, then helped me lie back down in my bed. She sighed, the air of guilt creeping back on her face.

"You warned me that you needed to stay in hiding or that human male would find you and cause much harm. I dismissed your concerns, thinking he couldn't get to you," Talin explained. "Instead, I should have been proactive in finding ways to ensure your safety, from alarm systems, security cameras, having his description and those of his known acolytes on the watch list in our various ports of entry. There was so much we could have done."

I nodded in understanding and gave her a reassuring smile. "Yes, there is much we could have done. I should have requested such security measures. But truth be told, a part of me also thought he could never get to me here."

"Really?" she asked, surprised.

"Yes, really. Many women in my situation are completely alone and isolated. I was a lot more careful then. But being surrounded by so many strong people, having a support system allowed me to let my guard down."

"A big error," Talin said dejectedly.

I shook my head. "Each situation is different. Sometimes, fully going into hiding is the way to go. Other times, taking the bull by the horns is the appropriate response. Liam had the means and the determination to find me. He would have stopped at nothing. Instead of facing him on his terms, which landed me in this hospital, we should have been the ones to set the trap and have that confrontation on our own terms. So yes, lessons learned. Humans say that it takes a village to raise a child. But it also takes a village—in this instance a clan—to build a safe future. Instead of hiding, I should have relied more on all of you to help find a solution."

"And this we shall all do should any new challenge arise in the future," Talin said in a firm tone.

"This, we shall all do," I echoed with a smile.

She returned it, caressed my cheek one last time, and dropped her hand. All softness suddenly vanished from her face, the return of her commanding expression giving me whiplash.

"For now, we must get you back on your feet. My son cannot go on being half-married to his human. I will see that weird ceremony you two want to have set in motion sooner than later," she said in that beloved grumpy tone that had me chuckling.

Yeah, I loved my prickly mother-in-law.

I remained in the hospital for one more day of observation, then finally returned home. My clan took pampering to an insane new level. Belle had warned me how overwhelming they could get in their need to take care of you, but I never expected it to be to this extent. The wretched woman laughed at my dismay when clanmates nearly fought each other for the right to come check in on me and help with my physio exercises.

When I started walking around the city again that following week, every eye was on me, making sure I didn't falter or need assistance. I now realized Ugrul wasn't exaggerating at that first assembly with his warning that once Krogal and I had children, people would be even more rabid in their need to look after them than they were with Belle's and Bayron's.

As annoying as it felt at times, it also made me feel amazing to have so many people concerned about my welfare and ready to have my back.

I truly had my village, my extended family.

It took a little over two weeks for me to feel like I was back to my old self. Krogal continued to handle me as if I was as fragile as a quail egg. The silly man refused to properly get frisky with me again before the third week, despite the doctor giving us the go ahead right after the first week. And even then, he held back on me.

As much as I loved his protectiveness, I wanted my husband back.

At first, I made subtle hints. When that failed, I expressed my wishes a bit more clearly. When that still failed, I sat him down and told him I wanted him to fuck me into next week. His horrified expression felt like a slap in the face and pissed me off to no end. Granted, he was just terrified he might hurt me, knowing how wild he became once he unleashed his passion. But enough was enough.

Tonight, it was make or break.

I returned home early from my store and prepared us a nice Haitian meal. I hesitated between our national dish called griot made of pork spiced to perfection, braised, then fried, and lambi, which was conch meat prepared in a spicy sauce. Since Haitians considered lambi an aphrodisiac, it was an easy choice. As he couldn't get enough of those, I added fried plantains and fried white sweet potatoes with the other sides. Once done, I got myself dolled up.

There was an assembly tonight.

I proudly watched Krogal gorge on my food, and especially get a double serving of pain patate for dessert—a sweet potato bread with raisins—before he hopped in the shower. I hurried into my old bedroom's washroom to remove my makeup, slip into a frilly negligee, and grab my secret weapons.

The poor man wasn't prepared for what I had in store for him.

He stepped out of the hygiene room to find me putting down a large rectangular box on the nightstand on my side of the bed.

"You're going to bed?" Krogal asked with confusion while still drying his hair with a towel.

"In a way, you could say that," I replied nonchalantly.

"Are you feeling unwell? Are your injuries—?"

"No, Krogal, I'm fine," I said gently, interrupting him. "I'm feeling great!"

He blinked, his confusion cranking up another notch while I smiled at him with an air of pure innocence.

"You… do not wish to attend the assembly with me?" he asked carefully.

"Initially, I was going to. But I've decided to go with

different plans for tonight. I'm sure you will have a blast, even without me," I said in the same conversational tone.

"Different plans? Such as what?" he insisted.

"I'm going to spend the evening with Bob... and his friends," I said, matter-of-factly.

My husband froze, shock, confusion, and a hint of outrage mixed with disbelief fleeting over his features in quick succession.

"Bob and his friends?" he repeated, his voice dangerously calm. "Dressed like this?"

I glanced down at myself, pretending to be surprised to be so lightly covered. "Hmmm, right. It's okay. They won't mind, and I'll be in bed anyways."

His mind appeared to go blank while he tried to make sense of my words. As offended as he obviously felt at the thought I might choose to spend the evening with another man, and worst of all in our home and in such a skimpy outfit, Krogal knew he was missing something. He knew I wasn't having an affair and was trying to read between the lines of what he perceived as a riddle.

"I see," he replied, although he clearly didn't see anything. "And who is that Bob? Have I met him?"

"No. He arrived yesterday, but we haven't had a chance to make a more intimate acquaintance just yet," I replied in a singsong voice.

He narrowed his eyes at me, the spark of anger fading, replaced by a playful curiosity. I loved that he was always willing to play along with my silly games. However, I doubted he would like the big reveal as much as he anticipated.

"Well then, I would like to meet this newcomer... and his friends, before I go. I will not be deemed a poor host to guests visiting my dwelling," he said with a dare in his voice.

"Of course!" I replied enthusiastically. "But I'm not sure you guys are going to get along."

"Is that so? Now I'm even more curious."

I turned around, picked up the large square box from my nightstand, then held it in front of me like a waiter with a tray of food. It was black with an elegant, swirly logo embossed in gold on top. Unless you were familiar with the brand, the iconographic symbol wouldn't reveal anything.

Krogal's surprised and inquisitive expression would have been adorable if I didn't know what storm was about to sweep through the room. I lifted the lid the way bankers and jewelers did in movies to present the contents of a suitcase full of cash or of a case filled with an expensive tiara or diamond jewelry set.

Right on cue, Krogal's face fell, and his jaw dropped. His four eyes roamed over the full set of female sex toys. Bob—the Battery-Operated Boyfriend—was a thick, multispeed vibrator. His friends were the other accessories included in the kit: a rabbit sleeve, a nubby sleeve—with the type of soft spikes that greatly resembled those of an Ordosian peen—a swirly sleeve that could have belong to the merfolks called Thalans, anal beads and Ben Wa Balls.

Once more, a plethora of emotions flashed over his face, from shock to outrage, to disbelief, and hurt. The latter had my chest constricting. I didn't want to hurt my man, but this needed to stop.

"Why in Khivolt's name would you need such things?" he asked, sounding betrayed. "Do I not see to your needs?"

I hardened myself and lifted my chin defiantly. "Actually, no, you don't. Not anymore. You treat me like a collector's item in a museum."

"You've been hurt!"

"That was one fucking month ago!" I snapped, before shutting the lid of the box with a bit more force than necessary. "The doctor told us it was fine to resume as normal after the first week. You've been multiplying the excuses to delay. And when you finally get on with it, I might as well have been made of glass. I want a husband, not a babysitter."

"I always make sure to pleasure you!" he argued, sounding offended.

"What you have done is to frustrate me," I retorted harshly. "Every time I think we're finally getting somewhere, you pull away and hold back. So I'm done getting my hopes up only to systematically be let down because you're too scared and don't trust me or the doctor enough to know what I can and cannot handle."

"It's not like that at all!" he exclaimed, disbelievingly.

"It's *exactly* what it feels like to me. I've tried to reason with you, but you won't listen. So fine, have it your way. Since you can't be a proper husband to me anymore, I will manage without you. These toys may not be you, but with them, I know exactly what to expect, and they won't hold back on me out of unfounded misgivings. Until you're ready to be a proper lover, you can keep your hands to yourself… all four of them."

As my heart bled to see him so hurt and devastated, I steeled myself in my resolve. We needed to pierce this abscess.

"You should get dressed, or you will be late for the assembly," I said in a casual tone. "I'll be in my old room."

Without waiting for his response, I calmly headed for the bedroom door, still holding my box firmly between both hands.

"I watched you bleed out," Krogal suddenly said in a tortured voice, stopping me dead in my tracks.

When I turned around, he was staring at me without seeing me, a haunted look on his face.

"I held you in my arms while you were going into shock. I stood by helplessly as you died. The first responders had to revive you after your heart stopped. For three days, you hung between life and death. So many bone shards scattered through your spinal cord, that even if you survived, they didn't think you'd ever walk again."

"But I'm alive, Krogal," I said in a gentle voice. "I'm alive and well. All of you saved me. My spine is healed. I can walk, dance, even jump on a trampoline. You all gave me a second chance at life. What was the point, though, if it's just so you can put me in a different gilded cage?"

I closed the distance between us, putting the box on top of the dresser as I walked past it, and placed my hands on Krogal's sides. He immediately wrapped his arms around me. The tortured expression lingered on his handsome face while his eyes flicked between mine.

"Life is too short, sweetie," I continued in a slightly pleading tone. "That day proved that everything can be taken away from us in the blink of an eye. You hated my desire to stay in hiding as you felt this was giving him power over me. I was afraid to lead a normal life because he might find and hurt me. And here you are doing the same by allowing the near-tragedy of that day to rob us of our normal married life. Despite the doctor's reassurances, you keep us in limbo out of fear of hurting me."

"I... I know. It's just... I'm in love with you, Farah. The thought of losing you... of hurting you..."

"I'm in love with you, too, silly man! You won't hurt me! If I feel any discomfort, I'll tell you. Pain and I don't get along at all. Have you forgotten how loud I squealed that one time I banged my pinky toe on the corner of the island?"

He snorted and nodded slowly. I smiled and cupped his face between my hands.

"Give me my husband back. I would really rather not have to become better acquainted with Bob and his friends," I added, casting a sideways glance at the vibrator box set on the dresser.

"Fuck Bob," Krogal growled, menacingly.

I made a face at him. "Uh, the whole point of this intervention is specifically to avoid that," I said tauntingly.

"You know what I meant," he replied with false severity.

"Do I?" I asked with false innocence. "I'd ask you to show

me what you mean, but I don't want to make you late for the assembly."

"Fuck the assembly," he growled again. "If you get hurt, I will spank you raw."

I never got a chance to reply. His mouth crushed mine in a possessive kiss, and my toes instantly curled.

# CHAPTER 18
## KROGAL

My mate melted against me as I claimed her mouth with a bit more force than necessary. A part of me wanted to punish her for demanding I let go of my ridiculous hang ups. And they were indeed ridiculous. Although I wasn't a physician, I thoroughly examined her medical records and bombarded her doctor with an endless string of questions. Farah had indeed made a full—if nearly miraculous—recovery.

Yet, every time I touched her, the image of her bloodied, unconscious form flashed before my eyes. Even my hands caressing her skin covered by a thin sheet of sweat in the throes of passion would start feeling like they were touching blood.

It shamed me that *she* was the one who had been injured, but *I* was suffering from PTSD.

As much as I continued to worry my great strength could harm her if I allowed myself to lose control, I rejoiced that she had given me this ultimatum. I had been dancing around this for too long. Not only was I punishing her and myself, but I truly was allowing Liam to continue to interfere with our lives.

I'd spoken twice with a therapist about it. Clearly, I needed a few more sessions. More importantly, I should have shared that information with Farah—an omission I would rectify in the morning.

For now, I wanted to reclaim our lives, and show her just how much I loved her.

I lifted her slender body and pressed her against mine. Kromor's teeth, she was made for me. As was her wont, Farah wrapped her legs around my waist. Her hands explored my body with an eagerness that both aroused and shamed me. My woman hungered for a passion that was rightly hers to enjoy but that I withheld out of fear.

*If she knew, Mother would chop off my braid.*

And I would deserve it, too.

I slipped a hand under the hem of the see-through top of her negligee. She shivered in the most delicious fashion as I caressed her back. To my dismay, my palms once more rubbed over the small of her back and left shoulder blade, in the areas where she had been shot. I'd instinctively done this more times than I could count over the past few weeks. Even knowing I would find the skin smooth and flawless, the traumatized part of me needed that reassuring confirmation.

I carried my mate to the bed and laid her down on the mattress without breaking the kiss. Our tongues pursued their sensuous dance for a while longer. My mate was a kisser and a biter, two things I could never get enough of from her.

I eventually released her lips and covered every inch of her body with gentle kisses and caresses. As I sucked and licked her right nipple, Farah lifted her chest for greater contact and fisted my hair on my nape. She raked the nails of her other hand on my back. I couldn't repress a smile at that less-than-subtle hint that I was being too restrained.

That wasn't the case, but I'd withheld so much of late that she'd forgotten I always proceeded with long preliminaries, even before this entire mess went down. Under the current circum-stances, I yielded to her unspoken request and sped things up a little. Instead of spending the next eternity worshiping every inch of her body, I kissed a path down to the apex of her thighs. The delectable scent of her musk and growing arousal had my cocks perking their heads up.

I parted her folds and circled her clit with my tongue, drawing a needy moan out of her. I repeated the motion a few more times before sucking on the little nub. She sighed with approval and tightened her grip on my hair. With her free hand, my mate fondled her breast.

In no time, her slit glistened with her essence. I slipped two fingers inside her, and the wet warmth of her sheath greedily squeezed them with each movement. My cocks jerked in response, and my abdominal muscles contracted with anticipation at the memory of how her inner walls felt around my lengths.

As I continued to voraciously feast on my woman, reveling in the tart taste of her essence, I intensified the speed of my fingers dipping in and out of her. I scissored them, stretching her in the process. Although Farah now required less preparation to receive me, I still devoted time to it. Considering her current impatience at getting things back on the rougher side, I wanted to further reduce the risks of any discomfort she might feel.

In no time, Farah was grinding against my hand. Her labored breath and voluptuous moans heralded her imminent climax. I accelerated the motion of my fingers inside my woman, crooking them so they would graze her sensitive bundle of nerves. She emitted a strangled gasp followed by a flow of encouraging—if not pleading—words, telling me not to stop, to touch her right there.

I gladly complied.

Her legs jerked violently around my face as she cried out. My primary left hand wrapped around her leg to restrain its movements as she shook with bliss. I didn't stop sucking her clit while she rode her orgasm. But I pulled the fingers of my primary right hand out of her. They were slick with her arousal, providing the perfect lubricant as they probed her forbidden entrance. Simultaneously, the fingers of my secondary right hand picked up where they left off, keeping her flying high for a while longer.

Zamorian females possessed two vaginas and two uteruses—the second one smaller and mostly used as a backup in case the primary one got damaged. While anal sex wasn't uncommon among my people, I'd assumed Farah wouldn't have been too keen on it with me, especially considering my size. To my surprise, she proposed it. At first, I feared it was out of a sense of obligation since I have two cocks. But she reassured me that she simply wanted us to fully be one.

To my delight, she enjoyed the experience. We didn't do it every time we coupled, which was entirely fine with me. Sex with my mate, however we went about it, was always phenomenal.

I relented on my ministrations when Farah started to come back down. After one last lick on her clit, I leisurely kissed a path back up her body. I settled over her, leaning on my secondary four arms not to crush her. My woman caressed my back and pressed her chest to mine. The look in her eyes nearly undid me. Farah didn't need to tell me she loved me. Her feelings radiated with the brightness of the sun at its zenith. The way she touched me, said my name, and even just smiled at me expressed it more powerfully than any word could.

I leaned forward and reclaimed her lips, pouring into it the depth of my adoration for her. Using my primary hands, I spread her legs wider and rubbed my lower cock against her slit, coating it with her essence. Eyes locked with hers, I slowly pushed it inside her. She adjusted quickly, and I immediately set a fast pace but with gentle thrusts. I ground my pelvis against hers so that my primary cock would massage her clit with each stroke.

Kromor's teeth, her wet heat around my cock was setting my

loins ablaze. Farah dug her nails in the small of my back and started lifting her hips in counterpoint to my movements. The message couldn't have been clearer. Forcing myself to silence my resurfacing fear of harming her, I started taking her deeper and harder. I studied her features for the slightest sign of discomfort and found nothing but pleasure on her beautiful face. Her feverish caresses and her words of encouragement between two moans spurred me on.

As she began to crest, I shifted my angle to strike her sensitive spot with each thrust. I peppered soft kisses over her face while whispering words of love. Just when I felt her on the verge of toppling over again, I crushed her lips in a greedy kiss and swallowed her shout of ecstasy.

My abdominal muscles contracted painfully with the need to unleash my passion on her, but I reined myself in and continued pumping in and out of my wife until the tremors of her orgasm receded. Farah gasped when I pulled out, flipped her onto her stomach, then pulled her hips up—her face still pressed against the mattress—before burying my primary cock inside her slit. It took every bit of my willpower not to ram myself in. I would eventually get back to that one day when my overprotective self wouldn't still feel so skittish about her recovery.

Once again, I set a fast pace. Farah pushed herself up on all four and started rocking back, meeting me thrust for thrust. The force with which she backed into me made her desires clear. Despite my lingering worries, I yielded to her wishes, and followed her lead. I tightened my hold on her hips and let go of my restraint.

"Yes!" she said in a throaty voice, as she threw her head back.

I slapped her left butt cheek—something I'd never done before. My mate gasped, and her golden-brown skin erupted in goosebumps. She turned her head to look at me over her shoulder. Lips parted, eyes hooded, she stared at me with such a lascivious expression that something broke inside me. I started pounding into her.

A lustful frenzy took me over as an inferno started raging in my loins. With a will of its own, my primary right hand smacked her rump a few more times at varying intervals. Judging by her reaction, Farah wholeheartedly approved. My mate's exquisite shouts of pleasure, the frantic sounds of our flesh meeting, and her throaty voice chanting my name were acting like the most potent of aphrodisiacs.

By Khivolt, how I had missed this!

Both my primary hands slipped in front of her, the left one fondling her breast while the right one settled on her clit. In no time, my mate detonated again. She collapsed face first against the mattress. Her inner walls contracting around my cock almost made me spill my seed. Grinding my teeth, I continued pumping in and out of her for a moment longer, while my thumb probed her rosette.

I pulled my main cock out of her and carefully inserted my smaller lower cock in her rear. Still flying high from her latest orgasm, Farah didn't display any sign of discomfort. Although her body resisted me at first, it only took a few shallow thrusts before it yielded to my invasion.

Without slowing the speed and strength of my thrusts into her, I bent my woman backward until her back pressed against my chest. I covered her nape and the curve of her shoulder with kisses while giving her time to adjust to me. Tilting her head to the side to grant me better access, Farah raised a hand over her shoulder to sink her fingers into my hair.

My hands were all over the perfection that was her body. To my relief, the thin sheet of sweat making her skin slick didn't trigger the blood flashbacks that had plagued me since the attack. I whispered words of love as I fondled her, and finally started carefully moving inside her when she ground her rear against my pelvis to signal she was ready.

Kromor's teeth! I could die with pleasure. As much as I enjoyed giving in to my more primal urges during sex, there was something magical, almost divine in this slow and tender lovemaking.

We pursued this dance for a while. Despite the intense pleasure each stroke provided me, it was the intimacy, the closeness of our bodies as I held her tightly against me that made this moment perfect.

After one last soft kiss on her nape, I gently lifted Farah off me and laid her back down on the mattress. She spread her legs and opened her arms, beckoning me. I came willingly to my mate… my love. With infinite care, I inserted my main cock in her sex, and my smaller one in her rear. It was a tight fit that once again required a moment for her to grow comfortable.

At the first thrust, I thought I would die from the pleasure overload as my wife simultaneously squeezed and stroked both of my cocks in her burning heat. A deep growl vibrated through my chest and up my throat as an inferno erupted in the pit of my stomach. I started moving faster, my primary hands fisting the bedsheets with a deadly grip as I fought a losing battle with lust.

When my woman began to writhe beneath me, clawing at me and begging for more, I threw all caution to the wind. I unleashed my passion, taking her deep and hard. And endless flow of growling moans—almost beastly in nature—tumbled out of me as liquid flames surged from my loins and spread outward through every inch of my body.

The world vanished around us. The only thing that mattered was the feel of my woman all around me, her taste on my tongue, her hands on my skin, and our bodies joined as one.

I was too far gone in a whirlwind of bliss to even notice Farah's orgasm creeping up on her. This time, when she cried out and her inner walls clamped down on my primary cock before contracting spasmodically around it, my own climax swept me away. Lightning struck me right in the middle of the spine with a violence that left me reeling. I roared as my seed erupted in a torrent of bliss. Shaken by the tremors of ecstasy, I kept rocking over my woman with erratic movements until the last of my seed was spent.

I felt dizzy and completely disoriented as I collapsed on the bed. I rolled onto my back, my wife still held in my embrace. She was trembling, her breath labored as she clung to me like a drowning woman. I gently caressed her back as our heartbeats and the room settled.

"Thank you for giving me my husband back," she whispered, her cheek resting on my left heart.

"Thank you for demanding I do," I whispered back.

I felt her smile and so did I.

# EPILOGUE
## FARAH

Saying that mess with Liam turned my life around would be the understatement of the century. In the weeks that followed his attempted kidnapping, much more drama unfolded.

I still had mixed feelings about what had led him to discover my presence on Xoccoris to begin with. Although the planet's Hall of Records had indeed shared the information about our wedding to the intergalactic records shared by all the members of the United Planets Organization, that wasn't how Liam found out.

Agent Benton, who had been in charge of my case after I first escaped, voluntarily leaked the information to my ex. From the beginning, he questioned my innocence, only caving in after a Temern confirmed I truly had no knowledge of whatever shady business Liam was involved in. What I didn't realize was that, even after I went to the refuge, Agent Benton kept tabs on me. He hoped to nail Liam if he once more came after me and violated the restraining order I obtained against him.

Moving to Xoccoris pretty much ruined any chance the agent had of this occurring. Therefore, he used me as bait. Naturally, I lost my shit after finding out how he put my life in danger.

However, Benton had not believed Liam would harm me, only attempt to kidnap me. As much as I hated to admit it, he'd been correct in that. I didn't doubt for an instant that my ex shooting me had been an accident. He meant to shoot Talin. Even as I lay dying, I heard his distress, first when his shots hit me, and second when he shouted for Talin to let him in so that he could care for me.

But Benton still put my life in danger.

His unit had been waiting at the docking bay, ready to arrest Liam the moment he tried to get me onboard his vessel. He didn't want to risk coming to the Penlam complex and getting detected as arresting Liam over there wouldn't have allowed Benton to lay more serious charges at his feet. But once he got me on that ship against my will, then the agent could accuse him of not only violating the restraining order, but of kidnapping and of intergalactic people trafficking.

Naturally, all hell broke loose once he found out how things had gone belly up. They put him on administrative leave while running an investigation for reckless endangerment. Krogal and Talin made a mighty stink about it. But even as the Enforcers apologized and promised accountability, I easily recognized their lack of sincerity in this instance.

Yes, they felt horrible about his actions putting me in danger. But Liam's arrest, and the heavy charges they were able to slap him with, got them the type of unlimited warrants they wanted to be able to dig through his homes and businesses.

And did they ever hit the jackpot!

Their discoveries were largely aided by the confessions of his two goons who survived their encounter with Krogal and Demar. The one Krogal tossed across the parking lot to knockout his companion suffered extensive fractures and injuries, including a crushed vertebrae. The basic medical care granted to convicts would leave him permanently disabled. When the Enforcers offered him a plea deal that would provide the advanced medical treatment he required to make a full recovery, he spilled his guts without hesitation.

I couldn't even blame him.

Between spending the next ten years on Molvi with a healthy body, or the rest of your life in that dreadful prison planet, surrounded by the vilest criminals while disabled, the choice was a no brainer. He gave them all the goods, prompting others to also seek plea deals.

Overnight, Liam's empire was no more.

Not only did he get a life sentence on Molvi, they sent him to Warden Dakon's Sector—the most savage and unforgiving holding area of the prison planet. The Obosian judge who presided over his case awarded me an obscene amount in damages. On top of that, all my money he had seized control of was returned to me.

Being filthy rich in his own right, Liam had no use for my money. Aside from negotiating good contracts for me when he was managing my career, he invested my earnings wisely. Even without the damages award I received, that money sufficed to guarantee a life of comfort and luxury for the rest of my days. No wonder he kept me from accessing it. Then, he wouldn't have had any control over me.

As I didn't crave a lavish and extravagant lifestyle, I didn't need all that wealth. Therefore, I found a brilliant way to use the punitive damages money I received.

Considering what a powerful man my ex had been, and in light of the nature of his crime, it made a huge scandal. Stories of Joree's heroism spread like wildfire. Pictures shared by the media of the crime scene prominently featured the mural Belle had painted of Joree and me. The young Nulia—and her species as a whole—became an overnight sensation.

Every planet of the alliance tried to acquire these wondrous creatures, with many civilians wanting them as pets. This prompted the Zamorian government to place a moratorium restricting the off-world sales of Nulias until strict rules and guidelines could be instated to protect them.

Unlike most other companion animals, you couldn't just waltz up to a breeder, check out his inventory, and pick the pet whose color or demeanor appealed to you the most. With Nulias, *they* picked *you*. Krogal never would have been able to get her for me had Joree not also chosen me.

Nulias were more like people than animals, with a great need to nurture and care for others. They weren't rescue animals for nothing.

Accordingly, I used my damages award to set up a foundation that would match Nulias with charitable organizations mainly on primitive worlds and refugee colonies that didn't have the means to acquire such wondrous creatures. Joree opened my eyes with her interaction with the other injured pets in Krogal's clinic, and then with other patients in the hospital. During my recovery and physiotherapy, Joree realized how her comforting presence could help some of the patients who didn't require isolation.

Needless to say that after the mural of Joree and me went viral, Belle put her foot down about tweaking the other pieces she had been working on featuring me so that my face would no longer be hidden.

I was fine with that.

Talin was over the moon. The events granted her and both her sons the same type of intergalactic heroic status that her nephew Bayron had achieved after saving the Atreall Queen—another momentous event immortalized by Belle. As I didn't care much for fame, I gladly let her give all the interviews that we kept being bombarded with.

All that drama also served as the best possible publicity for the fashion business I was putting together. I barely even started building my collection that people were already trying to place orders. While I totally gave up on singing, except for pleasure and in casual settings, I pursued my dancing projects on the side. Not only had dancing helped accelerate my recovery during physiotherapy, I was truly enjoying merging my Caribbean culture with the Zamorian traditional dances.

Both of those passions played an important role in my wedding planning.

As she couldn't have the traditional wedding she would have preferred, Talin went all out making sure it would still be the most memorable celebration on Xoccoris. The upside of it all was that she happily did most of the heavy lifting. My mother-in-law had connections everywhere. Anything I wanted, she knew someone who could get it done. As I always dreamt of a fairy tale wedding, her excessive enthusiasm didn't bother me in the least.

With Talin handling most of the wedding preparations, I got to work on a side project to get my husband the best wedding gift I could come up with. Thanks to Bayron's and Belle's assistance, we sweet talked the Ordosians into granting Krogal a private internship. We wouldn't be allowed inside one of their villages, but we could stay at the Hunter's Federation basecamp on Trangor. For two weeks outside hunting season, Szaro would take Krogal around the forests of his homeworld so that he could experience firsthand some of the local fauna, as well as give him some technical training directly in the Hunter's basecamp lab.

If things went well, his wife Serena suggested that private mentoring could continue remotely through vidcom since Szaro was impressed with what Krogal did for Ferach before they took over his care. But the best part was that she even hinted that the Ordosians might be open to holding veterinary summits on their homeworld. Anything related to promoting the welfare of animals, local and otherwise, held their interest.

I couldn't wait to present that gift to Krogal on our wedding night!

In the end, we didn't have the slaying of a wild beast, but a war dance to claim me.

In accordance with Zamorian traditions, I became a Vaika—a sacrificial bride—and wore the typical white sacrificial gown, although one of my own design. Adding a human element to it, I had a long veil, which Joree held between her front paws, flying behind me. Hovering would be a more accurate term as she maintained the proper distance with me.

Following Talin who led the way, I walked through two rows of single females forming a path on each side of the entrance of the arena. They sang while showering me with shabira petals, a flower which symbolized luck and fertility.

My heart fluttered with an odd thrill as she took me to a set of pillars framing a rectangular altar. Embedded in the stone platform in the center of the arena, the altar acted as a bench that the bride could sit on if she started feeling weak in the knees. I gladly submitted myself to being shackled to the pillars, the long chains granting me quite a bit of freedom of movement.

On a dais overlooking the arena, Feidin, her mate, sons, and their wives, looked on approvingly from their VIP box. Shortly after I regained consciousness in the hospital, the Clan Matriarch returned Krogal to Talin upon his request, reinstating the mother-son bond.

It pleased me tremendously. As much as I loved Feidin, Talin was the birth mother of the love of my life, and more than just my mother-in-law. A true bond had also formed between us. And I intended to nurture it in the future.

The cushion in the inner lining of the shackles prevented them from chafing my wrists. However, there would be no cause for me to strain against them as no harm could potentially come to me.

In a normal Zamorian wedding, they released a feral beast in the arena—usually a grummoll. I would have been sprayed with brumar sweat, a potent pheromone to entice the beast, so that it would come directly after me. To prove his worthiness as a husband and protector, Krogal would have been expected to single-handedly defeat the creature, keeping it from ever reaching me. Obviously, security measures were set in place to protect the bride in case the groom failed.

For our wedding, the traditional Thasnak dance that the males performed before the battle became one of the main events. Instead of the single males trying to impress me by outperforming the other men in the choreographed war dance, warriors of all ages joined in on the action. It became a symbolic representation of the battle between good and evil, with my man as the hero.

Krogal was magnificent as he flawlessly executed acrobatic battle moves that would put the most proficient martial artist to shame. It boggled my mind that a man so massive could show such dexterity. He stomped his feet, slapped his chest, and mimicked a plethora of powerful attack moves while shouting and grimacing.

He was terrifying… in the sexiest ways.

The other men warred each other in a savage dance that electrified the audience. I stared in awe at the spectacle before me, still struggling to believe the entire clan had answered the call to celebrate my formal union with one of theirs.

With a final war cry, the men dropped into a one-knee kneeling position, the tip of their spears stabbed into the packed dirt of the arena. The beating of the bamurs—giant drums similar to the Japanese Daiko drums—filled the arena.

The single women, also dressed in my reinterpretation of the traditional Zamorian gowns, spread around the arena. They danced in between the men. My throat tightened when I recognized the typical movements of my Haitian heritage. I had played no part in the choreography, only in the women's outfits and mine. Tears pricked my eyes when even the song the women sang as they danced and the rhythm of the bamurs took on a distinctive Caribbean edge. That they went out of their way to integrate my culture like this told me more than anything how completely they claimed me as one of theirs.

A collective gasp rose from the crowd when streams of flames shot through the sky. At first, I thought it was some kind of fireworks. But then I spotted the dark little creatures called Bitris. They resembled Indian flying foxes, with the same bat wings, but a leathery body instead of fur. They accompanied the women with their own aerial dance while spitting streams of fire. It took me a moment to realize they were forming Zamorian letters which spelled 'Soulmates.'

My chest constricted again. Krogal regularly cared for these circus pets. But it made sense he would include a part of himself in the ceremony as well.

With a final shout from both the men and women, silence descended over the arena. The Bitris landed in pairs facing each other and formed a path towards the altar. Each pair took turns spitting fire in the air, forming an archway under which Krogal marched towards me.

I couldn't wipe the silly grin off my face as I stared at my man with adoration. He stopped a meter in front of me, and I drowned in the dark depths of his obsidian eyes. Movement at the edge of my vision startled me. I'd been so lost in my man that I didn't notice his parents as well as Feidin and Ugrul approach us.

The Clan Matriarch always oversaw every wedding. While the birth mother could deny her children a marriage she disapproved of, so could the Matriarch. In fact, she could override the decision of the birth parents.

Here, her presence was merely a formality.

"Krogalsenyiek Skortheatis, you are here to claim the Vaika as your bride," Feidin said in a commanding voice. "As no male dared to issue a challenge, you may proceed."

Krogal puffed out his chest. He was shirtless as always, his braid bared of any adornment for the first time since our contractual wedding. Closing the distance between us, he accepted the key Ugrul extended to him and freed me of my shackles.

"Farah Toussain," Talin said in a solemn voice filled with pride, "my firstborn son Krogalsenyiek has proven himself over the past few months as a worthy protector for the family he desires to build with you. Does he meet your approval? Will you have him as your mate?"

"I do," I said, my voice filling with emotion. "I wholeheartedly do."

"Then yours he shall be," Talin replied.

Ugrul turned to the large stone altar behind me and activated a hidden mechanism. Had Belle not warned me of what would follow, I would likely be freaking out a little bit right now. The altar rose from the ground by close to a meter, giving it a proper height rather than that of a bench. The top slid open, revealing a small basin filled with purifying water, a short staff, and clean cloth on the other side.

Feidin retrieved a bowl—which she filled with the purified water—and a few cloths before going to stand next to her sister. Talin immediately began to undo Krogal's braid. It was silly, but I couldn't help a pang of jealousy to see her touch it. In the few months since my arrival here, I indeed grew to see a male's braid as something as off limits as any other naughty bits.

Meanwhile, Ugrul retrieved the staff which he brought to Krogal's father, Orym. My pulse picked up when he approached me and removed the custom-made medallion around my neck. Krogal had asked me to choose a symbol that represented me, or which held significant importance to me to be engraved on it. I chose a Nulia. To me, she had become the symbol of freedom, hope, compassion, and second chances.

Orym placed the medallion at the tip of the staff. My stomach knotted knowing what I'd have to do with it in a minute. But Talin washing Krogal's hair with a cloth dipped in purified water reclaimed my attention.

"Krogal, my firstborn… I carried you for ten months. I gave you birth, raised you, and nurtured you into the formidable male you have become. A male who fills this mother's hearts with pride and joy. Today, I release you."

My throat tightened at the powerful emotion those words stirred in my husband. Those two had come such a long way…

Talin turned to me and gestured for me to approach. I complied, feeling inexplicably nervous as she placed Krogal's braid in my hand.

"Farah Toussaint, I give you my son," she said. "From this day forth, no female but you shall touch his braid—for real this time—or have any claim over him."

All of us couldn't help a snort at her snarky remark.

"Plait it while repeating after me," Talin continued.

I nodded. Just like I did with Feidin on the day I arrived on Xoccoris, I repeated the vows after Talin while plaiting Krogal's hair. When I finished, Talin stepped aside so her husband could approach. He extended the staff to me. The medallion had turned red and was emitting scorching heat.

I accepted the staff, swallowed hard, and cast an apologetic look at Krogal. Although I should have known he would be proudly grinning and impatient to have me permanently brand my mark of ownership in his flesh, it still messed with my head. Belle having gone through it previously and confirming it wasn't torture for them was the only reason I didn't argue about proceeding with it.

I gave him a shaky smile and brought the brand to his chest, right above his left heart and pressed. The sizzling sound of burning flesh and the scent of charred meat had my stomach roiling. Where I would be screaming bloody murder, Krogal's face split into the widest grin as I continued to press the brand until the red light on the staff turned blue, indicating the process was complete. After burning the symbol into their flesh, four tiny needles poked out of the head of the staff to inject the male with antibiotics that would prevent infection and accelerate the healing process.

As soon as I removed it, Krogal emitted a victorious roar. His four arms spread wide, he rotated in place while the crowd went berserk. I couldn't help but laugh, my heart filling with happiness and love to see him so ecstatic to finally be officially bound to me before his people.

"Welcome to our family, Daughter," Orym said with a paternal affection that moved me to the core.

"Yes, welcome to our family," Talin echoed. "You are now officially ours. You are home."

Krogal smiled at his parents before turning his gaze towards me. With an air of pure adoration in his black eyes, he opened his arms to me.

A silly grin plastered on my face, I went to him willingly. He leaned down and gave me a tender kiss.

"I love you," I whispered against his lips.

His forehead resting against mine, he tightened his embrace around me. "I have waited for you my whole life, my Farah. I am yours, now and always. You are my hearts, my love, my eternity."

## THE END

# JOREE

# GRUMMOLL

I Married A Birdman
I Married A Minotaur
I Married Wonjin
I Married A Merman
I Married A Dragon
I Married A Beast
I Married Krogal
I Married A Dryad
I Married An Incubus
I Married A Mothman

**THE MIST**
The Mistwalker
The Nightmare

**DARK TALES**
Bluebeard's Curse
The Hunchback

**THE SHADOW REALMS**
Destined to the Wraith

**BLOOD MAIDENS OF KARTHIA**
Claiming Thalia

**VALOS OF SONHADRA**
Unfrozen
Iced

**EMPATHS OF LYRIA**
An Alien For Christmas

**OTHER**

# ABOUT REGINE

*USA Today* bestselling author Regine Abel is a fantasy, paranormal and sci-fi junkie. Anything with a bit of magic, a touch of the unusual, and a lot of romance will have her jumping for joy. She loves creating hot alien warriors and no-nonsense, kick-ass heroines that evolve in fantastic new worlds while embarking on action-packed adventures filled with mystery and the twists you never saw coming.

Before devoting herself as a full-time writer, Regine had surrendered to her other passions: music and video games! After a decade working as a Sound Engineer in movie dubbing and live concerts, Regine became a professional Game Designer and Creative Director, a career that has led her from her home in Canada to the US and various countries in Europe and Asia.

**Facebook**

https://www.facebook.com/regine.abel.author/

**Website**

https://regineabel.com

## Regine's Rebels Reader Group

https://www.facebook.com/groups/ReginesRebels/

## Newsletter

http://smarturl.it/RA_Newsletter

## Goodreads

http://smarturl.it/RA_Goodreads

## Bookbub

https://www.bookbub.com/profile/regine-abel

## Amazon

http://smarturl.it/AuthorAMS